ANGEL CITY SINGLES

ANGEL CITY SINGLES

A NOVEL

RALPH CISSNE

Library of Congress Control Number: 2018902138

ISBN-13 978-0-9998537-0-2 (paperback)
ISBN-13 978-0-9998537-1-9 (hardcover)
ISBN-13 978-0-9998537-2-6 (ebook)

BISAC: FICTION / General / Marriage & Divorce / Women

Cover and interior book design by Wendy Saade

Published by Morgan Road
www.morganroad.com

For David, Elizabeth,
Shelly and Louis.

During college David Bishop channeled his grief and passion into the stoic purity of cross-country running. In the spring of 1973 Noreen Unger, the coed he would marry, invited him to her apartment.

"Have a seat," she said. "Make yourself at home."

Noreen's reddish brown hair fell softly on her shoulders. Measured amounts of Jack Daniel's sour mash whiskey were poured. She took a sip, gathered the folds of her sleeveless summer dress and pressed her hips into the well of David's lap. A perfumed arm coiled around his neck.

"So," she whispered. "Why haven't you tried to kiss me?"

"I was being a gentleman," he said.

"Well," she purred. "Enough of that."

—

ONE

David Bishop discovered it was unwise to date the ex-wife. He paced between the moving boxes stacked in his empty apartment and considered what to say to her. It was dark when he zipped his leather jacket. Outside, streetlamps flickered to life. A cool breeze swept down from the north, rare for Dallas in late September, and stirred the leaves in the stand of live oak trees across the way.

He thought about that night in July when a casual conversation and the relentless summer heat rendered their bodies unrestrained. The mix of alcohol and biological reflexes fueled an ill-fated encounter worthy of a Leonard Cohen song. Unlike the beginning, back at North Texas State, that humorless evening was void of innocence. Early the next morning Noreen's ceiling fan offered a measure of relief as they lay naked, sheets twisted about their ankles.

Noreen pressed her lips to David's shoulder. "Tell me," she said. "What does this mean? What difference does it make?"

After ten years of marriage, their divorce and four years of bachelorhood David learned to choose his words carefully whenever a Texas woman asked an existential question or confessed that she carried a concealed weapon.

"It's been awhile," he said. "Since I had a hangover."

Noreen shook her head and turned to the glass of whiskey on her nightstand. The ceiling fan whirled above them. David untangled the sheets, pulled on his jeans and T-shirt, wandered to the bathroom and washed his face with cold water. Noreen's antique looking glass revealed lean boyish features, dark eyes and unruly brown hair. He examined his face, thought about what was revealed and what lay hidden. Noreen slipped on a robe and walked him to the door.

"Good luck finding work," she said.

Two months had passed. David drove the Buick Century he purchased from a used car auction. Central Expressway choked with traffic as he slogged south toward Marvin Gardens, a new club on Lower Greenville Avenue, to meet Noreen. She had selected this place for their farewell as an affirmation of her independence, something he never questioned during their marriage.

He parked the car. A long minute passed. David weighed the burden of goodbye and clutched the steering wheel until the scars on his knuckles turned white. Deep breaths filled his lungs. Years of training as a runner had reduced his resting heart rate to 56 beats a minute. He knew how to focus and the consequences of losing control. Outside, the cool wind whipped his face. The night sky yielded a tarnished haze. He searched for the North Star until it became clear.

"Looking for something?" a voice said.

A young woman approached dressed like a refugee from a vintage resale shop. She celebrated the pervasive and provocative '80s look, a product of the post-disco MTV fashion craze that compelled women to tease their hair, sport leather brassieres, and chew gum in public. David appeared younger than his thirty-five years yet he preferred the mature sensibilities of Highland Park women. They were less likely to get drunk on cherry vodka and throw up in your car.

David pointed to the sky. "There," he said. "The North Star. It's difficult to see in the city sometimes."

"Wow, you're right," she said. "I see it."

"It's called Ursa Major. That's Latin for 'who needs a compass.'"

The young woman's friends whistled and waved as they hurried across the street.

"That's funny," she said. "Ursa Major. I'll remember. Have a good one."

The clutch of women huddled like conspirators then went into the club. At the door David acknowledged Julio the bouncer, a weightlifter he knew from training at the gym. The DJ played Madonna's *Get Into the Groove* to the delight of the happy hour crowd. Men drank Lone Star beer and flirted with women who swayed to the beat and stirred straws through frozen Margaritas.

Noreen waited perched on a stool near the end of the bar with her legs neatly crossed beneath a tight black skirt. David recalled her sunny eagerness when they first met, how her fair skin revealed faint blue veins just below the surface. Noreen squared her shoulders when she saw him. She touched the delicate Celtic cross that hung from her neck then raised a cigarette to her lips. Beside her a flushed-face man in a finely tailored blazer flicked his lighter to life.

"Hello Noreen," David said.

The man was not pleased to see David. Noreen pursed her pink lips, exhaled smoke in a tight column then raised her bourbon and soda.

"David," she said. "This here's Charlie."

"It's Charles," the man said.

David focused on Noreen's cool gray eyes.

"You've been drinking," he said.

"It is happy hour." Noreen looked at Charles. "Guess I've had my share."

"And who are you?" Charles asked.

David refused to acknowledge him. Charles fingered his Rolex watch. A tense thirty seconds transpired as Noreen inhaled and exhaled then crushed her cigarette into the ashtray.

Noreen grabbed her drink. "Charlie," she said. "Thank you for the hospitality. David and I must tend to business."

They found a table away from the music. David pulled a check from his jacket and placed it on the table. Noreen slipped it into her purse without looking.

"Is that all of it?" she asked. "I don't have my reading glasses."

"Yes, two thousand," he said. "We're square."

"So you say." Noreen rapped a knuckle on the table. "I'm glad Travis helped you land a project and that you've made some money. Maybe your luck has turned. Maybe it was meant to be."

David had never been superstitious. He did not believe in luck or fortunetellers. When Noreen, or other women he knew, spoke of astrological signs or Mercury in retrograde he would nod agreeably and consider what he wanted for dinner. Although he gazed at stars and pondered the vastness of a chaotic universe he did not believe in a fate influenced by distant constellations. He didn't believe in much beyond himself. In high school he ran well enough to earn a track scholarship to NTSU in Denton, south of

Gainesville where he grew up. In college he met Noreen, but didn't consider this luck or as she liked to say, "Meant to be." They were both young and needed each other. That's just how it happened.

"I appreciate your help with the loan," he said. "Thank you."

"You're welcome." Noreen paused to light a cigarette. "Sometimes your pride is a devil that won't be denied."

"Please, don't start with that."

Noreen sipped her bourbon and puffed on the cigarette. "I can only hope that you've learned something along the way," she said. "That's all."

"Yes. I've learned not to date my ex-wife."

Noreen coughed. "That's a rich thing for you to say." Her voice strained. She extinguished the cigarette. "Is that what you call dating?"

"Noreen, I appreciate the loan. It was hard for me to ask, but I've paid you back. You know I'm grateful for everything. Let's not get personal."

"Personal?" Noreen's eyebrows went on tilt. "You're the one who mentioned dating. Our little one-night thing back in July should never have happened."

David flinched. He would not argue. Through his years with Noreen he had come to know the price of vulnerability. He recalled his shyness in college, how Noreen's apartment smelled of incense, burned toast and sex. He appreciated that Noreen encouraged him to finish business school and move with her to Dallas. He valued their love and that they had been the best of friends. He also knew how quickly she could turn.

"Drinking doesn't help anything," he said. "And the smoking is worse. What are you doing?"

"Whatever I damn well please." Noreen pushed the ashtray aside. "Right now my life suits me fine. I'm not the one slinking off to California."

"I'm not slinking anywhere."

Noreen took a drink and stared at David. "And why wouldn't you leave?" she said. "You have no one. Not me, not family, not anyone I know. I'm the one living out in Plano selling Mary Kay to make my mortgage. But if you want to live in California with the fruits and nuts, have at it."

David swallowed whatever protest he would mount and considered Noreen's verbal jabs added interest on the loan. He recalled an unsuccessful job interview in August. Frustrated, that afternoon he jogged in the heat around White Rock Lake. Distracted by a stray Beagle he tripped over a tree root. As he tumbled to the ground he experienced a moment of clarity in which he realized, through the yelp of a wayward hound, that he had nothing. With this realization he felt almost happy because he knew that he was free.

"You're right," David said. "I don't have anyone. I don't have a family or a home or a job in some cubicle. Once you leave the corporate grind there's no turning back. It's taken awhile to accept, but I would never say that I'm a loser. The truth of it, and what I would say, is that I am alone."

Noreen's gray eyes softened. "Seems you've always been lonely that way," she said. "I've done my best by you. But you're not a team player. Like when you worked in marketing at *The Morning News*. Your boss wanted to groom you for management. He even invited you to join Toastmasters."

David averted his eyes to the crowd at the bar. "You know I hate public speaking," he said. "I'd rather shovel wet cement."

"Right, because you're afraid of people. You'd rather be running circles around the lake or scribbling in your diary."

"It's a journal. There's a distinction. And running is therapy for me. At least I don't play golf. At least you weren't a golf widow."

"That's right," she said. "You don't play golf and you're certainly clever enough."

David stared into the lines of his open palms. "We've been over all of this," he said. "It never changes anything."

Noreen gnawed her lower lip. Pink lipstick marked the edges of her teeth. She drank the last of her bourbon and rattled the ice in her glass.

"I'm sorry you're wounded," she said. "I'm sorry you lost your parents. You've had some rough knocks, but aren't you a bit old to be going off to find yourself?"

David recoiled. He knew Noreen never intended to hurt anyone, but to mention his parents was an assault on his most vulnerable defenses. For a moment he couldn't breathe.

"We've said too much," he said. "Goodbye Noreen."

She reached across the table. Their eyes locked. David withdrew his hand and considered the difference between this moment and the first one they shared. He closed his eyes, embraced the passage of time and the ocean of experience that separated them. Noreen's image faded, her once dear face barely recognizable as she drifted toward a far horizon. The moment ended when a fresh bourbon and soda arrived on the table. David opened his eyes.

"It looked like you could use one of these," Charles said. He winked at Noreen then looked at David. "Sorry pal, nothing for you."

David rose to face Charles. "You picked the wrong time to

make that play," he said. "She's had enough."

Noreen reached for David's arm. "Please David," she said. "Don't do it. Don't make a scene."

David did not flinch.

Charles' face turned red. "And exactly who the fuck do you think you are?" he said.

Adrenaline coursed through David's body. He welcomed the sensation and recalled the instant he realized, like a stray animal, that he had nothing to lose. Now, in this moment, he embraced a rush of serenity and smiled at Charles as if he truly loved him.

"Back off," David said.

Charles' eyes grew wide. David clenched his fists. Charles hesitated then extended his arm and pushed. David struck Charles once in the stomach then followed with a right fist to the face that dropped Charles to the floor. Blood trickled from the corner of his mouth.

A crowd closed around them. Julio the bouncer wrapped his arms around David.

"Be cool, man," Julio said. "Just be cool."

Noreen knelt beside Charles and glared at David. "Damn you," she said. "What's your problem?"

The DJ played *Rock This Town* by the Stray Cats. Julio escorted David through the bar. He did not speak until they were outside and clear of the music.

"Charles is a dick," David said. "He wouldn't back off."

"Man, I believe you," Julio said. "But he's one of the owners. With guys like that you can't win."

"Fuck it," David said. "None of this matters. I'm leaving town in the morning."

"Good. That's for the best."

David stopped in front of his apartment to listen to the leaves stir in the live oak trees. Autumn leaves would eventually turn gold and brown and surrender to the change of season. He imagined a child at play beneath barren trees, oblivious to hunger or thirst, crushing dead leaves until evening came and his mother called him home. David remembered the chill of the night he lost his parents, how he became filled with the awareness of an undeniable void.

He examined the raw knuckles of his right hand and recalled what Uncle Buck had told him many years before, "A man's got to make a stand. And to know when to cut his losses." David understood what Uncle Buck had said. He understood what it meant, at last, to be moving on.

TWO

David maintained a deliberate pace as he drove west on Interstate-40 with what remained of his life loosely packed into a U-Haul trailer. The cloudless desert sky presented a postcard worthy sunset. He removed his aviator sunglasses and savored the fading tangerine light until it faded to black.

The Buick headlamps transformed the highway into the specter of an endless tunnel. The rhythm of the road and the blur of passing mile markers set his mind to wander. Thirty-five was not too old to find what he wanted. He was neither dead nor hobbled by the inevitability of middle age and whatever crises may ensue. The dull, steady beat of time had quickened into a great pounding like the heart of a mother giving birth to her first child. Time had delivered him into the slippery world of his dreams, onto the road to California and the haunting childhood memory of a sunny Santa Monica beach where he and his parents once walked. David recalled their laugher, the cool ocean breeze, and how seabirds hovered.

David's mother was a high school English teacher loved by her students. His father was a pharmacist who worked long hours, filled prescriptions and offered health advice to anyone who asked. The narrow drugstore aisles were stocked with sundries, soaps and shampoos, vitamins and remedies, racks of magazines and comic books. In the winter flu season David and his mother would often bring dinner to the drugstore in a picnic basket then return home so she could finish grading papers. David spent many evenings on the couch beside her with a *Flash, Fastest Man Alive* comic book or his *Weekly Reader*, falling asleep to the sound of her pen marking papers.

On a starry winter night in North Texas, only a few months after their California vacation, the Rangers called Uncle Buck from Highway 82. David remembered the bitter cold and how he collapsed when he heard the words.

"Your mom and dad are gone," Uncle Buck said. "They'll not be coming home."

David recalled the Fairview Cemetery and the cold gray afternoon. A winter wind carried the smell of red dirt and evergreen, the muffled sounds of sorrow. White rose pedals blew from bouquet-covered caskets and skipped across the frozen ground. He felt small among the crowd of students, friends and neighbors. He was only nine years old.

"Such a tragedy." He heard them say. "They were so young."

A preacher David did not know offered kind words and blessings then read from the book of Psalms. "How long, O Lord? Will you forget me forever? How long will you hide your face from me?" A final prayer was said and the caskets were lowered into the ground.

The mourners gathered around David, reached out to somehow soften the magnitude of his loss. Sadness swallowed him until he felt the reassuring weight of hands upon his shoulders. "Come along son," Uncle Buck said. "Let's go."

David's eyes grew tired. As the headlights pierced the darkness he thought about how, after his parent's death, he went to live with Uncle Buck, his father's older brother, and Aunt Mary. Good-hearted and thoughtful people, they had converted their three-story Victorian home into a bed and breakfast. Guests would come to admire the high ceilings and stained glass windows, antique furnishings and Tiffany lamps. Each morning the guests came down for country breakfast and conversation about the glory days of Gainesville cattle and Texas oil.

By the age of twelve, with his household duties done, David began to run. He entertained his own thoughts as he ran through the historic neighborhood, past the Bomber Bait Company and the State Theater, along California Street and the Butterfield stagecoach route. He ran on the brick streets around the Cook County Courthouse and on Commerce past the small shops and the drugstore where his father once worked.

In the beginning he would be forced to stop, heaving and gasping for air. But he ran until his stomach settled and his lungs stopped burning, until the strength of his heart allowed him to think he could run forever. As he ran he thought about comic book heroes like The Flash and Green Lantern, about their inner demons, the villains they challenged and the innocence they vowed to protect.

David parked the Buick near a row of eighteen-wheelers in an Arizona rest stop. He attempted to curl up in the front seat, soon realized he couldn't sleep and climbed out of the car. His breath formed small clouds. The night sky hung like a yawning canvas drawn tight across the desert. Here, far from a city, the heavens came alive. Stars danced and winked, pulsed energy out into a universe charged with light traveling since before his birth and before his parent's birth, fading remnants of life that once was.

David stretched, but the muscles of his back and shoulders refused to yield. He checked the padlock on the U-Haul. In the adobe style men's room, he paused at the sink for several long seconds and stared into the dullness of an aluminum mirror. The faint reflection revealed his fatigue. David rubbed the tips of his fingers across the metal surface, but it made no difference. Beneath his eyes hung shadows deepened from a lack of sleep and the uncertainty of his journey.

His body and mind ached for rest, for the blissful refuge of a lucid dream. David cranked the towel dispenser. Nothing. His muscles reacted instinctively. He smashed a fist into the empty dispenser. The sound echoed off the concrete block walls and set his ears to ringing. David closed his fist. Blood trickled from a gash in his knuckles. He washed the hand, nursed his wound and combed wet fingers through his hair.

Outside waited an elderly man with a leathered face and braided silver hair. David noted the concern in the old man's eyes. "It's okay," he said. "I slipped. That's all."

Diesel engines idled as David walked between the trucks. From a cab window a German shepherd bared its teeth and growled. The dog guarded while the master slept. David could not sleep. He stretched and looked back to the east and the expectation of a coming dawn. In Texas, the morning had already arrived, but that was well behind him. He started the Buick and drove west into the darkness.

THREE

The late September sun came up hot behind him as David crossed the Colorado River into the great California desert. With the trailer in tow he moderated his speed and by 10 a.m. approached Barstow where Interstate-40 merged with I-15, the route from Las Vegas to Los Angeles. The crossroads convulsed with commerce: The Diesel Time Truck Village and Love's Country Store, gas stations with mini marts, a Denny's Restaurant and Burger King, Super 8, and Days Inn motels.

A billboard announced construction of a designer outlet shopping center, "Opening Spring 1988." This scene could be anywhere in America, David thought, except this was the Mojave Desert, barren except for rocks and cacti and lizards, only civilized by the confluence of interstate traffic.

The weight of the trailer strained the engine. David did not run the air conditioner. Sweat glazed his neck and shoulders. Even in the heat, he admired the authenticity of the natural world, the emptiness of the bone-dry desert, the distant mountains, and the cloudless blue sky.

David wiped the sweat from his neck. He considered his former business partner Travis and how they lost their largest client, Flip's Home-Style Burgers, the year before. The corporate culture of mergers and acquisitions had fueled an economy of consolidation. What work remained did not support both of them. When the partnership ended David began to think about California, about trips he'd made on business and how the ocean breeze filled with possibilities. He struggled with the thought of leaving Texas until the moment of clarity when he tripped on the tree root at White Rock Lake.

David recalled, after his sudden realization, how quickly a project came to finance his move. Travis hired him to produce an industrial film segment on real estate development in Valencia, north of Los Angeles. During production David networked for jobs and found an apartment. He returned to Dallas, sold his furniture and packed what remained in the U-Haul trailer.

A convoy of tanker trucks thundered past and set the trailer to sway. David checked the rearview mirror and veered toward the shoulder. Beyond Barstow waited an expanse of baking desert. David took the last exit for fuel and breakfast.

The Wagon Wheel Diner sat between a Chevron station and an abandoned tourist store that resembled a teepee, the cone-shaped structure's bleached purple paint blistered by the sun. Gray dust from the gravel parking lot enveloped the car like a lowland fog. When the dust settled David locked the Buick and stared back across the highway into the late morning sun. Cars and trucks raced past. David squinted and wiped the sweat from his brow.

On the far side of the highway, through the dust and the rippled heat, David saw a small boy in a blue Hawaiian shirt. David took a step toward the highway. A truck roared by in the eastbound lane. The draft from the truck blew the boy's blond hair and lifted the tail of his shirt. The boy did not move or seem concerned. David checked the westbound lane. Another truck screamed past.

The way cleared. David removed his sunglasses and looked up and down the road. He rubbed the dust from his eyes, but the boy was gone.

The diner greeted him with an aromatic fusion of fresh-brewed coffee, fried bacon and disinfectant. Cold air blasted against the back of his neck. The place was empty except for a heavy-set man slumped over his breakfast at the far end of the counter. David noted the man's crew cut hair and Los Angeles Dodgers jersey wrinkled as if he had slept in it. In the men's room David washed the sweat and dust from his face and hands.

Sunlight sliced through the venetian blinds and glared off the countertop. David took a seat. The waitress approached with two pots of coffee.

"Name's Doris," she said. "Regular or unleaded?"

David didn't drink coffee. "Regular," he said.

Doris served his coffee with muscled forearms toned from years of pouring.

"Coffee's free with the special. $5.99 for two eggs, bacon, home fries and toast." Doris grinned. "Plus tip."

David smiled for the first time in days. "The special," he said. "Scrambled. Hold the butter. Hold the bacon. Substitute pancakes for the toast."

"Short stack's two-fifty extra."

Hunger and fatigue muted any interest in haggling. David had enough money to get where he was going. "Okay," he said. "That's fine."

A tanned face made Doris appear older. David guessed her to be about his age. The edges of her uniform were frayed. Gummed shoe soles squeaked against the polished linoleum floor as she pivoted for the kitchen.

David passed a spoon through the black coffee and recalled mornings in Aunt Mary's kitchen and the aroma of fresh-baked biscuits, scrambled eggs and Canadian bacon, waffles and pancakes. As an adolescent David would eat his fill, drink his milk and rarely speak a word. After breakfast he would help with the yard work, the laundry and cleaning. On warm summer days he'd often return to the arched window of his third-story bedroom. There he read from some of his mother's books or gazed across the elm trees and rooftops to watch mountains of cumulus clouds transform in the Texas heat.

David nursed his coffee and wondered about the boy on the highway. Doris returned with breakfast and filled David's cup.

"Anything else?" she asked.

"Yes, there is." David looked down the counter, past the heavyset man, into the light beaming through the blinds. "I saw a small boy next to the highway in a big blue shirt. Have you seen a boy like that this morning?"

Doris wiped the counter with a towel and stared at the highway. The wrinkles around her eyes deepened as she strained against the sun.

"Sorry darlin'. We don't get many kids in here even on a good day. Parents would rather take them to McDonald's for the Happy Meals."

"I wouldn't know."

"Don't worry yourself. Probably the Mojave sun dancing off the asphalt."

David ate his breakfast. Unlike the desert, in north Texas autumn was unmistakable. Leaves turned from green to yellow and gold and the wind came down cold and hard from the north. Days grew short, tree limbs barren and fallen leaves covered the ground with a carpet of maize and burnt sienna. In the desert autumn was the relentless sun, empty spaces and transient people passing through.

Like so many others, David was passing through. He had grown up fast it seemed, became a man running alone through the streets of Gainesville, through the wind and the rain, across the cinders alongside the tracks of the Katy Railroad, on frontage roads past the new Wal-Mart superstore and the Ford truck dealership. As he ran he would recall stories from the books his mother left behind. She had encouraged him to read at an early age and when he read those books he felt close to her knowing she had also turned those pages: *The Red Pony, Of Mice and Men, The Catcher in the Rye, The Red Badge of Courage, The Old Man and the Sea, A Tale of Two Cities, The Grapes of Wrath, A Farewell to Arms.*

He recalled his reluctance to turn the last page, to read the final paragraph, to say goodbye. After class in high school, while other teenagers cruised in their Chevy Novas and Ford Mustangs between the Dilly Dip and the Sonic drive-in, David ran for miles around the track and daydreamed about the stories of Hemingway, Fitzgerald and Steinbeck. He remembered his mother's tender touch and the care with which she turned each page.

The man from the end of the counter swiveled on his stool and walked to the cash register. David sipped his coffee, watched as the man searched his pockets. Doris waited until the man produced a rumpled bill. She opened the register to make change.

"Keep the rest," the man said. "It's not much, but you're welcome to it."

David noticed the man's unshaven face. A harmless guy probably down on his luck, David thought as he finished his pancakes. And with that the man approached.

"Excuse me, but are you headed for Los Angeles?"

David looked up into the round face. "You're not shy, are you?"

"Shyness doesn't pay," the man said. "Are you going my way?"

"Yes I am."

"Hey man, I could really use a ride." He shrugged, lowered his eyes to the floor. "I need to get back into town today."

"I've never given a ride to a stranger."

"Come on, man. I'm not that strange." He glanced around the empty diner. "No more than anyone else."

David spun on his stool. Breakfast was complete and his stomach full. He was tired of thinking. The solitude of the road had taken a toll. Something about the unkempt man made him want to laugh.

"Okay." David extended his hand. "I am David Bishop."

The man smiled. "Rocco Manelli," he said. "Glad to meet you."

They went out into the heat. Rocco waited beside the Buick. David folded the road map and lifted his Smith Corona from the floorboard of the passenger seat. He cradled the typewriter in his arms and secured a place in the trunk.

"Just so you know, Rocco Manelli is my stage name. I'm really Polish. You know, like Copernicus. I'm not ashamed of my heritage or anything, but no one could pronounce my name. An agent said I needed the right image. 'Rocco Manelli.' What do you think?"

"You don't look Italian." David walked to the front of the car. "Are you a prize fighter or a lounge singer?"

"No, man." Rocco pinched his thumbs and index fingers together in a clumsy gesture. "I'm a comedian."

David smiled. "That makes sense."

Rocco eased into the passenger seat. He wrenched his chin from side to side and surveyed the rack of clothes in the back seat.

"You have suits. Are you a business guy?"

A cloud of gray dust swept across the gravel parking lot. The last difficult years flashed through David's mind, the sluggish economy and the failed partnership with Travis. He didn't want to get into it.

"I used to be in business. Not as much anymore."

Rocco stretched the seat belt across his stomach.

"You're moving to Los Angeles?"

"I've always wanted to live there," David said. "My parents took me on vacation when I was a little kid. I loved everything about it, the ocean and the mountains, the palm trees and sunshine."

"Why now?"

David adjusted the side view mirror. "The opportunity for work," he said.

"Hey man, what happened to your hand?"

David examined the gash on his right knuckles. "It's nothing."

"Sorry for all the questions," Rocco said. "I had too much coffee. So, you got a job?"

The interrogation did not annoy David. "No. I'm keeping my options open."

"That's good," Rocco said. "You and everybody else."

The heat approached 100 degrees as David and Rocco turned south onto Interstate-15. The Buick strained under the burden of the trailer and two passengers. Heat reflected off the highway like mirrored slate. Northbound traffic appeared to float toward them on slick sheets, the highway a ribbon of mercury. They drove slowly across the desert toward the San Gabriel Mountains that separate the Los Angeles basin from the rest of North America. As they approached the mountains barbed wire and crooked wooden posts bordered the highway.

Rocco twisted in his seat. "Man, it is hot. I am sweating like a freaking sumo wrestler."

"Sorry Rocco, I can't run the air conditioner."

"I know, I know. What's this, a four-banger? Engine's pretty small to be pulling a trailer."

David wondered about Rocco, a sweating comedian with a belly too big for his seat belt. Normally, he would not have asked.

"Tell me if it's none of my business," David said. "How did you end up in Barstow?"

"Are you kidding? I don't mind." Rocco scratched his unshaven chin. "This guy Turner and me drove to Las Vegas to audition for a variety show at the Tropicana. His old Datsun got a flat. We missed the audition. To console ourselves we went through the Barbary Coast buffet line three times because, as you may have noticed, I love to eat."

"You'll drop a few pounds today."

"Man, you're right about that."

Rocco patted his stomach. He extended his right arm through the window, flattened his hand and let the air flow over it. A semi-trailer truck passed on the left and rocked the Buick. David checked the rearview mirror, clutched the steering wheel and hugged the right shoulder.

"So, what happened?"

"Turner insisted we sit down at this black jack table to soak up free drinks and try to win some money. We're lucky enough to play until we're both about trashed. They change dealers. The new one wiped us out in ten minutes."

"When the dealer changes and your cards turn, it's smart to move to another table."

Rocco opened his hand against the wind. "Yeah, but we were wasted. Thirty minutes later we're cruising the strip. The police busted us when Turner drove his Datsun onto the sidewalk in pursuit of a couple of young women dressed like hookers. I'm not saying they were hookers, but they looked the part. Turner is nuts. Believe me, those girls weren't that great."

Rocco withdrew his hand from the window. "I shouldn't hang out with Turner. He's trouble. Fortunately, the police acknowledged my innocence. I slept some in jail then I made Barstow hitching two rides. The last guy spotted me ten bucks for breakfast."

A succession of vehicles passed on the left. The Buick's temperature gauge approached red. David checked the mirror.

"What happened to your friend?"

"Turner? The booking clerk said he made a telephone call. Someone wired money to pay his due. They held him anyway. Probably needed to sober up. I couldn't wait around. With that guy anything could happen."

Interstate-15 widened. Rocco yawned, lowered his chin and nodded off. His head bobbed with the rhythm of the road. Every few minutes he snored. David continued a deliberate pace. The volume of traffic increased by mid-afternoon as they began the slow climb up toward the mountain pass. The incline increased. The engine strained. Rocco bolted upright when the load shifted hard to the back of the trailer. The Buick began to overheat. David turned on the emergency blinkers.

"Should we pull over?"

Rocco checked the dashboard gauges. "No. Don't stop," he said. "I think we're okay. Run the heater. That'll pull heat away from the engine."

This advice seemed to work. Their clothes became soaked with sweat as the Buick struggled. When they reached Cajon Summit the San Gabriel Mountains came into view. The mountains rolled off to the north and west like the shoulders of giants, heads bowed in reverence to the afternoon sun. Seduced by the beauty of the moment, David forgot about the heat and the traffic and the laboring car. In that instant all he knew was the majesty of the mountains and the deepening shadows, the realization he had arrived in California. He wanted to savor the moment, but that was impossible.

The Buick and trailer accelerated as the road swooped downward in a wide s-turn. The heater blasted. Emergency blinkers blinked. Cars and trucks roared past and honked their horns. The Buick picked up speed, faster down the mountain. The load in the trailer pitched forward and the car lurched hard to the right.

"Give it gas," Rocco shouted. "Whatever you do, don't hit the brakes. The trailer will flip. Give it gas."

David pressed the accelerator and gripped the steering wheel. Faster and faster they rolled downward into the shadows. Cars and trucks roared by and cut into the open lane ahead of them. The Buick swerved. The trailer swayed. Faster down the mountain. David's throat tightened, his mouth went dry. No time to think. No time to swallow. He clutched the steering wheel with a death grip and held on until they passed through the last curve and the road leveled out into the flatlands.

Rocco pressed his palms together in prayer, chanted something under his breath several times and clapped his hands. "That was a rush." He snapped the seat belt against his stomach. "Better than Mister Toad's Wild Ride. I'd go again."

Sweat dripped from the tip of David's nose. His heart pounded. "Not me," he said. "Once was enough."

Rocco provided directions as they merged from I-15 to I-10. The late afternoon traffic slowed to stop-and-go as they made their way through the seamless sprawl of suburban development, shopping malls and supermarkets, franchise restaurants and multi-screen movie theaters. Suburbs in the Texas heartland advanced on a comparable scale, but here development stretched across the flats and into the foothills where rows of new homes and retail complexes consumed the open land with an urgent sameness. Above the construction an auburn haze hung like a soiled curtain, obscured the mountains and the sky.

They continued west on I-10. When they neared downtown Los Angeles the last remnants of the setting sun disappeared behind the polished concrete and glass buildings. David was well past downtown when he exited and headed north on La Brea.

"Know where you're going?"

"I think so," David said. "The place I rented is off Sunset, through Laurel Canyon and up the mountain."

"That's great, man. You can drop me at Razor's Comedy Club. It's right on the way."

David drove north. He knew his way around town well enough, to and from the airport and production houses. On business trips he had enjoyed the perfect weather, the proximity of the ocean and the mountains, the distinction of cultural diversity.

They crossed Wilshire Boulevard, Sixth Street and Melrose Avenue. The shadow of night crept over the hills to the north. Magna-face outdoor bulletins beckoned with larger-than-life promises. Palm tree silhouettes swayed in the cool air. Traffic moved quickly when it moved. Pedestrians made their way along sidewalks past ethnic restaurants, retail stores and mini malls. At bus stops people waited and clutched their bundles. At La Brea and Santa Monica a couple begged, rattled change in their plastic cups as motorists stopped for the light.

When they reached Sunset Boulevard Rocco asked David to pull over. He shook David's hand then presented a sweat-stained calling card.

"I owe you, man." Rocco backed onto the sidewalk. "What a ride. I probably lost ten pounds. Call if you get bored or want to see a show. My number is on the back."

"Thanks," David said. "Take care of yourself."

David slipped the card into his shirt pocket grateful for the company, but doubtful he'd see Rocco again. Headed north on Laurel Canyon he passed the entrance to Mount Olympus and the Canyon Country Store. Lights across the hillsides sparkled as the Buick twisted and turned up the narrow streets of Lookout Mountain to his new place on Wonderland Avenue. The Buick struggled near the top as the incline became more severe. He parked in front of Mrs. Howell's garage. Best to let the engine cool off overnight, he thought.

David climbed out of the car weak-kneed and road weary. Mrs. Howell opened her door dressed in a leopard print housecoat with a matching turban. She seemed kind enough when David rented the place and he welcomed a kind word or two. She turned on a floodlight and stepped gingerly on the heart-shaped stones across her neatly trimmed lawn.

"Look what you've done." She scowled. Her hollow cheeks glowed. She thrust a crooked finger at the back wheel of the trailer. "You destroyed my delphiniums."

David walked to the back of the trailer. He'd only nipped a couple of plants.

"I'm sorry," he said. "It's dark. I couldn't see them."

"My gardener just planted these." Mrs. Howell shook her turbaned head. "Here you come and drive right over them."

"Really, I'm sorry. I need some sleep. It would be great if I could leave the trailer here tonight"

Mrs. Howell set her hands on her hips. "No. That's impossible," she said. "I won't have it. You can't leave the trailer on the street. Unload and move it."

At their previous meeting, when David presented the security deposit, Mrs. Howell had acted like peaches and cream. Now she stood defiant and recited the rules.

"There's no street parking. Your car goes beside the garage and never on my driveway. I pay for the water and utilities so keep your showers short. I'm sensitive to noise and never rent to people without proof of employment. I've made an exception in your case. I won't put up with any nonsense."

David managed a smile. She must be off her medications, he thought.

"That's fine." David unlocked the trailer. "Don't worry Mrs. Howell. Everything's going to be okay."

With an odd twist, Mrs. Howell gazed back into the floodlight toward her house then up into the boughs of the pine trees. She turned to David and wrapped her leopard print housecoat tight around her waist.

"I was a stunt double for Joan Crawford," she said. "A stunt coordinator once told me 'everything would be okay' right before I fell off a balcony and broke my hip. The director cut the scene."

"That's tough," he said.

Mrs. Howell handed David a set of keys. "Enough chit-chat. Get busy and move the trailer off the property. And for God's sake, be quiet."

"Yes, of course."

"Welcome to Los Angeles."

Mrs. Howell turned and navigated the heart-shaped stones like an egret wading through a marsh.

"Yes," David repeated under his breath. "Welcome to Los Angeles."

David unloaded the trailer and thought about the moment he decided to go, how any burden had slipped from his shoulders and he could run full out for the sheer joy of moving in a new direction. But now, carrying boxes up the wooden stairway, he felt the weight of each load, especially his mother's books.

After the final trip David took a shower and savored the comfort of the steaming water. The muscles in his back and neck relaxed. For two nights he had attempted sleep curled up in the front seat of the Buick, but tonight he could stretch out on his air mattress. He dressed and opened a box of books, welcomed Albert Camus, John Steinbeck and Anton Chekhov.

In another box he found a framed 5 x 7 image he placed in

the tiny window above the kitchen sink. His father took the photograph of David and his mother as they waded in the surf near Santa Monica pier, his father's shadow visible in the foreground. David remembered the cold water, how the wet sand sucked at his feet, how tightly his mother held his hand.

The Buick overheated on the way down Lookout Mountain. David turned up the heater. He left the trailer at a U-Haul dealer on Melrose then stopped at a Union 76 station on Sunset to let the engine cool and top the radiator with water. David kicked a tire. The trailer was too much for a 1,600-mile trip. He should have known better.

Red taillights on Sunset flowed westward and disappeared beneath an illuminated billboard. The Marlboro man dominated the intersection, an American icon of god-like irony. The Marlboro man stared down at David, smoked with immunity and the promise of self-determination.

Exhaust fumes mixed with the cool damp air. David checked the radiator then started up the mountain. His stomach growled. He had forgotten about food, about his last meal, and stopped at the Canyon Country Store. Hunger made him edgy and tight. He bought bottled water, orange juice, bananas, apples and bagels, the makings of a simple breakfast. He grabbed a bag of Famous Amos chocolate chip cookies. In the parking lot he ate a banana then drove with the windows down. The street twisted and narrowed near the top where homes on either side of the road began to turn off their lights.

David parked beside the garage. With paper bag in hand he was drawn up along a path through a Japanese garden and stopped on the dirt fire road that crested the mountain. To the south rolling hills and treetops obscured the hazy city lights. To the north spread the San Fernando Valley with its streets lit up like runways stretching north and east until they reached the foothills.

On a ridge forty feet away stood a fence post crowned by a strange shape. David moved closer, his footsteps muted in the dust. The hulk perched motionless except for a head that surveyed the mountainside with great precision. David felt invisible in the darkness. He took another step. The owl glared with fierce yellow eyes. The raptor spread its wings to full width, pushed off the post and sailed down into the valley without a sound.

FOUR

David met Richard Knox at Quincy's Snack Shack on Western Avenue near Korea Town. President of Knox Consultants, a public relations agency, Richard offered David work if Quincy's became a client. They agreed to have lunch at the restaurant before the presentation.

The young man behind the counter formed his words carefully. "Pardon me," he said. "Could you repeat the order?"

Richard Knox bristled and turned to David. "Can you believe they hire people who don't understand English?"

The manager approached. "Is there some problem?"

David preempted Richard. "We're having a difficult time deciding what to order. That's all."

The manager surveyed the bins of condiments and utensils then went back into the kitchen.

"Thank you sir," the young man said. "This is my first day taking the orders. I am nervous."

"You're welcome," David said. "You're doing fine."

Richard paid the bill and they settled in a booth at the front of the restaurant so Richard could watch over his new Jaguar XJ6.

"I don't like parking my car in this neighborhood," Richard said. "I don't like parking it outside my garage."

Of average size, Richard Knox possessed an uneven smile and

the pampered aging features of a man in his early fifties. His thinning black hair was slicked back into a short ponytail. The fashion conscious man's mullet, David mused to himself noting Richard's Armani suit and diamond signet ring.

When the server brought their food Richard tucked paper napkins into his shirt collar and explained how Quincy started with one drive-up window on Wilshire Boulevard. Now thirty-six Snack Shack locations served barbecued ribs and beef brisket, chicken and hamburgers.

Richard lowered his chicken sandwich and wiped sauce from his fingers. "I despise eating with my hands," he said.

"Barbecue is supposed to be messy," David said. "It's part of the experience." He tucked his necktie inside his shirt and sampled a sparerib. "Excellent sauce."

"They've done a few things right. But this down-home country thing is behind the curve. They need an identity overhaul. You'll see when I make my presentation. They're going to love it."

It was too late to make adjustments or excuses. Not knowing Quincy, David accepted this was Richard's pitch to win or lose.

"My partner Travis and I produced the Flip's Home-Style Burgers commercials for four years," David said. "Our campaign increased sales every year. We won ..."

Richard cut him off. "Swell, but they sold the business. Today, keep it simple. Give a quick set up and I'll pitch the concepts. Don't say anything about where you've been. If I get the account, I'll need help managing the work and you'll have a job. Okay?"

David swallowed his pride and noted the restaurant interior, the wooden tables and chairs, the working-class customers eating burgers and steak fries, baked beans and apple pie. When he watched people eat David often imagined a grazing bovine heard, jaws grinding, tails swatting flies, heads lowered into their food with mindless contentment. If people could only see how they ate, he thought.

After lunch David and Richard took turns in the men's room to wash their hands and straighten their neckties. When David got into the Jaguar the smell of fine leather filled the car.

"This is a beautiful automobile," David said.

Richard adjusted the climate control then checked the vanity mirror for chicken lodged in his teeth. "You should snag one," he said. "L.A. women love it."

Noreen had driven an older Jaguar, a source of contention in their marriage. David knew about classic Jaguar beauty and performance, the questionable reliability and high maintenance.

At Quincy's corporate office David and Richard waited for almost an hour. Richard checked his watch several times. A buzzer eventually sounded and they were escorted down a hallway lined with file cabinets into the executive office.

Quincy was an enormous man with red hair and a freckled complexion. Much darker than his face, the bulbous nose appeared to have been broken many times. Quincy sat behind a conference table stacked with computer-generated reports, assorted restaurant trade magazines and *The Wall Street Journal*.

An impressive woman with thick silver hair, Quincy's wife Alice smiled as she made the introductions then asked the secretary to hold their calls.

"Well boys." Quincy slapped a plastic ruler into his open hand. "Alice says you got something to show us."

"Yes sir." Richard forced a smile. "It's a pleasure to be here. At

Knox Consultants we have a solid reputation for creative marketing solutions. I'm confident you'll be impressed. David."

David wasn't enthusiastic about improvisation, but committed to do his part.

"We don't have to tell you about competition in the restaurant business," David said. "Consumers have many choices. It's tough, but essential to create opportunities to refresh your product line and service offerings, increase market share through upsell and broadening your customer base."

Quincy and Alice exchanged looks. Alice made notes on a legal pad.

"Richard has developed some creative concepts," David continued. "Our objective here is to build on your considerable success with Quincy's Snack Shacks, increase brand awareness and leverage customer loyalty."

Quincy placed the ruler on top of the computer printouts and tugged at his nose. "Okay." He snorted. "How do we do that?"

Richard seized the presentation boards. "Knox Consultants has won many awards," he said. "And Alice said you were open to entertaining new ideas."

"Always open for ideas," Quincy said. "Every time a customer walks into one of our restaurants, it's a new idea. Let's see what you got."

Richard lifted the flap of the first board to reveal Mr. Q's trademark logo: a letter Q with a beard, a smile and a chef's hat.

"For many years this has personified your brand. I think it's time to break new ground and introduce a new look. It's time to take your brand to the next level."

Quincy and Alice sat stone-faced.

"I propose expanding your budget and advertise exclusively on television and radio." Richard paced a few short steps. "Why is cigarette advertising banned from broadcast? Because television and radio are the most effective means to deliver compelling messages people cannot forget."

Proposing budget increases was never wise, David thought. Quincy resembled a lion prepared to pounce on prey.

"I know we can do better." Richard turned the next board to reveal a cheerful pig peeking through the letter Q, beneath the logo: *Quincy's World Famous Food.*

Quincy began to speak. Richard raised his hand. "Before you say anything, let me present the television commercials. I'm not suggesting real celebrities. We'll use actors who look like they would be famous. We'll have fun with it."

The storyboards featured renderings resembling Sylvester Stallone, Madonna and Eddie Murphy. Each commercial featured a celebrity-like character and concluded with the animated pig logo graphics. Richard sang the closing jingle with conviction: "You know who, eats at Q's."

Quincy and Alice studied the renderings. David didn't know if they would laugh or applaud, if he should wait quietly or run.

"I appreciate what you've done here, Mr. Knox." Quincy squeezed his nose and breathed deeply. "But do you know how much it costs to change signage for thirty-six locations?"

Richard straightened his tie. David eyed the door.

"You don't have to do everything overnight," Richard said. "But this isn't just about the logo. It's about creating the right image. The world loves celebrity."

"Mr. Knox, have you eaten in one of our restaurants?"

"Well, yes I have."

"Had our rib dinner?"

Richard's tanned face faded. "No, I'm sorry. I don't eat red meat."

Quincy's eyes widened.

"I've had your spareribs," David said. "Your sauces are delicious. I sampled all three: mild, hot and triple-x. You could market the sauces as stand alone products."

Quincy nodded agreement, picked up the ruler and slapped it against the stack of reports. "Exactly the point," he said. "Our sauce is great. Our customers lick their fingers. They don't lick their fingers before they eat. So, it must be the sauce."

Richard regrouped. "Mr. Quincy, I understand. These are only ideas. If you see something you like I can expand on it. If not, I can change it. Tell me what you need."

"What we need is a vacation." Quincy narrowed his eyes on Richard. "You help with that?"

Richard buttoned his suit. "No. I'm not in the travel business."

"And we're not in show business." Quincy relaxed into the squeaky chair. Alice stopped taking notes. "This is a small company that got bigger because we treat people right and serve great food. We've had eight straight profitable quarters and it is not because of advertising. Mr. Knox, we appreciate your time."

Alice opened the door. "Thank you Mr. Knox. Mr. Bishop," she said. "We appreciate you stopping by."

Richard fumbled with the boards. "What about next steps? When should we get back together?"

Quincy swiveled in his chair and reached for the telephone. "Alice has your number," he said over his shoulder. "If we decide to make a change, Alice will call you."

The afternoon sun was low in the west when Richard and David reached the parking lot. "They're fools." Richard snarled and unlocked the Jaguar. "I should have known they were a waste of my time. I thought it would be a snap."

David contained his disappointment. "It's rarely that easy," he said.

Richard reached for his lip balm. "They're just ignorant rednecks."

The only thing worse, David thought, would have been if Quincy had approved the concepts. In that case he was committed to work with Richard Knox. David didn't consider himself a redneck. He respected people who worked with their hands, like Uncle Buck and Aunt Mary and others, and considered rednecks a vulgar slur like any other. The so-called rednecks David knew wouldn't hesitate to say hello or help a stranger or to share whatever food or good fortune they had.

Richard drove to the Quincy's restaurant. David had left the Buick parked on Western Avenue. Nothing was said until they arrived.

"Thanks," David said. "For including me in the pitch."

"Forget about Quincy's," Richard said. "I'm sure something will shake loose for you."

After Richard drove off David sat behind the wheel of the Buick for several minutes holding a $54 parking ticket. He had cleared $5,000 on the Valencia film project. Now it was early October and he was in Los Angeles with few prospects. Caution would stretch what he had maybe three months.

David went into the Quincy's restaurant to use the men's

room. He returned to find his car keys hanging from the ignition, doors locked and windows rolled tight.

"That's perfect," he said. "Now what?" Muscles contracted, he slammed his open hand on the roof.

The sun descended. Along this stretch of Western were small shops, a liquor store, and a discount futon and furniture outlet with heavy security gates pushed to the sides. Signs painted in Spanish hung in windows, others with Korean symbols. Rush hour traffic belched exhaust. The breeze scattered discarded yellow handbills that tumbled into his ankles. Down the sidewalk women at a bus stop clutched bags from the 99¢ Store.

The alley across the street had stacks of flattened pasteboard boxes beside the dumpsters. Fresh graffiti tainted brick walls: WEER PIST, JESUS LIVES, FUCK U2. Two men in soiled clothing drank from bottles wrapped in brown paper bags. Down the block a group of tattooed youth in chinos and tank tops smoked cigarettes in front of an electronics store.

A kind woman at a Korean dry cleaner provided David with two wire coat hangers. "Please come back," she said. "Bring suits. Bring shirts."

The wire hangers twisted easily. David worked on the passenger side window for five minutes. Light faded. The boys down the block watched, entertained by David's lack of skill. He managed to extend the hangers toward the dangling keys when the LAPD patrol car pulled behind the Buick.

"Trying to steal that car?" the first officer asked.

"No, sir," David said. "I locked myself out."

The second officer exited the car and slipped a baton into his utility belt. "This isn't exactly your neighborhood," he said. "Are you lost?"

"No officer. I had a meeting nearby."

"Let's see your I.D."

He examined David's Texas license and returned it. A wrist rested on his gun. He scanned the street while his partner grabbed a locksmith tool. The officer slid the metal device between the window and the door, yanked three or four times and released the latch.

"You're lucky we came along," he said. "It's getting late."

The boys and the men in the alley across the street had vanished. Pedestrians hurried along. Women waited at the bus stop. Shopkeepers closed their security gates.

"I get the picture," David said.

"Good. You'll live longer that way."

When David returned to the top of Lookout Mountain, he saw Mrs. Howell on the ridge above the Japanese garden watching the sunset with a neighbor couple. He climbed the path and joined them.

"Isn't it wonderful?" the neighbor said. "Look at the colors."

The afternoon onshore breeze had cleared the haze to reveal a thin layer of clouds reflecting shades of pink and orange. On the horizon a sliver of the Pacific shined like polished granite.

"Yes, beautiful," said David. "Sunsets in Texas are like this. Except, of course, there's no ocean."

The neighbor couple embraced. It was almost dark when the four of them started back down the path. The neighbors turned toward their home. Mrs. Howell struggled on the slope. David offered his arm, but she refused.

"Have you found work?" she snapped.

"Not yet," he said. "But I'm learning my way around town."

When they reached her yard, Mrs. Howell stepped onto the heart shaped stones. "Don't waste time being a tourist," she said. "A man needs a job."

FIVE

An uneventful week passed. David settled into the garage apartment as a sense of despair crept over him. One evening he intended to rise for an early start, but slept until noon. When he rolled off the air mattress he devoured a can of tuna then showered and dressed. At the Canyon Country Store he bought *The Los Angeles Times*, turned past news of corporate downsizing and looming stock market corrections to the classified ads.

David studied the job listings and noted possibilities. Back at the apartment he opened his journal and wrote how the sunny California weather contrasted with a growing financial unease, how street people on Hollywood Boulevard panhandled to survive, how the Pacific Ocean transformed from blue to green to gray throughout the day.

He closed the journal and focused on the ceiling tiles. The walls around him seemed too close. It was eight o'clock in the evening when he dialed the telephone.

A sleepy voice answered, "Uh, hello."

"Rocco, this is David Bishop."

"Uh, David Bishop?" There was a long pause. "Oh yeah, David, the highwayman with the rolling sauna."

"Were you asleep?"

"No, man." Rocco yawned. "I was catnapping. Best time to catch me. Otherwise, I'm not here. Hang on a second."

The receiver rattled against a hard surface. David heard running water and a voice humming *Stairway to Heaven*. In a minute Rocco returned to the telephone.

"Thanks for hanging on. I'm awake now."

"How's your comedy career?"

"In development. How about you? Heard any good jokes?"

"Not me. I'm no comedian."

"Stop right there," Rocco said. "Everyone is a comedian. I know how to get your creative juices flowing and it doesn't cost a dime."

David braced for a sales pitch. "I have no interest in multi-level marketing."

"No, man. This isn't about money. I'm talking about your life. We're starting a comedy workshop at Razor's. You'll laugh your ass off. Norman Razor teaches the class himself. There's a free preview this Sunday."

"I don't know."

"Come on man. What have you got to lose?"

A fair question, David thought. David scanned the small room, at his air mattress bed, and the boxes of books stacked along the wall. He didn't have much.

At five o'clock the next Sunday afternoon David met Rocco on Sunset Boulevard near the side entrance of Razor's Comedy Club. A crowd of about twenty odd people milled about and talked, smoked cigarettes or scribbled in notebooks.

"Hey, David. Glad you showed." Clean-shaven, Rocco was more animated than the day they met in Barstow. "How you doing?"

"Not bad," David said. "But what's the story with this class? I thought you were already a comedian."

"I am. Norman Razor, however, is the guru of stand-up comedy. This is all part of my continuing education. I'm his assistant." Rocco lowered his voice to a whisper. "I get free coaching and stage time."

David laughed at Rocco's delivery. "So, you're working on commission?"

"Not much to it. The workshop sells itself."

Rocco waved to new arrivals then rested his arm on David's shoulder. "Hey man, I wouldn't sell you. This is for fun, honest. If you want, we'll hang out afterwards. You can buy me a beer."

At the appointed time Rocco unlocked the door. Hopeful comedians filed into the room and sat in folding chairs in front of the stage. David took a seat in the back near the door while Rocco ushered the crowd. Once everyone was settled Rocco checked for stragglers then shut the door and distributed a flyer and questionnaire. A quiet tension filled the room like the first day of high school. David never considered himself funny and had no interest in performing. Minutes past as David and the others completed the questionnaires.

Knuckles tapped against the door. "Hey, open up," a faint voice called. "Let me in."

Rocco and the students looked at David and the door.

"Should I open it?" David asked.

Rocco grinned. "Wait a minute," he said. "Let's see how bad they want it."

Knuckles tapped again. "Come on, open up," a female voice

shouted. "I know you're in there."

Rocco stroked his freshly shaved chin. "Okay," he said. "Let her in."

David opened the door.

"Thank you," the woman said. She smiled when she looked at him. "What took you so long?"

Her voice struck a common chord. The familiar accent hung in the air with a trace of her perfume, something soft and floral. Dressed in blue jeans and a suede jacket, she approached the stage with a self-assured stride, blond hair falling freely past her shoulders.

"You're late babe," Rocco said.

The woman dropped her oversized purse to the floor with a thud and took a seat on the front row. "Babe yourself, Rocco." She turned toward the audience and flashed a blue-eyed smile. "Sorry everyone. Hollywood traffic. You know the drill. I got here as fast as I could."

David sank into the shadows at the rear of the room struck by an overwhelming recognition. He had never seen the woman before, but the tenor of her voice and Ingrid Bergman features seemed as familiar as his own reflection. Instinctive male impulses channeled blood away from his brain. He resisted the temptation to fantasize about sweeping her up in his arms like a testosterone-crazed caveman.

"Hello, hello." A tall man burst through a curtain and walked onto the stage. Strands of wild hair escaped from beneath a black Los Angeles Kings cap. He stopped under the spotlights and grabbed the microphone.

"So, do you think you're funny?"

A few of the students replied. "Yeah, we're funny."

"I don't believe you." The man cupped a hand behind an ear. "Let's do that again. Let me hear you."

"Yes," the group responded. "We think we're funny."

"Good, very good. First you have to believe it, then we'll make it happen." He assessed the room. "Welcome to our stand-up workshop, the Cutting Edge of Comedy. I'm Norman Razor and this, in case you are unaware, is the opportunity of your life."

Razor pointed to a short, chubby man in the front row with a balding head and thick glasses.

"Hello, what's your name?"

"El-el-elmer," he stuttered.

"Very good. Elmer, we love cartoon characters. Come up and tell us about yourself."

"Uhhh, uhhh. I don't know. I'm not sure what to say."

"Elmer, this is your chance. Are you going to take it?"

Norman Razor retreated to a director's chair at the edge of the stage. The microphone stood beneath the spotlights. The room waited. Elmer rose from his chair.

"Let's hear it for Elmer." Norman clapped his hands. "Come on, show him some love."

The students applauded. Elmer's hands trembled as he grabbed the microphone. He squinted against the spotlights. Thick lenses magnified the angst in his eyes. David and the others held their collective breath.

Elmer's face turned red. "I'm kind of a klutz," he said.

They laughed.

"I'm so nervous." Elmer's expression shifted from anxiety to embarrassment. "I don't know why I'm doing this. Except, I'm thirty-two and my mom still calls me her little cowboy."

The room erupted with laughter.

"I'm so nervous," he said. "I think I wet my pants."

Everyone laughed. Norman stood next to Elmer and clapped his hands.

"That was great," Norman said. "Thank him."

David and the others applauded. Rocco whistled through his teeth.

"How do you feel now?" Norman asked.

"Great." Elmer beamed with joy. "I feel really great. Thanks Mr. Razor."

Elmer hopped off the stage. Amazed by the transformation he witnessed, David considered the courage involved with the risk of public humiliation.

Norman Razor tipped his cap. "Comedy is more than telling jokes," he said. "Comedy is what our friend Elmer just demonstrated. Comedy is about making a leap into the unknown. It's about embracing your self. If your self is funny, and I believe life is inherently funny, then you can make people laugh. What is better than that?"

The students applauded. Rocco whistled.

"Now, I'd like to introduce a very funny fellow, a semi-irregular here at Razor's and a certified graduate of the Cutting Edge of Comedy Workshop. Please welcome Rocco Manelli."

Rocco thrust himself onto the stage greeted by thunderous applause. "Thanks Norman. Thank you. Wow, you guys are great. Last time I heard applause like that was when I got evicted from my last apartment." Rocco rolled his eyes. "There were no pets allowed. I was lonely. So, I got a flea circus. A big flea circus."

The room laughed. David shook his head, impressed by Rocco's command of the stage.

"The flea circus made me feel at home. Even when the glass broke." Rocco scratched his chest. "My mother worked in the circus, as the bearded lady. Fortunately, my father loved hairy women. As a child I was confused by television commercials. I got a headache and sucked on an Alka Seltzer. My parents found me foaming at the mouth. Made me get rabies shots, just in case I was lying."

David and the others laughed and applauded. Rocco took a bow.

"Thank you. Thank you. I could go on, but this is your time. So, why don't each of you come up and tell us something about yourself. Who's next?"

Everyone sat fixed in their chairs, arms folded across their chests. David's heart raced. He pressed his chair against the wall. Rocco shaded his eyes from the lights.

"Okay, I'll pick someone." Rocco looked down at the first row. "Sarah, why don't you come up? Everyone please welcome Ms. Sarah Fleming."

Her name was Sarah. She was not afraid. As David watched her step onto the stage his primal instincts yielded to rational admiration. Sarah bowed gracefully.

"I'll be brief. My name is Sarah. I'm normally punctual so please forgive my tardiness. I teach special needs education, which is similar to my relationships with men. I want it to be special, but I get an education instead."

The women laughed. David understood what Sarah had said. He'd heard this many times, a common complaint among single women, but his understanding ran deeper than her words or familiar accent. As he watched Sarah he experienced a profound awareness as if he had known her his entire life.

"Comedy is great for building self-awareness," Sarah said. "Being on stage is better than a twelve-step meeting. Here, we get a lot more laughs. I hope you come back. My name is Sarah. Thanks for letting me share."

The prospective comedians applauded. Sarah skipped off the stage. Rocco thanked her then called the next person. Norman Razor sat to the side and sipped coffee from a thermos. David didn't think the people were necessarily funny, but everyone had some peculiar point of view or weird story.

Finally, Rocco peered into the back of the room. "Hey David, you coming up?"

The question startled him. David had only come to observe. Everyone turned and looked at him. Fear clutched his throat. Suddenly, he couldn't breathe. He didn't consider himself amusing and didn't crave attention. Now the room watched and waited. He could have refused. He could have stayed put, but then Sarah Fleming smiled with expectation and in a few fleeting moments David found himself on the stage.

A deep circular breath filled his lungs. David attempted to look at the audience, but the intensity of the spotlights obscured everything. He fumbled with the microphone.

"Hello, I'm David Bishop."

His voice cracked. His mouth went dry. His knees weakened. He dropped the microphone, bent to retrieve it and banged his head on the stand.

"Damn." David grabbed his forehead. The students laughed.

"Obviously, I've never done anything like this."

Fear loosened its grip. David took another breath. "Many of you speak like this is group therapy. I guess that's healthy. I guess that's better than staying home and scooping cat litter."

A few people chuckled. David thought about growing up in Texas.

"When I recall my childhood, I'm grateful I wasn't forced to take accordion lessons. Polka music can cripple a child. Those accordions are heavy."

Norman Razor sprang onto the stage and clapped vigorously. "Okay. Good stuff," he said. "David. Rocco. Everyone. Good work. You're a great group. The workshop begins a week from Tuesday from seven to ten o'clock. I hope everyone participates. We'll have a great time."

The students applauded. Norman Razor consulted with prospects. David waited while Rocco and Sarah chatted with other students. When everyone was acknowledged they headed for the door.

David's eyes met Sarah's. "You're pretty funny," he said.

"You would know." Sarah smiled. "You're a natural. Great deadpan delivery."

"Deadpan?"

"Right, like that. You know, understated, dry."

Rocco wrapped his arms around David and Sarah. "Speaking of dry. David is buying me a beer. Want to join us?"

"Sure," Sarah said. "Where?"

"Barney's Beanery. I'll ride with David and show him the way."

"Okay," she said. "See you there."

David turned to Rocco. "You don't have a car?"

"No," Rocco said. "But I'm working on it."

They piled into the Buick. Rocco asked to stop at a 7-Eleven. David parked, his mind consumed with thoughts of Sarah. When Rocco returned he cranked down the window and opened a pack of Marlboro Lights.

"Mind if I smoke?"

"Yes I do," David said. "It stinks up the car."

"Okay, that's cool." Rocco tucked a cigarette behind his ear and stretched the seatbelt across his stomach. "So, what do you think?"

"She's amazing. Bright. Funny. I think I'm in love."

"Are you insane? I'm talking about the workshop."

"I'm talking about Sarah."

Rocco shook his head. "You've lost it, man. I've known Sarah for a good while. We're buddies. She's great and all that, but you're wasting your time."

"I know how I feel."

"Get a grip, man. You just met her. Besides, Sarah's a Hollywood woman. They'll roast your cashews. I wouldn't lie about something that important."

Traffic on Santa Monica Boulevard flowed like columns of a conscripted army marching toward daily rations. David circled the block around Barney's Beanery three times before he found a parking space. As they walked up the sidewalk Rocco lit his cigarette and stopped to admire a couple of Harley-Davidson motorcycles.

Rocco approached a man in a leather vest. "That's a fine looking bike," he said.

"You gotta ride?" the biker asked.

"No," he said. "Not at the moment."

Rocco offered the man a cigarette. For a few minutes David watched the westbound traffic headed toward Beverly Hills. Rocco's banter with the biker continued. David went inside.

In the barroom a thick layer of smoke hung three feet from the ceiling. The crowd roared with conversation as Jim Morrison sang *Riders on the Storm*. David made his way through the patrons, acknowledged inviting glances from a few women and men.

He pressed his way through the bar and found Sarah in a back room. She surveyed a pool table, chalked her cue with one hand and sipped a Margarita on the rocks. Her opponent, an athletic young man in a Nike T-shirt, slouched against a wall.

"You work fast," David said.

Sarah winked, set her drink aside then banked the four-ball cleanly in the side pocket. Her bridge was solid, her stroke firm.

"Nice shot," the young man said.

Sarah made the six-ball with a delicate touch down the rail. She didn't move her eyes from the table.

"David," she said. "This is Ed."

Ed watched Sarah work the table. She made the nine-ball, lined up the eight and rolled it in the side pocket.

Ed slipped his cue stick into the wall rack. "Good run."

"Thanks for the game," she said.

"No problem."

Ed lit a cigarette and walked into the bar.

"You're good," David said. "Want another game?"

Sarah laid her cue stick on the table. "Not tonight," she said. "I like to quit while I'm ahead."

The room was warm. Sarah removed her jacket, the sleeveless blouse revealed well-toned arms.

"The way you shoot pool," David said. "I would have guessed you had a tattoo."

Sarah raised an eyebrow. "Who says that I don't?"

Rocco slapped David on the back. "I warned you to watch out for her," he said then turned to Sarah. "Need a drink?"

"One is plenty," she said. "I work in the morning."

Rocco asked a waitress to bring two Budweiser's. They took a corner booth. The waitress returned with their beer. David paid the tab.

Rocco raised his bottle. "Here's to comedy."

Sarah licked the last bit of salt from the edge of her glass. "Here's to friends."

David countered, "Here's to tattoos the sun never sees."

They laughed. David listened as Sarah and Rocco recounted the pitfalls of living in Hollywood, a subject he was learning fast enough. Barney's ceiling and walls were covered with auto license plates from across the country. The symbols of relinquished roots formed a collective memorial to rusted metal and westward migration. Sarah said she was from West Texas, but David knew that. The accent betrayed her. An education major from Texas Tech in Lubbock, she had taken Norman Razor's workshop before.

"You want to be a comedian like Rocco?" David asked.

"Hey man." Rocco's tone was playful. "I don't like the way you said that."

Sarah stroked Rocco's hand as if he was a dog. "I don't want to be like Rocco." Her voice softened. "I'm a singer. I used to be uncomfortable in front of an audience, especially between songs. The workshop is fun and helps me relax. It also helps at work."

"You're a teacher?" David asked. "You mentioned education."

"I work at a small private school in Los Feliz," she said. "I teach music and vocals. Meager pay, but I love working with my kids."

Rocco downed his beer. "She's lucky, you don't get many hecklers in grade school."

Sarah checked her watch. "Sorry boys, I must leave. Early day tomorrow."

She finished her Margarita and scooted out of the booth. David held her jacket. She slipped her arms in the sleeves.

"A gentleman," she said. "How nice."

"Would you like a walk to your car?"

"Oh brother." Rocco moaned. "I'm going to be sick."

Sarah sneered at Rocco. "Thanks David," she said. "But I can handle it. Good night."

She walked away. Rocco set his elbows on the table and folded his hands as if prepared to bless a meal.

"David, I hate to say this."

"What?"

"No, I probably shouldn't."

"Come on."

Rocco sighed. "I think Sarah might like you."

"Really? So give me her telephone number."

"Don't be lame. You should've asked her."

"Come on. I didn't have the chance."

Rocco shook his head. "Hey man, it's not done. Besides, you have to wait. If you press your case, you'll blow it."

"What do you suggest?"

"Take Razor's workshop."

David scoffed. "This is such a con."

"Do the workshop. You'll get to know Sarah and see where it

goes. You'll have a blast. Like I said, you have nothing to lose."

Rocco tilted his empty bottle and made a sad face. Amused and engaged, David ordered another round of beer.

"Thanks man, I appreciate this," Rocco said. "I am so broke."

"I suppose you're hungry, too?"

Rocco slapped his belly. "Are you kidding? I'm always prepared to eat."

The waitress brought their beer. Rocco ordered a double cheeseburger, fries and baked beans. David requested a large bowl of chili and a tossed salad. Neither of them hesitated once their food arrived. As they ate David thought about how Rocco resembled Jumbo Jefferson, an offensive lineman he knew in college, who could eat a hamburger in two bites, drink a bottle of catsup on a dare, anything for a laugh. One day in the cafeteria Jumbo choked on a chicken bone and crashed to the floor, kicked chairs and wheezed for air. Everyone thought it was a prank until he turned blue. Six guys held Jumbo while one of the athletic trainers performed an emergency tracheotomy with a steak knife.

Rocco devoured the last few fries. "Man, I appreciate this," he said. "I've been delivering flowers for my Vietnamese friend Don Loc. The work's more off than on. I was really hungry tonight."

"You don't have a car," David said. "How can you deliver flowers?"

"They have a truck." Rocco lit a cigarette. "Delivering flowers is a risk-free job. Even gangbangers won't hassle you when you're holding a dozen roses?"

David thought about what Rocco said. "I could use some work." He took a long drink. "I haven't had a part-time job in fourteen years. Not since college."

Rocco blew a perfect set of smoke rings. His creations floated across the table. "Man," he said. "You're in L.A. now. With father Reagan in the White House, corporate raiders plundering and work scarce, you must adapt."

"I could work part-time until I found something that fits. I have a lot of experience."

Rocco sipped his beer. "Experience is good," he said. "So is a sense of humor. In fact, you got to have a sense of humor if you live in Los Angeles. There's no middle ground. Here it's either old money, new money or no money."

"But, where do I find short-term situations?"

"Check out *LA Weekly* classifieds. There's a place on Wilshire that specializes in odd jobs. They usually have an ad."

Outside Barney's Beanery the damp night air closed around them. They drove north to Sunset then headed east. Bright lights beckoned. Night transformed the meandering Sunset Strip into a blurred rush of neon signage and taillights. Hollywood locals, UCLA students and tourists cruised in their low-riders, BMWs and rental cars. David and Rocco rolled down their windows, listened to classic rock and laughed like schoolboys ditching class.

At Gower they turned south past television sound stages with super graphic sitcom marquees. On the wide sidewalk, three Guardian Angels wearing white T-shirts and red berets marched north on patrol.

"Hey brothers." Rocco whistled. "Watch your backs. Keep the peace."

The Guardian Angels saluted. Rocco pointed the way. A few minutes from the bright lights of Sunset Boulevard the street turned dark. David headed east on Fountain Avenue and stopped in front of an apartment building with iron bars welded onto the security entrance and ground story windows. A streetlamp sputtered above the Buick.

"This is your place?" David asked.

Rocco stepped out of the car. He lit a cigarette and stared up at the streetlamp. "Yes. The hood's shady. But rent's cheap for a security building. Like I said, my budget is tight."

"I hear you," David said. "If we don't speak before then, I'll see you a week from Tuesday."

"Man, that's great. Thanks for the beer and food. You're a regular guy." Rocco stopped in the middle of the street. "Have your brakes checked. They're squeaking pretty bad."

On Lookout Mountain, a fragrant breeze fluttered through the eucalyptus and evergreen trees. David crawled onto his air mattress lightheaded. For the moment, he wasn't consumed with thoughts of Sarah Fleming or hearing her voice. That night his dreams filled with blue skies and surrender.

SIX

The next morning, Monday October 19, 1987, The New York Stock Exchange plunged into a catastrophic collapse. At 9 a.m., unaware of the unfolding financial market disaster, David began calling. Within two hours had left messages for most of his job leads. He discovered that Southern California also suffered from the recession, the epidemic of leveraged buyouts and white-collar job losses. When he managed to penetrate the voice mail maze and spoke with a human, impatient screeners echoed a familiar refrain of "no" and "thank you."

"I'm sorry Mr. Bishop," a woman at an advertising agency reported. "Last month we laid off a third of our staff. There are no openings. Not even an entry-level position."

"What about free-lancers?" David persisted. "If you've cut back, you need free-lance support. May I meet with your creative director and present my work?"

The voice narrowed to a point. "That won't happen. She won't consider it. Send us your resume. Who knows?"

David couldn't wait. The law of supply and demand proved basic market economics that David knew well. His money would last three short months. In the classifieds he found low-wage jobs in retail sales, fast food and telemarketing. He couldn't, with a clear conscience, sell pet health insurance or herbal metabolic booster diet plans. David telephoned Richard Knox's office. The assistant said Mr. Knox was in New York on an extended business trip. David left a message he didn't expect to be returned.

David laced his running shoes. Downstairs he found Mrs. Howell rummaging through the garage wearing a green jumpsuit and a winter cap with fur flaps that covered her ears. She had moved a stepladder beside her Oldsmobile and eyed a shelf stacked with storage bins.

"Do you need a hand?"

"What?" Mrs. Howell lifted a furry earflap. "What did you say?"

"Do you want help getting something down?"

Mrs. Howell lifted both earflaps and tied them on top of her cap. "I can't find my rain hats," she said. "They're in one of those bins. I'll need them when it rains this winter."

David didn't ask questions. He steadied the ladder, climbed to the shelf and found two containers marked winter clothes.

"Are these the ones?" David asked.

"Won't know until I look."

He moved the storage bins to the floor. "These are too heavy for you," he said.

Mrs. Howell popped a lid. The stink of mothballs filled the garage. "You think these bins are too heavy?" she said. "How do you think they got up there?"

David crossed his arms and waited.

Mrs. Howell continued her search. "Go on," she said. "I'm sure you have things to do. I'll have the gardener put them back in the morning. Don't worry about little old me."

David waited.

"Here it is." Mrs. Howell clutched a yellow rain hat. "I knew I had it."

David headed up to the fire road. Each stride kicked up clouds of dust. A brown haze hung over the city below, shrouded the buildings and the neighborhoods and the broad streets that stretched west toward the ocean. An occasional flash of light reflected off a windshield. On the pavement he jogged along past homes that lined the mountain ridge. Their facades seemed solid, but beneath each structure a foundation had been cut into the hillside supported by steel and reinforced concrete.

His body relaxed into a comfortable rhythm. David thought about the roads he had run across north Texas, through the flatlands and the gentle rolling hills, the old neighborhood and the tree-lined suburbs of Dallas. The endorphins kicked in and he greeted the sensation of stillness he knew, from years of running, could be sustained as long as he kept moving. Arms and legs swung freely. A Doberman pinscher rushed an iron fence, barked and gnashed its fangs. David picked up the pace and crossed to the opposite side of the street.

A half-mile further he headed back. The Doberman growled when he passed the iron fence. David pressed until he reached the fire road where the incline challenged him. He wiped the sweat from his face. It was good to feel his feet connect with the earth and to empty his mind. The T-shirt hung wet and heavy as he plodded through the dust to the end of the road. Above him a hawk circled, scanned the mountainside for rabbits and squirrels.

The garage door was closed. Mrs. Howell, wearing the yellow rain hat, watched through a window as David crossed the driveway. He waved. Mrs. Howell tipped her rain hat and turned away. David took a shower, ate a peanut butter and banana sandwich then found the advertisement for Odd Jobs Incorporated in the *LA Weekly.*

David was stunned when he turned on the radio and heard the news. The stock market had experienced the largest crash in history. In a single day, the Dow Jones index lost $500 billion or 22% of its value. Stock markets around the world collapsed. Investors lost millions. Enraged clients murdered brokers. David did not own any stocks, but he understood the repercussions. Finding employment would be more difficult. All he had was the Buick, the money in his checking account and the thin promise of the classified ads.

The next morning David drove to Odd Jobs Incorporated where he met Olga Barnes, a middle-aged Eastern European woman with an oval face. A burning cigarette dangled from the corner of her mouth. The sole proprietor, Olga embraced capitalism with understated enthusiasm. She squinted through the cigarette smoke, presented David with a sample job binder and an application.

"Stock market crash? No worry. We have plenty of jobs," Olga said. "Fee is ninety-nine dollars. Only cash. No check."

"Ninety-nine cash," David repeated. "That seems fair."

Cigarette ashes tumbled onto Olga's desk. "As young girl I immigrate from old country with father and mother. We work hard to make life. Learn much work needed. It is good, America. You know?"

Olga swept ashes to the floor with the back of her hand. She took two puffs and perched the burning butt in an ashtray. Behind her a wiry young man with acne-scarred cheeks wore a Los Angeles Lakers visor and a headset, his nose buried in a *Silver Surfer* comic book. He answered the telephone without looking up.

"Odd Jobs Incorporated, all kinds of jobs for all kinds of people. Yeah, there's a fee. October special is ninety-nine dollars cash with unlimited access for ninety days. Yes, we're open until six."

He reclined, propped his Birkenstock sandals on the desk and flipped the page of his comic book. "Thanks for calling," he said. "Have a nice day."

A young woman entered the office followed by an older gentleman. Olga acknowledged them as they selected job binders and settled onto the sagging sofa. David reviewed sample listings that included movie extras, personal assistants, limousine drivers, bartenders, waiters, and television game show contestants. A $100 bonus was offered to chronically depressed subjects needed for psychological testing at UCLA Medical Center. With the volume of listings David figured he could make his fee back quickly. He presented Olga with the application and five twenties.

Olga presented an active job binder, scratch paper and a pen. "Thanks, Mr. Bishop," she said. "Note jobs. We update each week. Come back. I wish you well."

Two telephone lines rang. Olga and her assistant answered simultaneously, "Odd Jobs Incorporated."

David examined the listings, noted several projects and part-time positions paying $15 to $25 an hour. Olga Barnes and her assistant completed their telephone calls.

"Excuse me," David asked. "There's a job here for children's birthday parties. What's involved?"

Olga lit a cigarette. "You wear costume. Entertain kids."

"What kind of costume?"

She covered her mouth and coughed. "Whatever kid want, Big Bird, Paddington Bear, Spiderman, Superman."

"Superman would be okay," David said.

Olga and the assistant exchanged looks.

"Every guy wants to be Superman," the assistant said. "You have to be at least six feet tall. Forget Superman. When the little bastards figure out you can't fly, they go berserk."

David imagined third graders in party hats, high on sugar cake and ice cream. He could see himself dashing through a doorway with the shredded remains of his superhero cape flapping behind him. David studied the binder, made notes and excluded anything involving children.

Friday morning David reported to the Cunningham Fine Art Gallery on Rodeo Drive dressed in his oldest blue jeans and a gray sweatshirt. Slender and impeccably groomed, Mr. De Carlo, the gallery manager, resembled an animated caricature. He escorted David through stacks of wooden shipping crates to the rear of the gallery.

"Two contemporary Italian artists begin showing next week," De Carlo said. "A contractor painted the main gallery. We need you to finish the walls of the three smaller rooms so we may display other artists."

David examined the paint cans, rollers and brushes. "I can do this," he said.

De Carlo cringed. "One would hope," he said. "On the telephone you implied you knew what you were doing."

"Painting walls is not complicated."

"Very well." De Carlo tipped his chin toward the ceiling. "I appreciate you coming on short notice. Please be tidy and be quick. We'll pay you seventy-five dollars upon completion."

"Thank you," David said. "I'll get right on it."

David covered the floors, secured the drop cloths and painted the edges of the walls first. He took extra care around the crown moldings and rolled slowly to avoid spray.

When he finished the first room David took a break, removed his shoes and strolled into the main gallery where De Carlo hovered over two assistants unpacking a large canvas. De Carlo stepped back to check a painting hung on the opposing wall. The massive abstract held layers of modeled paste covered with broad-brush strokes. The painting resembled a convulsion at the edge of deep space, blended midnight black and swirling cobalt blues with flashes of titanium white.

"And what do you have to say?" De Carlo asked.

"This is intense," David said. "Almost disturbing."

"No, no." De Carlo pressed manicured fingernails to his temples. "When will your work be done?"

"Excuse me," David said. "I was taking a break."

De Carlo's eyes bulged. "Mr. Bishop, how much longer will you be?"

"I'll be done by four," David said.

"Please carry on."

David returned to the cans of paint and opened the rear gallery door to vent the fumes. Above the alley, miles from the ocean, a pair of seagulls hovered over the garlic-laced garbage cans from the restaurant next door.

At 4:30 p.m. Mr. De Carlo inspected the rooms and paid David. He scrubbed his hands in the gallery bathroom, checked the soles of his shoes and returned to the main gallery. Two additional paintings continued the tone and textures of the first, variations on a cosmic theme of chaos and creation.

On Rodeo Drive David strolled the sidewalk triumphant. Tall, fragrant and unaffected women paid no attention to him. Dressed in work clothes he was invisible, free to watch as they chatted with their companions swinging designer shopping bags.

David drove to Johnny Rockets on Melrose. The retro-style diner was packed with customers. Popular music played from the Fifties and Sixties: Frank Sinatra, Elvis Presley, Diana Ross and the Supremes. He found a stool and ordered a hamburger, fries and a chocolate shake. The eager young waitress wore a nametag, Louise from Reno. She presented his food and an empty cardboard plate onto which she poured catsup in the shape of a smile. She clapped her hands like a casino dealer changing shifts.

"Enjoy," she shouted over the music.

David ate slowly. Louise made her rounds, recommended a slice of pie or a sundae. Customers must adore her, David thought, certain Louise longed for a hot shower to rinse the smell of onions and grilled hamburger.

It was dark when David returned to Wonderland Avenue. He parked the Buick and climbed to the crest of Lookout Mountain to commune with the scattered stars, dulled by the city lights and patches of fog.

His memory funneled back to the loss of his parents, his mother's gentle touch and her voice reading childhood picture books: *Mother Goose, Peter and the Wolf, Jack and the Beanstalk.* As a child, and even now, he wrestled with the awareness of what had been ripped away. Uncle Buck and Aunt Mary had done their best. David managed to fit in, to make a few friends and to do his part yet his sorrow often turned to anger. In fifth grade a thoughtless boy called him "the orphan." David responded like a wounded beast, an animal that bloodied its fists on schoolyard bullies or wooden fences, whatever taunted him or stood in his way. Years later, as he ran the streets, he learned how to retreat from a growing rage, how a new life can be constructed on the foundation of what had been destroyed.

SEVEN

David presented Rocco with a check for three hundred dollars, a significant sum from his shrinking finances. He accepted the need to ground himself, and, if Rocco's pitch proved successful, discover if his infatuation with Sarah had merit.

Norman Razor stood center stage and spread his arms. "The bold, the dispossessed," he said. "Offbeat misfits seeking salvation. Welcome one and all. Welcome, to the experience that will change your life."

Eighteen anxious students waited. David recognized Elmer and a few others. There were several new people, but David sat beside Rocco with an eye on the back door.

"Where's Sarah?"

Rocco spoke without moving his lips. "Cool it," he said. "I told you she'd be here."

"That's good. Your mouth hardly moved. You should be a ventriloquist."

"And you could be a dummy."

Norman Razor glared. "Excuse me, am I interrupting something?"

"No sir," Rocco said. "Sorry."

The stage door opened with a groan. Sarah rushed to the front of the room.

Norman shook his head. "The first minutes of the first class," he said. "And I'm being heckled. Come on people, let's get started."

Sarah dropped into the seat next to David. He tried not to look at her as Norman demonstrated exercises to help develop the power of free association.

"Don't be afraid to say something inane," he said. "Comedy is not about looking good. It's the opposite. Trust your instincts. Learn how to make something out of nothing."

Rocco would demonstrate. "Lead us off," Norman said. "Don't think. Don't hesitate. What's your perfect job?"

"A cruise ship lounge," Rocco replied. "A microphone and a buffet line. A long buffet line."

"Heroes."

"Red Skelton. Ronald McDonald. Jerry Lewis."

"Fantasy."

"A massage therapist. A rubber sheet, whipped cream and cherry Jell-O. Vegas showgirls. Any combination."

The students laughed. Rocco saluted and took a seat. Norman asked them to choose a partner. The room buzzed with nervous chatter. David turned to Sarah, studied her face, and noted the color of her wide eyes, which at that moment leaned toward lavender blue. Sarah did not blink as she waited.

"Flowers," David said.

"Georgia O'Keeffe," Sarah replied. "Irises. Water lilies. Blue bonnets."

David imagined a field of blue bonnets growing wild along a sunbaked Texas highway. A warm wind caressed his face.

"David." Sarah shook his knee. "Next?"

"Sure. Sorry. Uh, rock stars."

"Joni Mitchell. Eric Clapton. Bono. Stevie Nicks."

"Favorite food."

"Caesar salad. Egg rolls. Lobster bisque. Crab legs."

"And for desert?"

"Chocolate mousse. Key-lime pie. Fortune cookies."

Norman Razor clapped his hands. Sarah smiled. David noticed the fine blond hair descending from the hairline in front of her ears.

"Okay," Norman said. "Switch."

David took a breath.

Sarah touched his knee. "Your favorite games," she said.

"The Olympic decathlon. Football, college or NFL, it doesn't matter. Seven-card stud."

"Cartoon characters."

"Rocky and Bullwinkle. Roadrunner. Mighty Mouse."

"Favorite films."

"Shane. Doctor Zhivago. Five Easy Pieces."

"In the summertime?"

"Thunderstorms. Fire flies. Homemade ice cream."

Norman applauded their efforts, called the students together and fixed his gaze on the front row. "David," he said. "You were eager to speak at the beginning of class, come up and tell us a funny story."

"About what?" David asked.

"We'll let you know when you get up here."

David couldn't think of a story. Rocco pushed him toward the stage where he stood under the spotlights. Someone yelled, "Trader Joe's."

David shrugged his shoulders and peered into the room. "I don't know Trader Joe."

The students laughed.

"No questions. No thinking," Norman said. "You're in a grocery store. Go with it."

"Uh, okay." David thought about fruits and vegetables. "A woman is stocking produce. I hold two melons and ask her if they're ripe. She slapped me."

The women groaned. David envisioned a vaudeville act, a hostile audience hurling tomatoes and cabbage. With the spotlights, he'd never see it coming. David attempted a defense. "It was an innocent question," he said.

"Cashier," Rocco said.

David hesitated. "The checker asked if I wanted a bag," he said. "I replied, 'Do I look that bad?'"

Rocco laughed, but that was it. Silence. David waited. His pulse elevated, his mouth went dry.

"Nail polish," Sarah said.

David thought. "The checker chewed the candy-red polish from her press-on nails. I say, 'Your nails do look good enough to eat.'"

A woman in the second row groaned. Again, silence. David imagined incoming tomatoes.

Someone shouted, "Boyfriend."

David stepped to the edge of the stage. "Her biker boyfriend collared me. 'Nobody insults my old lady. You bitch fucker,' the biker said. 'I'll kick your ass.'"

Norman clapped. Rocco and the others offered polite applause. David felt his heart thump like he had run wind sprints.

"Thanks David," Norman said. "Good work. You're my first student to confess a nail polish fetish. Also, I'm no prude, but for this workshop avoid foul language. When you're out in the real world fending for yourself you may say whatever you want. Words that rhyme with duck always work for a cheap laugh."

"Sorry," David said. "That biker had a foul mouth."

Sarah laughed. David didn't consider himself funny, but he realized the audience and his physical response mirrored a familiar pattern. His body reacted as if he had run a good distance where the endorphins kicked in, where he relaxed and no longer felt pain.

Joyce Levy, a redhead from Kansas City, took her turn. Sarah and Rocco applauded wildly when she took the stage. Joyce embraced the moment and tilted her hips in a seductive manner.

"Hey Joyce, tell us about your first job," Sarah said.

"I worked at a freaking Burger Queen." Joyce struck a pose. "Whoops, sorry Norman, I almost said fucking."

The students laughed. Norman Razor crossed his arms and said nothing.

"I lasted two weeks. A customer complained his flame-broiled patty was too small. I told him, 'You ordered it well done, didn't you?' Real men love big buns."

The students laughed. Joyce curtsied.

"Denny's," Rocco said. "Talk about Denny's."

Joyce rolled her eyes. "After Burger Queen, I worked at Denny's, which was better because you don't have to mop high school kid's puke in the drive-through. Instead, you get old drunks and truckers asking 'Honey when do you get off?' I replied, 'Not in your freaking life.'"

Several women applauded.

Joyce beamed. "I'm thirty-two and work in the restaurant business, but I've moved up. I haven't worn a hairnet in years."

Students took their turn on stage and vented. At the end of class Norman encouraged everyone to engage their stream of consciousness. "Don't force it," he said. "Allow your thoughts to flow. We generate material just being in the world. Consider your life is a joke. Take notes."

The students congregated outside. Sarah and Rocco introduced David to Joyce when Elmer interrupted.

"Rocco, last week I was so nervous." Elmer's eyes filled the frames of his glasses. His face flushed. "But tonight, I got really excited."

Rocco moved between Joyce and Elmer. "Stand back," he said. "Our little cowboy might explode."

Elmer bounced like a dog begging a biscuit. "No, I won't."

"Elmer," Rocco said. "You are one sick pup."

He stopped bouncing. The flush faded from his face.

Rocco hugged Elmer. "Hey man," he said. "We wouldn't tease if we didn't love you."

Sarah joined Joyce and Rocco surrounding Elmer in a group embrace.

"We like when you're excited." Joyce stroked Elmer's balding head. "It makes a woman feel effective."

Elmer's cheeks glowed. "Alright," he said. "Enough already. I'll see you next week."

Joyce offered Rocco a ride. David walked Sarah down to Sunset Boulevard. They stopped beside her Volkswagen beetle, the convertible top and rear window faded with age. The hubcaps were missing.

Sarah caught David's gaze. "'Bitch fucker'?" Her lips stopped short of a smile. "I haven't quite heard that one before."

"Nor have I," David said. "It just popped out."

"I'll remember that."

David stepped closer. "The workshop is fun," he said. "More than I thought."

Sarah opened the door and tossed her purse onto the passenger seat. "It's good to have a few laughs," she said. "Like I mentioned the other night, it helps me at school."

"How so?"

David watched the westbound traffic. Sarah slipped into her car. The window squeaked and rattled as she rolled it down.

"A few of the children are difficult," she said. "Some of the parents can be worse."

"I want to hear more about your work," he said.

Sarah checked traffic in her rearview mirror. Approaching headlights illuminated her eyes. "More about school or more about me?"

David considered his response. "Both," he said. "But more about you."

A surge of traffic passed. She looked off down the street. After several seconds she sifted through her purse and wrote her telephone number on a scrap of paper.

"Call me." She presented the paper, started the car and shifted into gear. "Let's go for a late lunch on Saturday. Nothing too serious."

David wasn't certain if he was ready to know a woman again, or to be known. He wondered about the prospects for happiness, about hearing a familiar voice call softly in the night.

EIGHT

They met at The Source restaurant on Sunset. David arrived early, took a table on the covered patio and ordered a Red Zinger iced tea. Nearby, an older gentleman turned the pages of *Variety*. In the corner a young rocker couple wore black leather. The woman drank coffee and read *Rolling Stone*. The man poured Tabasco sauce on his omelet. His companion lowered her magazine and dipped an index finger in the hot sauce. The man drew her sauced finger into his mouth.

Sarah arrived wearing dark sunglasses, a loose black sweater, blue jeans and boots. Daylight looked good on her, David thought as he held her chair and nodded to the scene in the corner. Sarah peeked over her sunglasses.

"Wonder what they're having for dessert?" David asked.

"They look creative." Sarah waved to the waitress and ordered iced coffee.

"I wonder," David said. "Do you think Tabasco is an aphrodisiac?"

"I wouldn't know," she said. "I'm not that kind of a girl."

"Sorry, I was ..."

"It's okay." She removed her sunglasses and touched the back of his hand. "I've never been crazy about Tabasco sauce. Not like that anyway."

David squeezed lemon into his tea. "What kind of girl are you?"

"Actually, I'm not a girl." Sarah lowered her voice. "I'm a woman."

David turned to the menu. "I won't argue about that," he said.

They ordered vegetable soup. Sarah suggested they split a free-range turkey sandwich with avocado and bean sprouts. She poured cream into her iced coffee, wrapped a paper napkin around the glass then sipped through a straw. Outside, a petite woman wearing a black shawl pushed a baby stroller up the sidewalk, another child tethered with a red plastic rope.

"How can they afford to have children?" Sarah said. "I can barely afford myself."

David assessed the woman and children. "Maybe that's all they have," he said.

The woman waited at a crosswalk, clutched the stroller and held the tethered child close to her side.

"I might be envious," Sarah said. "I'm not sure."

"Children are something to be sure about it."

Sarah nodded agreement. "Most of us are the result of raging hormones," she said. "Or failed contraception. Either way, the consequences of love are long term."

David weighed the conflict in her words. "The consequences of love," he said. "That sounds like a self-help book."

"Maybe I should write one. I've certainly done enough research."

David shifted in his seat. "Tell me about the first time you were in love?"

Sarah's lips curled into a gentle smile. "You're not much for small talk, are you?"

David shrugged. "Small talk is for people who have nothing to say."

Sarah glanced at the leathered couple. "You mean love like our friends in the corner?"

"I mean the very first time."

Sarah's brow furrowed. "You seem trustworthy. I wouldn't call this a love story, though. It was really my first crush. Every summer my cousin Mary Lou and I spent a week with our grandparents. They had a cabin on Lake Texoma near where you grew up."

David thought about Highway 82, the road to the lake. "I know it well," he said.

Sarah's blue eyes narrowed. "We were fourteen. Mary Lou was boy-crazy, but I was more cautious. One day near the cabin a Chevy van broke down with four high school boys in a band. The lead singer Buster was scruffy and cute. It was exciting to look at him, but what did I know? Grandfather wanted to call the sheriff, but grandmother telephoned a garage. Mary Lou and I talked with the boys until the tow truck came."

The waitress brought lunch. Sarah turned a spoon through the vegetable soup and took a small bite.

"Mary Lou and I decided we'd ride bicycles down to the garage at the bottom of a steep hill. I lost control and crashed into the side of the tow truck. Landed spread-eagle on the hood. The boys laughed. It may have looked hilarious, but I could've broken my neck."

"Were you hurt?"

"Scraped my knee and elbow. I started to cry. Mary Lou and Buster helped me off the truck. It was pitiful."

On Sunset Boulevard a Grave Line tour bus screeched to a stop. The engine idled. The light changed. The bus moved west toward the Beverly Hills homes of movie stars and celebrities.

"Buster apologized. He suggested Mary Lou and I meet him and the drummer later that night. At 11:00 p.m. we met the boys near the boat docks. The moon was bright. We sat on a retaining wall. Everything was fine until the boys started pawing and kissing us. Mary Lou and I had gone to church camp the summer before. We knew how to kiss and how to defend ourselves."

Sarah took her soup in measured bites.

"I grew tired of kissing and pulling Buster's hands off my shorts. I suggested we walk down by the water. He didn't want to stop."

David regretted he asked the question. The waitress brought fresh glasses of iced coffee and tea. Sarah finished her soup and took a bite of the sandwich. She sighed then poured cream in her coffee.

"You don't have to talk about it," he said.

"No, it's okay," she said. "It wasn't a big deal."

She wrapped a paper napkin around the iced coffee and continued. "Buster was unaccustomed to rejection, but I said 'no' loud enough he heard me. So did Mary Lou and the drummer, only a few feet away. Buster's mood changed as we walked onto the boat dock. The moon was shining. The water was still. For a second I thought Buster might be a regular guy then he kissed me hard. His fingers dug into my hips. I pulled away. He called me a bitch and shoved me in the lake."

Knots formed in David's stomach. He imagined his fists against Buster's face. "What a jerk."

Sarah squinted against the afternoon sun and gnawed her lower lip. "Yes, Buster was a jerk. Mary Lou helped me out of the water. I've never been one to cry, but that day I cried twice over the same boy. Mary Lou and I stood in the moonlight and sobbed. Then we started laughing. It wasn't funny, but we couldn't stop. Teenaged nerves."

Sarah's gaze drifted across Sunset, beyond the traffic and office buildings into the ashen sky. She appeared lost for a moment, then the trace of a smile returned to her lips.

"I learned why they call it a crush," she said. "It only felt like love until I got to know him. Fortunately, that didn't take long. Mary Lou and I swore we'd never date musicians."

David knew enough to listen. Sarah's smile widened, she sipped coffee and looked at him, her irises blue like speckled robin's eggs.

"My experience with Buster wasn't anything like real love," she said. "Six years and many boys later, Mary Lou reminded me the night I got engaged."

"To a musician?"

She took a bite of her sandwich, stirred her coffee and watched ice spin in the glass.

"Yes, a musician, but he wasn't anything like Buster. In the beginning he was sweet and attentive, wrote such soulful songs. To him making love was a ritual of reverence."

David didn't want to hear about her lovers, but he had asked the question. "I'd think you'd prefer reverence," he said.

Sarah looked David in the eyes. "It's nice at first, but you get bored with the routine. I've learned to appreciate spontaneity."

David summoned his best poker face and attempted to hold her gaze. A standoff ensued. Neither blinked. David held his position as long as possible then accepted he'd been bested. He lowered his eyes and took the last bite of his sandwich.

The black leather couple gathered themselves. The woman slid her hand onto the back of the man's pants and squeezed his ass as they walked to the door.

"Take that couple," Sarah said. "How long can they do each other before one loses interest?"

A teenaged boy in baggy pants clattered along the sidewalk on a skateboard. Arms hung by his sides. In one fluid motion the boy shifted his weight, altered course then jumped off, seized the board and walked across the parking lot.

"It is easy for relationships to get out of control," David said. "Like that bicycle you crashed into the truck."

Sarah smiled and watched the rush of cars on Sunset Boulevard. "You're right," she said. "Guess I needed better brakes. So, tell me about your first love."

The waitress brought their check. Sarah insisted they split the bill and proposed they drive up to the Griffith Observatory. David followed her east on Franklin. They left Sarah's Volkswagen near her apartment on Vista Del Mar. She pointed the way as they entered Griffith Park.

"It's your turn," she said. "My story was kind of lame. I want to hear about your first love."

The road turned through tree-covered hillsides. David was impressed by how quickly they were surrounded by nature, recalled his early childhood and how his parents took him on Sunday drives in the country.

"I was in second grade," he said. "Her name was Sally, a cherub with curly white hair and a turned-up nose. I was shy and didn't know what to say, but whenever I thought of her I felt happy. Near the end of the school year Sally brought a bouquet of flowers for show and tell. When it was her turn Sally went around the room and let everyone smell the bouquet. She presented the flowers to me and kissed my cheek. All of the kids laughed."

"You're making that up."

"No," he said. "It's the truth."

"So, what happened with your cherub?"

"Sally's father took a job with a big oil company in Houston. They moved that summer. I never saw her again."

The observatory parking lot overflowed with cars and buses. David circled the lot then parked on the shoulder of an access road. Adults and children crowded the entrance. Sarah slipped her arm through David's as they wedged inside. In the lobby a Foucault pendulum hung from the ceiling by a steel cable. Set in motion, the pendulum swung back and forth powered by gravity and the axial rotation of the earth. The crowd converged on the pendulum. Heads bobbed. Necks craned.

"I can't see," a child cried. "Help mama."

"Hold my hand," the mother answered.

Complaints echoed in several languages. People pushed to improve their position. It became difficult to breathe.

Sarah nudged David toward the door. "Let's get some air," she said.

They moved back to the entrance and away from the crowd. A walled walkway encircled the exterior of the observatory. On the southwest side they stopped to enjoy the waning light and the tree-covered hills below. Sarah relaxed against the wall and looked out toward the city, her face framed by the cloudless haze and the white stucco wall. A cool breeze brushed the canopy of trees beneath them and lifted the hair from her shoulders.

David offered his jacket. Sarah wrapped it around her shoulders. When she turned he noticed a faint crescent-shaped scar in the fleshy curl of her upper lip. His reflection appeared in her sunglasses. The lenses distorted his face, made his cheeks appear fat and happy.

"Heliotropism," she said. The faint scar disappeared when she spoke. "Movement toward the light."

A group of children ran past, following the leader. Sarah and David stepped aside.

"Toward the light?" he asked. "Or away from it?"

"Toward the light." Sarah huddled in his jacket and fixed on the empty sky, her voice soft and sullen. "Dark and light don't exist without each other. We go in and out of the shadows moving toward whatever sustains us. With plants it is light. For people, the choice is too often darkness."

David never had much patience with the superficial. He wanted to touch Sarah's face, to acknowledge his understanding, but he knew better.

"Are you always so serious?" he asked.

Sarah shook her head. "I don't think of myself that way," she said. "I've been distracted. Some of it's personal and then there's work. I don't know if my contract at school will be renewed next spring. Looking for a new job is not the end of the world, but I'm concerned. That's serious enough."

Their shoulders touched. "I know how you feel," he said.

The breeze died with the sun. In the distance, streetlights came to life. Darkness prevailed as they crossed the lawn and parking lot.

When they turned onto Los Feliz Sarah checked her watch.

"Hey." Her voice brightened. "Want to go to a party?"

"Sure," he said.

Sarah's friends Grace and Peter lived in a loft warehouse off Venice Boulevard where they recycled cast-off furniture into up-valued pieces of art. In celebration of Grace's fiftieth birthday they decorated the space with black streamers and flashing yellow road-hazard lights. Dressed in a black sombrero, Peter escorted David and Sarah into the living area. Grace, eyes closed and body covered with a blanket, lay on a futon in the far corner of the room.

"Forgive us, but Grace came down with a bloody migraine," Peter said. "It just came over her. But what could we do? She wouldn't miss her own party."

A woman massaged Grace's neck and shoulders. Subdued partygoers gathered around a nearby service table, visited quietly, ate strawberries dipped in chocolate and drank Chardonnay from bistro glasses. Music by the Grateful Dead played softly on the stereo.

Sarah did not want to interrupt Grace's treatment. Peter led them to the kitchen where they found Rocco and Joyce filling plates with smoked Salmon and boiled shrimp, asparagus spears and crab cakes.

A woman with sun-ravaged skin and an abundance of turquoise jewelry waved her hand. "I had the most frightful experience in Sepulveda pass," she said. "Traffic slowed to a crawl. When I finally reached the Highway Patrol cars I thought a sack of potatoes had fallen in the road."

The woman took a drink. Her silver bracelet rattled against the glass. "It's not a sack of potatoes," she said. "It's a deer. The torso all twisted in a heap. I thought I would faint."

"You had it rough?" Rocco scoffed. "Think how that deer must have felt."

The woman grabbed her glass and headed for the living room. Peter tipped his sombrero and followed her.

"Look who's here," Joyce said. She embraced Sarah and David then handed them glasses.

Rocco poured wine. "What are you kids up to?" he asked.

"We had lunch," David said. "Then Sarah showed me Griffith Observatory."

Rocco slipped an arm around Joyce's waist. "The observatory," he said. "Let's toast to heavenly bodies."

"Don't listen to him," Sarah said. "Sounds like he's loaded."

"I'll drink to that," Joyce said.

The other guests were polite, none too loud or too drunk. The subdued behavior mirrored the host's condition. David expected more volume from a Hollywood crowd. They could have been snorting cocaine and playing charades.

An attractive woman with flawless features entered the kitchen dressed in a black silk blouse and faded jeans. Rocco mocked an English accent as he addressed her.

"Pardon me," he said. "But aren't you the star of that new 'Some Days' commercial?"

The actress blushed and struck a sarcastic chord. "Yes. Thank you," she said. "My parents are proud. I graduated from Juilliard and went straight to work promoting the finest feminine hygiene products."

"That's so great," Joyce said. "You look so fresh. Maybe you'll get a soap opera. You'd be great for daytime. You have perfect skin."

"Thank you." The actress nibbled a wheat cracker then turned away. "You're very kind."

Rocco waited until the actress cleared the room. "I auditioned for that part," he said.

"You liar," Joyce countered. "You did not."

"Okay, you're right. It was another hygiene product."

Sarah groaned. "Oh, no."

Rocco insisted. "Listen, it's not that bad. At the audition I waited almost two hours. By the time they called, my right leg is asleep. I fall on my face. The casting coordinator claimed I was drunk. I begged her to let me read. I got down on my knees for that woman."

Rocco crouched and wrapped his arms around Joyce's hips.

"Did you get the commercial?" Sarah asked.

"No," Rocco said. "The producer didn't like how I pronounced ointment."

After an hour of conversation, and two cups of black coffee, Joyce dragged Rocco away from the food. Sarah and David escorted them to the door then wandered among the partygoers. Grace remained reclined. When they approached David noticed the streaks of gray in her thick brown hair.

Sarah knelt and stroked Grace's arm. "Happy birthday Gracie," she said.

Grace opened and closed her eyes. "Thank you dearest," she said. "Forgive me for being in this awful state. I'm pleased you're here."

Sarah spoke softly. "I want you to meet my friend David."

David accepted Grace's hand, her skin moist with lotion.

"Hello Grace," he said. "I'm sorry you're feeling ill."

Grace closed her fingers around David's hand. "Are you new to Los Angeles?"

"Yes, I just got here."

"Are you an artist?"

David had never been asked that question. "I don't think about that," he said. "Perhaps in some ways everyone is an artist."

Grace opened her eyes. Sarah rested a hand on her shoulder.

"I agree," Grace said. "I've attempted to write many times. With me words start and then stall. I prefer painting. An unfinished canvas is easier to leave than a story. There always seems to be more to say."

"Yes, I can see that."

"I am pleased to know you," she said.

"Take care," he said. "And happy birthday."

David stepped back. Sarah kissed Grace's forehead and the two whispered for a few moments. David noted how carefully Sarah touched her friend. Finally Sarah stood, took David's hand and bumped him with her hip.

"Are you ready?" he asked.

"Yes," she said. "You may take me home."

On Venice Boulevard the night was cool and calm. A blanket of fog rolled in laced with the heavy air of the sea. Halos of mist encircled the streetlamps. The fog muted the sound of passing cars and brought everything in close.

David drove slowly, east on Venice then north on Highland. The fog thinned as they reached Vista Del Mar. An aging hacienda-style structure, the building was shielded from the street by towering evergreens. Sarah led David through a darkened archway and across a small paver-stone patio. Water gurgled in a fountain. Vines climbed stucco walls. A large wooden door creaked as they entered a narrow corridor with a succession of smaller doors spaced like a dormitory. Candle flame-shaped bulbs cast a dim glow against the plaster walls. Minor chords of a Spanish guitar floated through the air.

Sarah searched her purse for keys. "Years ago, this place was a monastery," she whispered. "The landlord says it's built on a powerful meridian. He claims the grounds are blessed."

"It's like from another world," David said.

Her apartment was a single room with a kitchenette, a bathroom and large closet. The vaulted ceiling and a narrow stained-glass window were illuminated from the outside by a security light that cast flecks of color across the wooden floor. The bits of color moved with the shadows of a restless young tree. On the wall hung an unframed print, one of Monet's water lilies. Sarah's furnishings consisted of a red love seat, a small café table, two chairs and a Yamaha piano keyboard. Her bed was tucked into a niche above the closet surrounded by gauze netting hung from the ceiling. The ladder leading to the niche seemed to rise into a chiffon cloud.

Sarah cleared a stack of sweaters from the love seat. David settled into the cushions while Sarah tended a kettle on the small range. Soon the kettle whistled and Sarah brought hot chocolate in china cups then sat cross-legged braced against the end of the love seat. Light played against the side of her face, half-visible and half-hidden except for her eyes. Clear and blue, her eyes penetrated the shadows. A clock ticked in the corner of the room.

"It was fun today," she whispered.

"Yes, great fun," he said. "You were kind of quiet by the time we reached the party."

"Sometimes I don't feel much like talking."

Sarah cradled the cup and sipped slowly, her upper lip glazed with chocolate. The faint rhythms of the Spanish guitar lingered in the hallway. They sipped chocolate. Minutes passed then Sarah gathered their cups and set them on the floor. She took David's wrist, touched the ridge of his knuckles and turned his palm toward the ceiling.

"I've noticed," she whispered. "You have nice hands."

When David tried to speak Sarah pressed fingers to his lips. His pulse quickened. He caressed her cheek. His fingers explored the smoothness, found the fleshy lobes of her ears and disappeared into the silky folds of her hair. Their eyes closed. Immersed in darkness, the first kiss was soft and sweet and tasted of chocolate. David grew bolder and she responded. Their lips joined in a delicate dance, their breath accelerated. Clothing tumbled to the floor. David found her skin smooth and warm and willing. His hands and lips moved slowly on her body, brushed the back of her knees, across the arch of her lower back and trailed down her stomach. Sarah pulled David to her breasts then to her face where she could see his eyes and taste his lips.

She was eager to have the weight of his body against hers. They pressed harder and harder, slipped further and further, one into the other. The love seat edged across the floor with each undulation. They folded again and again, one into the other. Hearts pounded. Toes curled. The love seat squeaked and groaned until, at last, they collapsed together.

Their hearts steadied as they shifted their bodies and withdrew to their own thoughts. Outside, the leaves of the restless tree fluttered in the breeze. Shadows played across the hardwood floor and scattered flecks of colored light. David touched Sarah's shoulder and pulled her close. She pressed her back against his chest, rested her hand on his and relaxed into the cushions. Sarah stared at the stained-glass window and the shadows beyond.

David braced himself against the silence. The clock ticked. Minutes passed. He longed for sleep and imagined the two of them climbing the ladder into her bed, up into the chiffon cloud, and dreaming quietly.

"Are you okay?" he asked.

Sarah touched the back of his hand as gently as she could.

"It's late," she said. "I think you'd better go."

NINE

David awoke at 3 a.m. The air mattress deflated, his hip and shoulder against the floor. Among the shadows on the wall he imagined Sarah's face, an illusion that persisted as he dozed too exhausted to inflate the mattress. As morning edged into the room hunger gnawed at the hollow pit of his stomach.

Illusions would not sustain him, David thought, as he washed his face. The dull aches in his body ascended to the base of his skull. Water did not quench his thirst.

"What have you done?"

The mirror did not respond. David did not need an answer. Sarah wasn't anticipated, but he acknowledged this possibility the moment he watched her enter that room.

Early that afternoon he called Sarah and left a message on her machine. Hours passed. Sunday evening turned to Monday without a response. He didn't know whether to feel shunned or concerned. By Monday night he resisted the urge to drive down to Vista del Mar. That would defeat his cause. He recognized the flu-like symptoms of his amorous affliction: glands swollen, loss of appetite, persistent headache. The only recourse was patience. He stared at the clock and the telephone and attempted to form a productive thought.

On Tuesday night David arrived for Razor's workshop and found Rocco outside the rehearsal room smoking a cigarette with Joyce and other students.

"Hey David," Rocco said. "How's it going?"

"I'm not sure." He scanned the street where Sarah would park her car.

Rocco stepped away from Joyce and the others. "You and Sarah looked like you were doing fine Saturday night," he said. "What happened?"

"I don't want to talk about that," he said.

"Hey man, I warned you. Hollywood is hell on love." Rocco crushed his cigarette into the lid of an ashcan. "Come on, let's go in."

Rocco corralled the students. Norman Razor waited on the edge of the stage. He began to explain the importance of comedic observation when the door opened. Sarah hurried to the front row and took the seat between Joyce and David.

Norman paused and cleared his throat. "Take whatever life gives you," he said. "Most of the good stuff is absolutely free. Be specific. Build your show from the details and bone crushing tragedy of your life."

Sarah pressed her knee gently against David's thigh. A tremor of enthusiasm reverberated throughout his body and settled just below the navel. He didn't look at her.

Rocco supervised a workout. Each performer received an observational topic. Rocco displayed an uncanny ability to pick the most appropriate subjects: Toilet training, traffic school, lactose intolerance. When David's turn came, Rocco didn't have to be psychic.

"How about it David? Tell us about dating life."

David took the microphone. "Thanks Rocco. You're such a pal." David didn't think about love or devotion or the tremor in his gut. Surprised by a sudden lucidity, he didn't think about redemption from his previous unsteady performances. He said what he thought as clearly as possible.

"I really don't care to meet women in bars. I prefer art galleries or bookstores. They're less likely to throw up on you."

A wave of laughter greeted him.

"Never date women who knit. They tend to be obsessive and unpredictable. Their mothers probably knitted, so they can't help it. Knitters will knit you an ugly sweater. If you wear this cable-knit nightmare, it will age you forty years. You'll look like you just escaped from a nursing home, without your walker."

David mimicked an elderly man and shuffled across the stage. The students laughed.

"If you refuse to wear an ugly sweater, a yarn lover may snap into a psychotic episode and puncture your lung. Knitting needles are deadly weapons."

Rocco, Sarah and Joyce applauded. David returned to his seat. Other students followed, wandered through monologues about the high rent in Los Angeles and how real estate defines worth, the perils of Beverly Hills pet sitters and what it means to love bean curd. At the break, most of the class went outside to stretch their legs or have a smoke.

David thought about the hours he had waited by the telephone and what he would say. Sarah appeared tired and David's reluctance yielded to the likelihood of some new reality about to unfold.

"Can we talk?" he said.

Sarah looked toward the door. "We should," she said.

David followed her down the sidewalk. They stopped near the corner beneath the buzz of Norman Razor's red neon marquee.

"You don't knit, do you?" David asked.

"No," she said. "No knitting. You're safe with me. That was good work. You've been practicing."

"I've given it some thought."

"Well, it shows. Keep it up."

"Thanks," he said. "I was starting to worry."

Sarah pushed a strand of hair behind her ear. "That's sweet," she said. "But there's no need to worry about me. Sorry I didn't return your call. But it's difficult."

"What, dialing?"

Flashes of red neon reflected in Sarah's eyes. "I can understand if you're upset," she said. "I'm sorry. I should have called you back. That's not like me."

David shifted from offense to defense without substitution. Somehow he wanted to set everything right. He touched her face.

Sarah smiled. "Saturday was a wonderful surprise," she said. "We were on a roll. I really care for you, but this isn't good timing for me. I just can't be in a relationship right now."

Gravity became an irresistible force. David dropped his hand. Sarah reached for it, but he pulled away. Anticipation yielded to a sharp pain that struck David's chest then moved to his throat. He swallowed hard, tasted the acid reflux of impending doom. Blood flowed away from his brain, charged his limbs to take a stand, to fight or run. For a moment he couldn't think and the words fumbled from his mouth.

"I think this could be good," he said. "For both of us."

"David, please. Don't."

It was too late for retraction. He had been careful and cautious. His only hope was to stumble on.

"Is it a crime to be honest?"

"No." Her jaw tightened. "If you weren't honest, I wouldn't be interested. Not at all."

David lowered his eyes to a crack in the sidewalk where a trail of ants busied themselves, crawling in and out of a hole.

"Look here." Sarah lifted his chin, her voice softened in apology. "We were on a roll. We shared a wonderful moment, but David, right now you have to let that go."

David considered the ants and the hole in the sidewalk.

"This may be a surprise to you," he said. "Because it was a surprise for me."

"What are you saying?"

"I risk sounding like a complete fool," he continued. "But I want to get to know you. Because I think I could love you. Is that possible? Would you allow such a thing to happen?"

Sarah recoiled. Her eyes widened. David thought she could punch him in the mouth.

"Are you out of your mind?" she asked.

Her condescension sobered him, but did not halt the momentum of his confession. "You can be a bit abrupt," he said. "I'm not complaining because I find that attractive. I like your attitude. I love the way you walk and your voice, the way you think and how you chew your food."

"Chew my food?" Sarah appeared confused. "Exactly how do I chew my food?"

"Gracefully, with your mouth closed like a human being, not like some barnyard animal. That's how most people eat. It's disturbing. Your table manners are impeccable."

"You're impossible," she said. "That's the most bizarre compliment I've ever heard."

"Thank you," he said. "That's how I see it."

They each smiled in declaration of an unspoken truce. A siren wailed in the distance. Sunset traffic raced along. Razor's neon marquee buzzed. David held Sarah as closely as he dared. She buried her face in his shoulder.

"I want you to be my friend," she said. "I could use a good friend right now. Isn't that enough?"

David didn't want to be her brother or faithful male companion. "Yes, of course," he said.

Rocco called from the doorway. "Boys and girls. Recess is over."

After the workshop Sarah and Joyce left arm-in-arm. "I'll call you," Sarah said as they reached the door. "I promise."

David nodded satisfied they had said all they could for the night. He helped Rocco straighten the folding chairs and offered him a ride home.

"Thanks man," Rocco said. "I can always use a hand. I'll buy some beer. You look like you could use one."

They stopped at Gower Gulch for a six-pack of Miller High Life, a large bag of pretzels and cigarettes. At Rocco's building David held the provisions. Rocco unlocked the security gate. They climbed the narrow stairwell to the second story breezeway and walked down to the apartment.

Rocco's living room smelled of sandalwood and cigarettes. The room was empty except for a stack of *LA Weekly* newspapers and a cardboard box filled with tattered paperback books. In one corner hung a simple Buddhist shrine with an incense burner and a Fruit Loops cereal bowl to catch the ashes. A circus poster for *The Greatest Show on Earth* was pinned to the far wall. A vintage 1950's chrome-legged dinette table and three chairs occupied the space beside the small kitchen. Dirty dishes filled the sink.

Rocco pointed to a chair. "Take a load off. I'll find some glasses." Rocco opened a cabinet and returned empty handed. "Nothing's clean. Let's drink from the bottle."

They drank beer and ate pretzels. Rocco cracked a window, lit a cigarette and attempted to blow smoke through the screen. The volume of discourse escalated when he finished the first beer.

"My friend." Rocco dropped his cigarette butt into the empty bottle. "Something you want to say?"

David sipped his beer. "I think the situation has stabilized," he said. "But thanks."

"It's your call, man." Rocco grabbed a handful of pretzels. "Like a told you, love's a pisser in this town. In Hollywood it's easier to date women you dislike. At least you know where you stand."

David laughed. "Maybe it's not love at all," he said. "Maybe sexual attraction is purely genetic predisposition? Our brains are programmed to respond to certain physical characteristics and behavioral signals. Maybe there's no love involved?"

Rocco chewed pretzels then lifted his beer. "Hey man, you're going in deep," he said. "Maybe love's a communicable disease. They should immunize us. Every spring the girls go to the mall. The boys get a booster shot."

"Spoken like a sexist pig," David said. "Want another beer?"

"Sure, I'm up for it."

Inside Rocco's refrigerator a green growth flourished, the origin a merger of rotten vegetables and leaked dairy products. He held his breath, grabbed two beers and shut the door.

"Were your parents really in the circus?"

"Hey man," Rocco said. "It's inappropriate to question the source of my material."

Rocco twisted the cap off the bottle then rummaged through a pile of mail. He unfolded a poster that read *Trust Life* and pinned it to the wall above the table.

"Okay, since you asked." Rocco admired the poster and took a drink. "My parents were Polish. Not exactly open-minded, but on occasion I made them laugh with one stunt or another. I learned how far to go before my father would smack the back of my head and tell me how tough he had it growing up. I'd swear I was going to join the circus. Plus, mom was a great cook. And I never had the bus money."

"What's stopping you now?"

Rocco's attention shifted toward the corner and the Buddhist shrine, the cereal bowl filled with ashes.

"Funny you'd ask, because I just submitted my application for clown school. It's a long shot. The competition is rough." Rocco propped his hands on his hips. "'Rocco the clown,' sounds good, huh?"

"Yes," David said. "But what about comedy?"

Rocco lit another cigarette and leaned against the wall. The chromed chair groaned. "Man, I love being on stage. Comedy is cool and everything. But I can't see hanging out in bars every night. I'd get in too much trouble. I'd rather be a clown. I'd rather make kids laugh. Their parents, too."

"What are you doing about money?"

"Money?" Rocco jumped to his feet. "Damn, I forgot. I got a job."

Rocco raised his Miller High Life. They clinked bottles.

"Starting Thursday, I'm the new service advisor at Larry's Hollywood Lube Job."

David couldn't help but laugh. "That's the real name?"

"Of course. I know my way around cars and have great people skills. Larry pays advisors ten bucks an hour."

"Congratulations, Rocco. Good for you."

They finished the beer. Rocco walked David down to the security gate.

"You okay to drive?"

"I only had a couple. Thanks for the company."

"Hey man, it was my treat for a change." Rocco closed the gate. "Good night."

The street lamp sputtered as David approached the Buick. The front left hubcap was missing. Two figures darted from the bushes. Chrome flashed and David started after them. The culprits kept low to the ground, dropped the hubcap and sprinted around the corner. David chased them for fifty yards then stopped, went back, and picked up the hubcap.

With a couple of beers in his belly, David wasn't up for a chase. The kids were fast. He'd give them that. He couldn't afford more problems. If he caught them there would be plenty.

He tossed the hubcap in the trunk and drove up to Sunset. David recalled how Sunset wound toward where the bright lights and asphalt stop at the water's edge. He imagined ocean waves pounding the shore. Through the somber mist mother ocean beckoned.

She waited patiently in the darkness, singing softly with her arms spread wide. David drove up through the winding inclines of Laurel Canyon anxious to surrender his busy mind to the fickle muse of sleep.

TEN

A bright sun burned through the marine layer. David's window framed a peaceful morning filled with evergreens and red tile roofs. A woodpecker pecked for breakfast grubs. Dogs yelped. A delivery truck shifted into low gear. David looked south across Wonderland Avenue where, below the mountain, the buildings of West Los Angeles sparkled in the haze.

Despite his emotional hangover David decided to be productive. He balanced his checkbook and counted the money in his pocket. The question about being an artist lodged in his mind. Advertising work proved creative, involved semantics, design and direction, the forging of marketable ideas into a commercial process. It served a purpose. He took pride that he had avoided clients with deceitful intent including a burial at sea business in Amarillo and a chain of Houston tanning salons selling anti-aging creams.

David opened a bag of Famous Amos chocolate chip cookies, sat down at the Smith Corona and rolled a sheet of paper in the typewriter. Fifteen minutes passed. David consumed the cookies. His attention strayed from a blank page to the treetops beyond his window. His fingers converged above the keys, but nothing happened. The heavy chains of practicality proved impossible to cast aside. He had no patron willing to support artistic indulgences.

In defiance of his doubts, a daydream ensued in which David

contemplated an artist's life. On a warm Champs Elysées, David shared a bottle of Bordeaux with a seductive woman in a sleeveless silk dress. She was French so her age was irrelevant. The wine proved effective. He admired her mocking laugh, pursed lips and tufts of mysterious armpit hair. With a flip of her wrist she opened a compact mirror and applied hot pink lipstick on her lips, nose and cheeks until she resembled an extra in Fellini's *Satyricon*.

They tumbled into a taxi. The French woman kissed him. The brown eyes of the voyeur driver filled the rearview mirror. At an intersection a horn honked. The taxi screeched to a halt and they slammed against the front seats. The woman bit David's lip. The French woman laughed hysterically, her face smeared with hot pink lipstick and blood.

The woodpecker rapped against a tree. David's thoughts returned to reality. He abandoned the typewriter, stepped to the window, and cursed his idleness. Fantasy and confusion could not be allowed. He shifted gears and sorted through Odd Jobs Incorporated leads. One assignment involved public relations and marketing for on-going social events. He reached Liz Edwards on his first call and was summoned for an interview. He showered and hurried down the mountain dressed in a gray chalk-striped suit.

Liz Edwards lived and worked in a grand high-rise building on Wilshire Boulevard. The doorman announced his arrival and directed him to the elevators. Ms. Edwards welcomed him with a spectacular tenth-floor view of the UCLA campus and the hills to the north. David guessed her to be mid-forties, tall and attractive with long jet-black hair that contrasted sharply with her well-attended complexion. David removed his shoes and followed her bare feet across the plush carpet.

She wore a black wrap-around dress and delivered a speech she had likely recited countless times. "Angel City parties start at eight unless it's a happy hour event and those begin promptly at six. You must arrive thirty minutes early. An hour early if it's a themed event so you can help with decorations. You must be well groomed and wear a coat and tie at all times. You'll help work the door, hand out flyers and make sure our guests are happy."

David raised a hand to ask a question.

"In a minute." Her dark eyes glistened. "I pay twelve dollars an hour for a three to four hour shift. That includes access to the buffet and the opportunity to work in the most exciting singles scene in Los Angeles. Are you ready?"

David stood and extended his hand. "How could I resist?"

Liz took his hand. "I can count on you?"

"Yes," he said. "When do I start?"

At 5:30 p.m. Friday David arrived at Gimlet's Bar and Grill in Century City. Liz Edwards introduced David to Harold Ames, a slight man with slick hair and a nervous twitch in his left eye. His head appeared unusually narrow as if, during his mother's labor, forceps had been aggressively applied during a protracted delivery.

Liz turned to David. "If you have questions," she said. "Direct them to Harold. He's number two tonight."

Harold ran his fingers down the lapels of David's suit. "Nice threads," he said. "Are you something special?"

"No," David said. "But thanks for asking."

Harold pressed his nostrils together with a thumb and index finger. "Since you look so prosperous, work the front door. Greet people. If they don't have tickets, send them to the line in front of me. I'll take their money and give them a nametag."

By six thirty Gimlet's banquet room was packed with people picking over cocktail sausages and raw vegetables, tortilla chips and salsa. A line formed at the cash bar. The crowd mingled and exchanged business cards. After a drink the volume of conversation amplified. Photographs in the Angel City Singles newsletter featured attractive couples with toothy smiles. In reality, most attendees were average middle-aged people, well dressed and weary from the workday, their eyes cast hopeful glances around the room.

At eight o'clock Harold Ames forced a thin-lipped grin.

"David, you did well on the door." Ames eyed a woman near the bar. "We got a hot crowd tonight. Why don't you take a break? Eat a bite. Be social. Ask people if they're having a good time."

"Thanks," David said. "I'll do that."

Harold was a carnival pimp, David thought, a person who'd hawk tickets to a freak show. The less conversation they had the better.

At the buffet David quickly learned he couldn't make a meal from leftover appetizers: sliced carrots and celery, tortilla chips, crackers and cheese cubes. He took his share and nudged through the crowd to a corner where less social guests occupied tables cluttered with abandoned paper plates and plastic cups. He cleared trash and acknowledged two older women drinking coffee.

David finished his makeshift meal and watched Liz Edwards sip from a generous glass of white wine as she walked toward him. "It's a nice crowd," he said.

Liz drew close to avoid straining her voice. "Yes, it's marvelous. Business is way up this month. I knew you'd do well. We have two or three events each week. Can you work that often?"

"Yes, of course."

The crowd pushed them together. David smelled her perfume.

"Excellent," Liz said. "Then I'll count on you for Wednesday." She dragged her polished fingernails across the back of his hand then turned into the crowd.

For two weeks David worked enough Angel City Singles events to buy groceries. His funds dwindled with each passing day so he restricted purchases to garner the most nourishment for the money: bottled water, whole wheat bread, bran flakes, non-fat almond milk, bananas, apples, pasta, kidney beans and broccoli. This commitment to conservation left few temptations in the cupboard. Austerity ruled.

In the mornings David reviewed his employment leads, and Odd Jobs listings, then called about marketing or sales positions. In the afternoons he waited for employers to return his calls, but in Los Angeles a returned phone call proved to be a rare occurrence. Every job opening received a flood of applicants.

One afternoon David paid homage to the lifeless telephone. He sat cross-legged on the floor beside the boxes that held his mother's books. Too many people and not enough work, he thought as he wrote in his journal. Had he misjudged himself? Had he made a terrible mistake?

He turned the page, scribbled in run-on sentences about how, before his parents died, he endured Sunday church services counting the colors in stained glass windows, about home-cooked meals and Thanksgiving sweet potato pie. He wrote about how, early in their marriage, Noreen took her morning coffee with cream and how she started drinking with her girlfriends when they moved to Dallas.

David closed his journal, rolled on the floor and fell asleep. The room was dark when he awoke, the floor hard beneath him. He stretched like a cat then looked out the window at the shadowy trees and the gloom that filled the valley. His stomach groaned. He longed for chocolate, a taste of sweetness, to experience something other than himself.

He laced his running shoes and took a long jog on the dark fire road then showered and prepared his dinner. David attempted to write some jokes worth repeating. Once a premise and a punch line conjoined, he went to the bathroom mirror and delivered them with a straight face.

"I refused to donate my disco-era clothing to Goodwill," he said. "I didn't want anyone to be caught dead in my aged polyester. Think no one cares about you? Be late with your rent check."

He polished his bits before the mirror and on Tuesday night they lived or died. His comedy comrades either laughed or did not. In rehearsal, rejection provided many reasons for laughter. Often the worst jokes were the most painful and the most amusing.

The following Tuesday Norman Razor and Rocco escorted the class through the editing process. The students provided critiques until what they delivered on stage represented some twisted observations about their lives. Long hours at Larry's Hollywood Lube Job appeared to agree with Rocco.

David tried not to dwell on thoughts of Sarah. It was simpler to restrain his urges and be cordial in class. It was easier to bury himself in his journal, to run along the crest of the mountain or take a shower. David's withdrawal proved to be short-lived. After class, Rocco and Joyce cornered him.

"Hey man," Rocco said. "I've got some big news."

Rocco displayed an eager grin and was about to speak when Sarah walked up to David.

"Do you hate me?" she said.

"Why would you say that?"

"Because you've been ignoring me." Sarah offered a sly smile. "I don't like to be ignored."

"But," Rocco said. "I was just going to say ..."

Sarah turned to Rocco. "Okay, what is it?"

Rocco couldn't contain himself. "I bought a car, a classic 1964 Ford Falcon Futura convertible," he said. "I practically stole it from one of Larry's customers."

Joyce shook her head. "More like salvaged," she said. "That car doesn't even have a top."

"Hey, it's a convertible," Rocco said. "This is Los Angeles. Who cares if the top is shot? There's no rust and it doesn't burn oil." Rocco stepped in front of Joyce, his face twisted in mock pain as he pleaded. "Listen, Joyce is making me go to the Whole World Expo on Saturday. Please don't make me go alone."

"What's the Whole World Expo?" David asked.

"She wants to hear this lecture about women who sleep with dogs. Please, I'll be the only guy."

Joyce elbowed Rocco. "Don't be dense," she said. "Faith Heartwell wrote Women Awaken the World. I have four tickets if you two want to go. It's on me."

"Please," Rocco begged. "Afterward we can cruise up the coast in the Futura and picnic on Zuma Beach."

"Excuse us a moment," David said and pulled Sarah aside.

"So," she asked. "You've been ignoring me?"

"No." David met her blue eyes. His reservations dissolved. "I've been preoccupied."

"Okay," she said. "Just checking."

Sarah offered encouragement. David sorted through her mixed signals and resisted the impulse to embrace her.

"Don't worry," he said. "Everything's fine."

Sarah shrugged. "So, let's tag along. Saturday sounds like fun."

The Saturday morning marine layer hid the promise of a warm fall day. Rocco, Joyce and David met in front of Sarah's apartment and tossed their swim trunks and beach towels into the Futura. Sarah and David climbed into the back seat of the topless car. Wind whipped their faces as they cruised along the Santa Monica Freeway. Sarah nudged her sunglasses up the bridge of her nose. When she turned to David, the world warped into an elliptical reflection in her dark lenses, his face distorted beyond recognition. Palm trees and concrete embankments whizzed by in a blur.

Rocco parked in the back of the Santa Monica Civic Center garage. David helped him hoist a nylon tarp over the car they secured with plastic rope. Joyce led them into the Whole World Expo. Faith Heartwell's talk was an hour away so they joined the congregation in the aisles of self-discovery to sample a New Age smorgasbord of organic foods, World music, hemp clothing, birthstone jewelry, books on tape and a virtual sea of self-proclaimed visionary authors and alternative healers. Exhibit booths and reassuring pitches offered hope with new explanations for the inexplicable and the obvious, new solutions for overcoming the inevitable.

Uncle Buck had warned David to avoid the commerce of miracle workers. David recalled Noreen's girlfriends in Dallas going on about their rising signs and numerology. How they'd consult horoscopes before accepting a date or a job interview. The unexplained interested David, but he believed the laws of nature prevailed over everything. He figured the Native Americans understood that certainty and they were well represented in the New Age bazaar.

After thirty minutes of drums and drumming, tofu snacks and incense burners, David turned to Rocco and said, "I bet people who believe in reincarnation are more likely to recycle."

"Good point." Rocco stopped to examine a chart of the intestinal track. "But what's with all the colon therapists?"

A delicate man in a white turban answered. "If you have a moment, I am most happy to demonstrate."

"No thanks." Rocco backed away. "I prefer prunes."

The exits were clearly marked. Joyce hovered nearby to keep Rocco in line. Sarah and David relaxed into a pair of meditation pods. The dual-action vibrating chair backs kneaded their shoulders and spines while the pods played soft music mixed with the sounds of running water and singing birds. Despite his skepticism, within a few minutes David fell under the spell of the electronic rainforest. He relaxed on the threshold of a dream when Joyce grabbed him.

"It's time for Faith." She pulled him from the pod. "We can't be late."

Sarah and David staggered to their feet, held each other for support and followed along. Joyce led Rocco by the hand. The auditorium filled quickly as women hurried to find seats. Many of them carried Faith's book.

Rocco hung close to David. "I told you it would be like this," he said. "I'm glad you're here, man."

Two women patrolled the room with stalks of burning incense. The room filled with the heady scent of sage. A man with long braided hair played a flute. With his first note the energy shifted as if the entire room had taken a singular breath. The flute played. The entranced assembly waited.

Curtains parted. The room exploded with applause as Faith Heartwell stood before them, a statuesque woman with thick white hair and eyes the color of a tropical sea. Her skin appeared ageless. The sleeves of her long golden gown blossomed as she raised her hands. An attendant presented a microphone.

Faith's voice was confident and soothing. "It's not an accident that we have come together. Understand this is a path we have chosen. It's important we are aware of this choice. It's important we exercise our intelligence and our intuition."

Faith crossed the stage and nodded in the direction of David and Rocco.

"It's encouraging to see brothers among us. Please know you are welcome. The sexes don't exist without one another. Wisdom rises from sharing and acceptance, from understanding and forgiveness."

Faith sipped a glass of water and surveyed the audience. Rocco sank low in his chair. Sarah edged closer to David and touched his fingers.

"Our needs are simple," Faith continued. "But it's easy to forget. Near the crossroads of harmony and mindlessness there's a clearing of truth. If those around you offer ideas with love and compassion, accept them. Hold on to them."

Faith raised her eyes toward the ceiling. She stood motionless for several seconds then crossed the stage.

"In the clearing you will find your truth. It's like the breath. We find wisdom through bringing in and letting go. There's no separation in this world. Your breath is like an ocean moving inside you. It's the power of this ocean that holds our planet and our universe together."

David held Sarah's hand and listened. He agreed with Faith, though he accepted the time spent in the meditation pod could have warped his cerebral function.

Faith placed a hand over her heart. Her chest rose and fell. "Please close your eyes," she said. "Breathe. And listen to the animated spiritual rhythm of your heart."

A drummer tapped a muted syncopated beat from the rear of the room. The flute began to play. A rush of movement stirred through the aisles and again the room filled with burning sage.

David accepted the wisdom of nature and the sounds and smells that surrounded him. He closed his eyes and breathed deeply. Minutes passed and time extended as the drum beat continued. The flute began to whisper. David sank deeper into thoughtlessness. Eventually, the music stopped and the room was immersed in silence. David opened his eyes and looked at Sarah. Her eyelids drooped. She smiled sweetly. Rocco began to snore. Joyce shoved an elbow into his ribs.

Rocco sat upright. "Hey," he said. "What's happening?"

Joyce placed her hand over his mouth. Sarah and David suppressed their laughter.

On the stage, Faith settled into a director's chair. The room remained still. After a few moments, a young woman in the front row stood.

"In your book you write about how relationships are like gardening," the woman said. "Can you speak about that?"

Faith tapped a finger on her temple. "Relationships," she said, "are similar to gardening yet somewhat more complicated. In either case, constant weeding is required."

The audience laughed. Faith smiled and lifted her head. The sleeves of her golden gown flowed beside her.

"We are part of the natural world," she said. "But we are not wild. Our inherent wisdom gives us the power to join the dance and to celebrate life. But we often confuse love with sex. Our sexuality is not an amusement park. It's a gift of self, an expression of love. If one theme signifies our liberation as women it is this: if you choose to marry and create a child, do it consciously with a partner who shares your commitment to raising a loving human being. Choose wisely."

David recalled Noreen and the early days of their marriage. How they were too young and too eager. People go through years of education without courses in relationships. There are few guides but the vagaries of upbringing and popular culture, peer pressure and vacuous love songs. Denial was a powerful force, he thought, as the questions and answers continued.

When the gathering concluded Rocco lead them back to the Futura. They drove north on Pacific Coast Highway. A brilliant afternoon sun turned the Pacific into a blinding mirror. Currents of cool air swept over the expanse of pavement and sand. Above the beach, gulls rode the thermal breeze searching for their next meal.

Rocco drove past Will Rogers State Beach, crossed the intersection where Sunset Boulevard reached the ocean and passed the entrance to the Getty Villa. Topanga State Beach was a snapshot of surfers, tourists and drifters watching the waves. Pacific Coast Highway narrowed as they approached Malibu where a row of beach houses hung precariously above the sand and surf. Across the road the Santa Monica Mountains rose abruptly in the sun.

In Malibu they stopped at a deli and bought sandwiches, chips and bottled water. A few miles further north they stopped at Zuma Beach welcomed by the gentle onshore breeze and an unseasonably warm sun. Sarah and David changed into their swimsuits. The foursome spread towels near the bathhouse, ate quietly, and watched the surf break up and down the shoreline. When they finished eating, David dug his bare feet into the loose sand. Sarah peeked over her sunglasses and winked at him.

"Let's take a walk," David said.

David took Sarah's hand. They stepped toward the ocean. Joyce wiped mustard from Rocco's cheek.

"You two go ahead," Rocco said. "Now that we've eaten Joyce and I are going to make out. I hate to make out on an empty stomach."

When Sarah and David reached the shore, sandpipers scurried back and forth ahead of them. Waves forced water across the smooth, packed sand. Up the beach, a red-haired girl and her father finished the walls of a sandcastle they would soon abandon. Above them, a pair of Chinese dragon kites climbed in the wind, pilots pulling strings to keep them aloft.

David and Sarah walked and watched the surf rise and fall. About half a mile up the beach they turned around. Sarah pivoted in the sand and bumped her hip against his.

"What are you thinking?"

David didn't look at her. Out on the ocean a pair of pelicans bobbed on a swell. "I'm trying not to think," he said. "Not too much anyway."

Sarah stepped out in front and walked backwards to face him. "You're being serious, aren't you?"

"That's almost funny." David moved closer. "Seems I'm serious whenever I'm around you. It must be contagious."

They stopped. A wave crested and thrust cold water around their ankles. The ocean breeze lifted the hair off Sarah's shoulders. Late afternoon sun illuminated the curve of her upper lip and the tiny crescent scar. David waited several long seconds then kissed her as gently as he could. His lips lingered on hers until she broke it off.

"We really shouldn't," she said.

David dropped his hands. Sarah pulled away and pointed at the water.

"Look," she screamed. "Dolphins!"

The waves broke close to shore and a pair of bottlenose dolphins navigated slowly through the swells. Sarah grabbed David's hand. They rushed down the beach, marveled as the dolphins glided effortlessly through the water. They followed the dolphins until they could see Rocco and Joyce.

In that moment David was compelled to embrace the forces of nature and join the dolphins.

"Come on," David said. "Let's swim out to them."

"Are you crazy?" Sarah stopped. "The water's freezing. We just ate and there's an undertow."

"Forget that," he said. "I'm going."

David tossed his shirt to Sarah and raced into the surf. The first wave broke when the water reached waist deep. David lowered his head, dove and the wave crashed over him. He pulled through the frigid water, came up for air on the other side then swam hard until the water was cold and deep beneath him. But there were no dolphins. He continued to swim, but all he saw was the rise and fall of waves. A four-foot wall crashed down on him. David struggled to the surface, gasped for air and felt the current seize him.

A succession of waves pummeled him. Another rose and collapsed. He took a deep breath and dove downward. Beneath the surface the water was cold and quiet. David exhaled and drifted for a long minute suspended in silence. He opened his eyes and watched the beams of sunlight penetrate and disappear into the darkness below. Above, the bright surface became a rippled window to another world. Beneath, the water shimmered, cold and serene and all consuming. Drawn to the seamless comfort of the quiet depths, David considered the ultimate serenity of letting go. He hung there suspended like an embryo. For a moment, everything remained perfectly still and silent and how he wanted it to be. David's lungs protested. The body's instinctive will to survive forced him up. Again, he ascended and broke the surface.

He gasped for air. The waves tossed and taunted him. He pulled hard until he moved beyond the breakers. Rolling swells lifted him as he treaded water. A chill reverberated through his limbs, his teeth chattered and the current pressed against him.

David looked to the shore, saw Sarah and then, suddenly, a small boy standing behind her. The boy's big blue shirt hung loose and flapped in the breeze. David wiped salt water from his eyes. The boy stood behind Sarah and reached for her hand, but they never touched. The boy raised his arm and summoned David.

A wave crested and fell. David took a long breath and started back, swam parallel to shore, across the current, until a wave lifted him then he kicked and pulled as hard as he could. He attempted to catch the surge and when the wave didn't take him he rested for a few minutes. He swam slowly, deliberately and caught one wave after another. The pace of his stroke increased to avoid losing what he had gained.

The waves rose and collapsed. The current forced him back, but he continued to swim and rode the waves until, at last, he touched the sand. The water surged and receded. The beach shifted beneath his hands. He crawled through the foam and stumbled to his feet. Sarah ran into the water and wrapped a towel around his shoulders.

"Damn it," she screamed. "You could've drowned."

David collapsed against her. "You were right," he gasped. "The water is freezing."

"Hey man," Rocco said. "You scared the crap out of us."

David raised his head. Salt water flowed from his nostrils. He looked up the beach. "Where's the boy?" he asked.

Sarah pulled the towel tightly around him. "What are you talking about?"

"The little boy in the blue shirt," David said. "He was standing right behind you. He waved to me."

Rocco lead their march away from the water. "Hey man, we were all waving. I thought my arms would fall off."

David limped into the bathhouse and took a shower. Sand and seawater poured from every orifice. He dressed as quickly as his fatigue would allow. When they reached the parking lot they sat in the topless Futura and watched the ocean swallow the orange sun.

David scoured the beach, abandoned except for an older couple, two young girls, and thin clouds an orchid pink.

"Feeling better?" Sarah asked.

David groaned. "I think I'll make it."

"I can't believe you did that," she said.

David rested his head against the back seat. "I can't believe it either."

David leaned forward. Residual salt water drained from his sinuses.

"I know just what you need," Joyce said. She held a freshly rolled joint between the seats, checked the parking lot, lit the joint and inhaled. "Have some of this."

David accepted the joint. "No, I better not."

He had smoked a few times in college. Marijuana never interested him. David offered the joint to Sarah. She shook her head. David passed it on to Rocco.

"Come on you guys," Joyce said. "Get high with us."

"Listen, man." Rocco inhaled, held the smoke, and spoke through clenched lips. "Doctors prescribe grass to ease the suffering of terminally ill patients." Rocco released a cloud of smoke and passed the joint back to David. "Come on man. Join the party."

Joyce and Rocco grinned like Cheshire cats.

"I guess we're all terminal," David said. He took the joint and inhaled as deeply as he could.

ELEVEN

Saturday night David worked the door at Bradley's Bar. An animated disc jockey played a blend of MTV Eighties pop rock and disco-dance track favorites. DJ John was popular with the partygoers, but not with Harold Ames. David learned doorman duty involved recognizing trouble before it happened.

On a break he approached the DJ booth. "Why the tension between you and Ames?"

"Jealousy," John said. "Harold hates that everyone loves me."

"I need more information."

John glanced over his shoulder. "After a marina party I go to the men's room and open a stall. Bingo, there's old Harold with his hand up this chick's skirt doing a line of cocaine off her breast."

"What happened?"

"I excused myself and went to the next stall," John said. "The chick freaked. Dumped a gram in the toilet. Harold was pissed. He's paranoid. Thinks I'll rat him out."

"Would you?"

"If he messes with me. Liz hates that shit. Drugs are not part of the program."

Harold Ames crossed the dance floor and snapped his fingers. "Okay Mr. Disco, play some music," he said. "When people get bored it's bad for business."

DJ John climbed into the booth.

Harold wiped his nose and glared at David. "What are you staring at?" he said. "Make yourself useful. Go dance with one of the fat girls."

DJ John made an announcement, "Hey everybody, there's a special request from old Harold, the boss man. Everybody jump up and shake your booty."

The sound system came alive with the Ohio Player's *Love Roller Coaster*. Dancers crowded the floor as John growled into the microphone. "Come on people. Let's party."

Harold blew his nose in three long honks then headed for the front door. David followed and found Liz Edwards rubbing lotion on her hands, a ritual she repeated in the waning hours of each event. Harold reached for his cigarettes and went outside. A tall young woman approached David, "Brenda" written on her nametag in cursive letters.

"Come dance with me," she said.

Liz nodded approval. David sensed displeasure. Brenda pulled him onto the dance floor and he did his best to mirror her movements.

"You're cute," Brenda said after the song. "But it looks like you haven't danced since the Seventies."

"Thanks Brenda." The music resumed. David attempted to keep up. "You must be clairvoyant."

"Not me," she said straight-faced. "I sell handbags at Neiman-Marcus. What do you do?"

"At the moment, I'm dancing with you."

"No," she said. "For a living?"

"My day job is marketing. I do some writing."

Her expression brightened. "Writing is so there," she yelled above the music. "In my true life I'm a poet."

"True life?" David moved closer. "What do you do with your poems?"

"Go to poetry readings. They have them all over town. You should check it out."

Liz Edwards waved from the landing.

"Sorry," David said. "Duty calls."

Brenda kissed his cheek. "Poetry is happening," she said. "Follow your heart."

Liz Edwards waited with her arms folded. "I don't mind a few dances," she said. "Remember the rules. No fooling around while I'm paying for your time. It's late, watch for drunks."

The crowd danced at a fevered pace. David took a position near the dance floor. Two men danced the gator, flopped on their stomachs like drunken fraternity pledges. The crowd encircled the men and clapped. The barrel-shaped woman came from nowhere, charged the bar behind him, and grab a short man.

"How 'bout giving mama some lovin'?" the woman said. She wrapped her arms around the man's neck. "Give mama what she needs? I'll make a man out of you."

David checked for backup. Harold was gone. The music blared. The dance crowd clapped. The woman held the man in a headlock. Liz Edwards rushed across the room.

"Let him go," David said. He grabbed the woman's arm. The woman tightened her grip.

"Excuse me," Liz shouted. "You've had enough."

The woman sneered. "I haven't had any."

She strengthened her hold, the man's face turned blue. She

tried to kiss him.

"Please," Liz shouted. "Release him."

With amazing quickness the woman dropped her claim and lunged at David. He dodged and thrust an arm between their chins. The woman used every ounce of strength to plant her lips on David's face. He held her off.

"You men are a bunch of fairies," she said.

The woman's frenzied breath reeked of rum and cola, onions and guacamole dip. The roily stench served as motivation. David pushed. The woman fell backward into a chair that collapsed beneath her weight. Stunned, she squatted on the floor. Liz and David helped the dazed woman to her feet, ushered her through the bar and out the front door. Her primary victim followed close behind, straightened his rumpled shirt and tie. The woman stumbled along the sidewalk then turned on them.

"You fairies." She flipped them off. "You'll never learn to show a gal a good time."

David turned to the disheveled man. "Your friend's had too much to drink," he said.

The man looked insulted. "Friend?"

"Sorry," David said. "I thought you knew her."

"I've never seen that awful woman before. Not in my life."

They watched the woman wander off.

Liz offered the man a pair of guest passes. "Please accept our apologies," she said. "These tickets are for our big South Bay party next weekend. It's always a great crowd."

"No thanks." The man was indignant. "I've had quite enough of your crowd. Good night."

Harold Ames opened the door and blew his nose. "What's

happening?"

Liz didn't hide her anger. "Where the hell were you?"

"Taking a break," Harold said. "No big deal."

"For you, maybe."

They followed Liz inside and closed the party, announced raffle winners and upcoming events. People headed toward the exit. David distributed newsletters and discount coupons. Liz settled accounts with the bar manager. When everyone was gone, Harold and David carted the supplies through the parking garage and loaded them in the trunk of Liz's BMW. She dismissed Harold with a nod and offered David a ride to his car. When they reached the Buick Liz touched David's hand, her fingers moist with lotion.

"I appreciate the way you handled that woman," she said. "Those situations can get ugly."

"Thanks, Ms. Edwards. It was purely self-defense."

"Please, call me Liz," she said. "It's nice to know you are there. Harold can't make it next week. I want you to be number two and work the front with me."

Liz Edwards' dark eyes turned misty. She leaned toward him with a sudden expectation. David opened the door.

"Sure," he said. "I'm glad to help."

On the drive home David's brakes started grinding. He remembered Rocco's warning. He didn't want to spend the money.

Late Monday afternoon David took the Buick to Al, the mechanic Rocco recommended. After the assessment, Al stood beside the Buick wiping his hands with a red shop rag.

David struggled for words. "Four hundred and seventy-five dollars?" His voice cracked. "Why so much?"

Al's manner was tempered by years of dealing with automotive misfortunes. "You need a complete brake job. Got to replace the front right disc. When metal grinds, it's going to cost you. That's the best I can do. Anybody else in town would charge seven hundred."

"I understand," he said.

David accepted Al's offer, sunk his hands into the pockets of his leather jacket, and walked east on Hollywood Boulevard. Shadows were long. The Walk of Fame swarmed with costumed promoters and social outcasts, teenagers and off-season shoppers buying T-shirts and movie posters. Tourists poured from a bus to take pictures in front of Grauman's Chinese Theatre. Storefronts proudly displayed larger than life images of Marilyn Monroe, James Dean and Elvis Presley. Dead Hollywood idols presided over the parade. An older woman in Bermuda shorts stopped on the star-splattered sidewalk to scrape discarded chewing gum off her sneakers.

In front of a pawnshop pedestrians maneuvered around two young musicians. One sported long bleached blond hair and wrap-around sunglasses. He shook his mane and clutched electric guitar cases.

The taller one tugged at the cases. "No way," he said. "We're not pawning."

"We'll play acoustic," said the blond musician. "We'll play some gigs and get them back."

"Acoustic sucks. Why not sell your fucking hair to a wig shop?"

"We can't get three hundred for my hair."

Further east on Hollywood Boulevard there were no tourists or musicians or street performers. Beyond the Walk of Fame, the carnival midway yielded to blocks of run-down buildings crammed between new mini malls and security access offices. To the north, homes climbed up into the hills. The afternoon sun faded in the west.

David marched down the sidewalk. An empty stomach growled when he passed shady Chinese restaurants and pizza joints. A shopkeeper stood watch in his doorway. Handbills floated in the air. A man in a tattered army surplus poncho rummaged through a trashcan then extended his hand to David.

"Spare change?"

David clenched his teeth. "It's a bad day to ask me for money," he said.

"Spare change?"

David gave the man a dollar.

"Bless you," the man said. "Bless you."

At Larry's Hollywood Lube Job David waited for an hour reading a shopworn *People* magazine with Madonna on the cover. When Rocco finished work they took the Futura back down Hollywood Boulevard.

Neon signs accented an ominous gloom that bright lights do not penetrate. The evening sideshow wandered aimlessly to the droning beat of soundtracks that poured from passing cars and discount electronics stores. Daytime tourists surrendered the streets to nocturnal creatures, ragged beggars, gangs of restless teenagers, the occasional prostitute, and recruiters from the Church of Scientology.

Rocco parked in front of the Two Guys from Italy restaurant where a biker club mingled and admired their motorcycles. Rocco ordered a large sausage and mushroom pizza and a pitcher of beer. A small boy came through the door with a box of candy. The mother waited outside. The boy flashed a gap-toothed grin.

"Hey mister, may I sell my candy?"

The manager wiped the counter with a towel. "Sorry little one," he said. "I can't afford to share my customers. You'll have to find your own."

"Please, mister."

Rocco left the booth and bought four bars.

"Having any luck?" he asked the boy.

"Not much. I need to sell this whole box. It is for my school."

"You and your mother go down by the theaters," Rocco said. "There are more tourists."

The boy and his mother headed west. David and Rocco ate the pizza and drank the beer. Rocco ordered a second pitcher, lit a cigarette and set the ashtray between them.

"So," Rocco said. "What's the damage?"

David stared into his beer. "Four hundred and seventy-five," he said. "That's a lot when you're broke."

Rocco blew smoke rings toward the ceiling. "That's a lot any time."

"I'm screwed." David set his empty mug on the table. "All I've found are odd jobs. About enough to eat."

Rocco chewed pizza crust. "Food is important."

"After I pay Al for the brakes it's going to be tough. Then what do I do?"

"It's all right, man." Rocco filled their mugs with beer. "Don't sweat it."

They finished the pitcher and drove up Lookout Mountain in the topless car. The cool air slapped the back of David's head. When they reached Wonderland Avenue, Rocco pulled into the driveway.

"Thanks for referring me to Al," David said.

"Forget about it. When's your car ready?"

"Wednesday morning."

"Then I'll pick you up tomorrow night for the workshop. Our final rehearsal before the showcase."

As Rocco backed into the street his headlights exposed three coyotes trotting up the hill.

"Nice neighbors," Rocco said. He shifted gears. His taillights disappeared around the corner. David stood in the dark and listened to the eucalyptus leaves stir in the night air. A dog howled from the road above.

Mrs. Howell watched from behind a curtain as David climbed the steps to his apartment. The curse of the lonely landlady, he thought. Perhaps solitude served to temper the soul for greater service. He opened the refrigerator and found his last beer, took a long drink. Shadows played on the back of his hand. He imagined walking through a field of summer grass and cheerful wildflowers beneath a bright sun. The telephone rang.

"Hello."

"Hello yourself," Sarah said. "What are you doing?"

"Thinking."

"About some good jokes I hope."

"It's more involved than that."

"Better lighten up. Our showcase is a week from tomorrow."

David finished the beer in a gulp. "Frankly, I'm not concerned about that."

"You don't sound worried about anything. Are you loaded?"

"Yes, I probably am."

"Rocco told Joyce you're having car problems."

"Yes, it's bad enough."

"Well, here's some good news. Thanksgiving is a week from Thursday. The restaurant where Joyce works is closed. We're preparing a little feast. We want you and Rocco to celebrate with us."

David reflected on holiday meals, turkey and dressing, cranberry relish. "Thanks," he said. "I'm in no position to refuse a free meal."

"Okay mister enthusiasm. We'll plan on it. Write something funny. That'll be good for you."

David opened his journal. Empty pages soon filled with words. He felt a tremor. Vast spaces existed within him. Age was incremental. Wrinkles slowly deepened. Gravity pulled. The bond that sustained him proved elusive. He could not stop the advance of time. Perhaps in a universe of constant change, common ground was an illusion. Perhaps love was merely a seductive opiate, an addiction to biological impulses or a fleeting dream. People cast aside their winter clothes. Anoint their scars with oil. They beg forgiveness. Heal their wounds. A heavenly chorus announces their ascension. Above the clouds they embrace, create a world of their own where infinity stretches out in all directions.

At dawn a bulldozer roared to life. David staggered to the window and watched the machine attack the hillside. The diesel engine grunted as the bulldozer raked the ground, pulled loose the vegetation and rocks then scooped and dumped and raked until the dirt separated. Workmen sprayed water to control the dust. A stream trickled down the street. Piles of brush and roots and rocks were lifted into a dump truck. In his half sleep hangover David was fascinated until he realized the work would continue all day.

David returned to his air mattress serenaded by the roaring diesel engine. He covered his ears and longed for sleep. A prisoner of his own making, he served his sentence and plotted escape from impending financial doom.

TWELVE

The Word Wizards game show paid the biggest prize money in Hollywood. David's audition was scheduled early in the afternoon of Razor's comedy showcase. He figured there would be plenty of time to audition then rehearse before he went to the club. David waited with thirty hopeful contestants and completed the application. A production assistant answered the telephone with unbridled zeal.

"Thank you for calling Word Wizards, the show that pays you back." She tilted her head. "That's so great. Bye now."

David thought about the comedy showcase and performing in front of an audience for the first time. He should have been nervous. He should have been running his lines. But if he got lucky on Word Wizards he could be flush in a week. $10,000 could be won on a single show.

A haggard woman with a stopwatch and a whistle ushered them into an adjacent room.

"Okay people, let's get started." She clapped her hands. "Grab a prompt sheet. Take a seat along the wall. My name is Mary. The secret to Word Wizards is speed and accuracy. When you are called, speak clearly. And be quick."

"Your prompt sheets have several categories. Pair off, prepare to ask and respond. When I call your name, you and your partner stand. Your partner asks the question. You have seven seconds to respond. Any questions? Okay, let's get going."

David's partner was Sue from Big Bear Lake, an earthy woman wearing a plaid flannel shirt, hiking boots and shorts that revealed a healthy growth of leg hair.

Sue whispered to David in a breathless clip. "I can't believe this. I'm going to be on Word Wizards. I've watched the show my entire life. My family runs a lodge near the lake. We watch every day."

Her breath smelled of coffee. Hyperactive and caffeinated, Sue manifested a behavioral profile David found particularly loathsome. He wanted to relax, but Sue demanded undivided attention. David sat politely and absorbed the impact of every word.

"The family says I can do it." Sue's whispered rant continued. "Now I'm here. I'm so nervous I can't see straight. Aren't you excited? Of course you are. You're here and they're about to call your name. Maybe they'll call me first. Who knows? Don't worry. I'm your partner. Is this exciting or what?"

Ten prospects were quizzed before Mary called Sue's name. Sue crossed her fingers, squealed with manic delight and fixed her eyes on the floor.

David read the question, "Prompt forty-five: Name breeds of dogs."

Sue launched her caffeine-fueled assault: "Husky, golden retriever, greyhound, poodle, dachshund, Dalmatian, chow, cocker spaniel, collie, Chihuahua, schnauzer, boxer, beagle, bloodhound."

"Times up." Mary clicked her stopwatch and scribbled on her clipboard. The hopefuls applauded. "Well done."

Sue sat and grabbed David's arm. "Yes, yes, yes," she said.

David prayed he wasn't next.

"David Bishop," Mary said.

He stood and squared his shoulders. The bitter taste of fear and digestive fluids bubbled up into his throat.

Sue read, "Prompt nineteen: Name things that are yellow."

David's mouth went dry. "Bananas, a canary, uh, the sun, the moon." He closed his eyes. "Butter, uh, corn, squash, lemons."

Mary clicked her stopwatch. "Times up."

David slumped into his chair. Sue squirmed in her seat. The rest took their turns. When the quizzing was complete Mary left to review her notes. The room erupted with nervous chatter.

Sue consoled David. "You got a tough break," she said. "Colors are difficult. They're so impersonal. But dogs are easy. I love animals. Isn't this exciting? Being on television is my dream. It's going to be great. All of my family and friends will be watching."

David turned to Sue. "Do you ever stop talking?"

"No," she said, unfazed. "Not really."

Mary returned and announced the picks with routine inflection. When Sue's name was called she vaulted from her seat and screamed, "Oh my God! Oh my God!"

David headed for the exit with the other rejects. The crowded elevator made a silent descent. When the doors parted they dispersed into the Hollywood afternoon with their heads bowed. David crossed the side street with a slight hatchet-faced man named Felix. David was compelled to speak, to somehow break the spell of their collective loss.

"Word Wizards is a lot easier when you're watching on TV," David said.

"You have to be fast and perky," Felix said. "They always pick the most energetic ones."

"You've auditioned before?"

"Many times."

"Are you an actor?"

"No," he said. "I'm a mime, but I also play the oboe. I perform at Venice Beach. Mostly I play the oboe. People don't care much for mimes these days. I think the silence bothers them."

Felix presented a business card. "Call me if you need an oboe player. Or a mime."

On the rear window of Felix's rust-spotted Dodge van a peace sign was spray painted above a sun-bleached sticker that read: SHIT HAPPENS. Felix drove off leaving a trail of exhaust fumes.

The bitterness of defeat coated David's tongue. There was no time for regret. More immediate issues consumed David as he turned the Buick onto Sunset Boulevard. Razor's showcase was only a few hours away. David accelerated, began to rehearse as if cramming for a final exam. The worst that could happen was he'd make a complete fool of himself.

A super-sized Angelyne billboard demanded his attention. The iconic sex goddess loomed above Sunset Boulevard with her massive milk-white breasts. A flatbed truck swerved in front of the Buick. David slammed on the new brakes, but it was too late. The over-burdened truck tilted. Produce crates catapulted skyward. Hundreds of artichokes and tomatoes became airborne. David veered. The Buick jumped a curb and crashed into a *Los Angeles Times* newspaper rack. Produce rained down. Tomatoes splattered. Artichokes rolled across the street.

In Hollywood the police are never far away. LAPD arrived by the time David unbuckled his seat belt. He climbed out of the

Buick careful not to trip on artichokes or mashed tomatoes. The front right bumper and grill were dented, the newspaper rack wrecked.

David slammed a clenched fist on the newspaper rack. Late editions slid onto the sidewalk. He leaned against the Buick. The truck driver and passengers hurried to clear the street of broken crates and produce. A witness told police the truck had lost control. There were no injuries or other vehicles involved. One officer directed traffic while another spoke with the truck driver in Spanish.

An officer approached David. "You're not injured?" he asked.

David was slow to respond. "Not physically."

"The driver doesn't have insurance. Does your car run?"

"I'm not sure."

"You need to move it off the curb."

David signed the police report. The Buick started, but when David shifted into reverse the transmission slipped. There was a loud scrape as he backed off the curb. The transmission surged. He shifted to park. The transmission lurched as he drove away. At each intersection he begged the Buick, "Please don't die. Please go on." He caressed the steering wheel and coached the crippled car to Al's Brake Shop.

"We don't do transmissions," Al said. "But this doesn't sound good."

David pressed his temples. "What's the verdict?"

"Best you will do is a rebuilt transmission."

"How much?"

Al lit a cigarette. Smoke hung in front of his face. "I got a buddy that'll give you a deal," he said. "Probably be at least a grand.

Maybe fifteen hundred."

David choked. A grand for a rebuilt transmission would be cheap. "A thousand dollars? Fifteen hundred?" he said. "That wipes me out."

Al crushed the cigarette under his boot. "It's a shame," he said. "But what are you going to do? In Los Angeles you got to have wheels."

Al would have the Buick towed in the morning. David retrieved his briefcase and leather jacket and started off. Razor's showcase began within the hour.

Al called after him. "You need a ride?"

"No." David didn't look back. "I'll walk."

David hurried west on Hollywood. He didn't look at the star-covered sidewalk. The inhabitants of the neon midway stepped aside. His thoughts vacillated from rage to despair. He maintained a frantic pace. The briefcase swung by his side. At La Brea David turned south down to Sunset then back toward the west. Mini malls filled with young people buying music and renting videos. Security guards watched convenience store shoppers stopping for beer, cigarettes and rolling papers. In restaurants, couples lounged at window tables, drank wine and ate their evening meals.

"Just keep going," David said. "Don't slow down."

He crossed Sierra Bonita, Stanley and Genesee. He attempted to rehearse. He couldn't remember the order or the punch lines. Everything morphed into a maze of haste and misfortune.

"You are funny," he said. "Funny. Funny. Funny."

When David reached the club Rocco and Sarah waited near the side entrance. Joyce and Elmer and the rest of the class stirred about, referred to note cards or chewed fingernails.

"Hey, David." Rocco's eyes filled the frames of his new wire-rim glasses. "Man, you look like crap."

"Lower than that," David said. "I'm subterranean."

Sarah touched his shoulder. "What's wrong?"

David clenched his teeth. "I wrecked my car. The transmission is toast. That means I'm a week away from taking up residence in my car or a pasteboard box."

"Hey man, calm down," Rocco said. "You're going to burst a blood vessel."

"Come on," Sarah said. "It can't be that bad."

"Yeah," Rocco said. "It can't be worse than going up in front of that crowd and blanking out."

"Thanks Rocco," David said. "That's just what I needed."

"I'm only messing with you."

"This isn't funny," David said. "The transmission is trashed. I'm screwed like a mongrel dog."

Rocco laughed. "That's good man. Tap those emotions."

"I'm unhinged." David demanded. "This isn't funny."

"No," Rocco said. "It's hilarious. Keep it up."

"Everything's going to work out," Sarah said. "You'll see. It always does."

Rocco slapped David's back. "Man, get ready to go on," he said. "We start in fifteen minutes. Elmer's first and you're second."

The club filled with regulars, friends of performers, a few white-legged tourists in shorts and prospects for Razor's next workshop. Waitresses in logo T-shirts rushed to take drink orders. People huddled around small café tables and waited for the show.

David and the others gathered in the back of the club for a pre-show pep talk. Norman Razor went down the line and shook their hands.

"I'm proud of all of you," Norman said. "Don't be afraid to abandon your script and engage the audience. It's okay to just be yourself. Go up there and have fun."

Norman turned and went up onto the stage. The spotlights cut through the darkness and cigarette smoke. He raised his arms to the audience like a preacher calling on holy spirits.

"Hello and welcome. I'm Norman Razor and some of the comedians you're about to see have never performed before. Ever."

A man in the first row howled. Another booed. Norman wagged a finger. "Please, brothers and sisters, reserve any cruelty for your house plants. These are funny people. Have a few drinks and be considerate. Now let's have a big welcome for the emcee of tonight's comedy extravaganza, Rocco Manelli."

Rocco grabbed the microphone. His thick body cast a wide shadow. The audience applauded.

"Thank you. Thank you very much. I haven't heard that much applause since I was evicted from my last apartment."

Laughter rumbled through the room as Rocco recounted the hardships of growing up in a circus family.

"Some kids dream about running away to join the circus. My dream was to escape the clowns I called parents. As a twelve-year-old I couldn't run very fast in balloon pants and size 28 shoes."

The audience laughed. Rocco glided effortlessly through his monologue. David shrank in the corner. Elmer chewed his fingernails until Rocco called his name.

"Hello, Elmer?" Rocco tapped the microphone. Elmer withdrew the fingers from his mouth and crept toward the stage. "Elmer? Come out wherever you are. Please welcome Elmer."

The spotlights magnified the fright in Elmer's face. "Hello." His voice cracked. "My name's, uh, Elmer." Nervous laughter filled the room. "Sorry, I almost forgot my name."

Elmer attempted to lower the microphone stand. His foot became tangled in the cord. "I don't know why I'm doing this," he said. "Except I'm thirty-two and mom still calls me 'her little cowboy.'"

The audience laughed. Color returned to Elmer's face. David pressed his back into the corner like a prizefighter hanging on a turnbuckle. He took a breath and closed his eyes. Minutes passed. He didn't recall what was said. A burst of laughter brought him back. The audience applauded. David opened his eyes. Elmer stepped off the stage and romped through the crowd with his head held high.

"Oh, we're having fun now." Rocco raised his eyebrows. "Thanks Elmer. Hey, you're a great crowd. Ready for more?"

Rocco shook his head and asked again, "I said, are you ready for more?"

"Yes," the audience responded with conviction.

"Okay, that's better. Next, please welcome a very good friend with a serious sense of humor, Mr. David Bishop."

Rocco stepped away from the microphone and clapped. David hesitated. The room began to spin.

Sarah reached out to him. "Go for it," she said.

"I will not be humiliated," David said under his breath. "I will not fail."

A surge of adrenaline carried David forward. For a few brief seconds he felt confident then weeks of frustration overwhelmed him. Panic raced through his body, but he continued until he found himself on stage.

Rocco offered a goofy grin and backed away. The spotlights obscured everything. Out in the darkened room, ghostly shapes shifted in a cloud of cigarette smoke. David adjusted the microphone stand. Long seconds passed. He gazed down at the faces in the front row and cleared his throat.

"What do you do when your life sucks?" His question floated in the air and was greeted by silence. "What do you do when you're broke and need cash?"

Someone shouted, "Call Elmer's mom."

Laughter rocked the room. David regained his composure.

"Thank you for the audience participation." He ran his fingers through his hair, felt the sweat on his brow. "No, you don't call Elmer's mother. You audition for a game show."

David lifted the microphone from the stand, paced the stage and exposed his angst. "Today, I auditioned for big bucks on Word Wizards." He slapped a palm against his forehead. "They dumped me for a caffeine-junky lumberjack named Sue, who doesn't shave her legs."

A spit of laughter started in the back of the room. Blank faces stared from the front row.

"Forgive me. I've had a really bad day. I crashed my car into a truckload of artichokes."

There was a chuckle or two. David picked up the pace and spoke as quickly as he could.

"In fact, I've had several bad days. My California dream has become a nightmare. This is the Eighties, but last night I had a Sixties flashback, a nightmare from the Twilight Zone. The Fugitive strangled the one-armed man. I Dream of Jeanie broke her bottle over master's head. Ed Sullivan wore a mini skirt on Gilligan's Island. Ginger got jealous. Eddie Munster was adopted, as the poster child for Hair Club for Men."

David imitated Dennis Hopper. "It's a weird dream, man." He pressed his palm to his brow and roamed the stage. "Jimi Hendrix joined Peter, Paul and Mary singing *Puff the Magic Drag Queen*. Hendrix put the torch to little Jackie Paper. On American Bandstand, Sonny and Cher joined the Beach Boys. They sang *I Got You Dude*."

Tourists in the second row laughed. Someone whistled. David paused to collect his thoughts.

"Thank you," he said. "The dream jump cuts to Christmas. I'm going steady with a young Donna Reed. She explains the performance features of her new waterbed. It's *A Wonderful Life*. And a very weird dream."

Silence. David's heart pounded. A man in the first row handed him a bottle of beer.

"Thank you," David said. "Going home for the holidays? That's a great way to spend some quality time. Did your mother smoke during pregnancy? Thank her for those preschool withdrawals. The other kids cried for juice and cookies. You craved milk and Marlboros."

A few chuckles followed by sympathetic groans. Someone tossed a cigarette on the stage.

"Yesterday on Sunset, this drunk drops his pants and urinates on the sidewalk. I said, 'Where's your social decency?' The drunk said, 'That's why I don't piss my pants.'"

A woman in the back yelled, "That's Rocco's cousin."

The audience laughed. David slipped the microphone into the

stand. "Think about this. If you're still single, would you date your-self?" He waved. "Thank you. Enjoy the rest of the show."

Rocco lead the polite applause. When David reached the back of the room Sarah greeted him.

"Good job," she said. "You had some good laughs."

"Right, a couple," he said. "Probably those drunk tourists from Toledo. That was awful."

"Stop it. That was your first time. You were great."

"I completely sucked."

David relaxed into the warmth of Sarah's embrace. He pressed his face into the folds of her hair, soft and thick with the smell of smoke.

THIRTEEN

Thanksgiving Day David didn't feel like shaving. He showered and put on blue jeans, a white dress shirt, and his leather jacket. Weeks had passed without a hint of rain. The air was cool and dry. Rocco arrived at noon unconcerned about the weather or his topless car as they wound their way down Wonderland Avenue.

"Ready for the big feast?"

"Sure," David said. "I can eat."

Hillside homes became a blur. Rocco lit a cigarette and negotiated the turns. His body swayed like a child on an amusement park ride.

"Bummed about your car?"

David braced for the next turn. "After I pay for the transmission I can't make rent. Mrs. Howell will probably evict me. I can't blame her."

"Hey man," Rocco said. "I can spot you a couple hundred."

"Thanks, but I couldn't let you do that."

Rocco stuffed his cigarette in the ashtray. At the Wonderland School children played dodge ball. Rocco stopped at the Laurel Canyon intersection and lit another cigarette.

"Hey man, don't get sideways." Rocco exhaled a plume of smoke. "You can always crash at my place."

David stared into the hillside. "Thanks," he said. "I appreciate the offer."

When they arrived at Joyce's house Sarah opened the door wearing a powder blue blouse and faded jeans, her hair rolled up into a neat twist. Bronze drop earrings dangled against her neck. David handed her a bottle of Cabernet.

"Thank you," she said. "You didn't have to do that. Come on in. We're almost ready."

The house was filled with the smell of turkey and fresh-baked pies. Rocco and David followed their noses to the kitchen where Joyce and two young men drank Chardonnay and daubed dough on baking sheets. Joyce made the introductions. Manuel and Fernando cooked at the restaurant where Joyce was the hostess.

Rocco circled a finger above a pie. "What is this?"

Joyce glanced at the Kit-Cat wall clock and seized Rocco's finger. "Pumpkin," she said. "And it's worth the wait. Control yourself."

"A constant battle," he said.

Sarah turned to David. "Let's have a glass of wine."

David opened the bottle and poured. They leaned against the counter and watched Fernando carve the turkey. Even with the cooking, David noted the trace of lavender rising from her skin.

David emptied his glass. "I feel better now."

Sarah refreshed their wine. "It's Thanksgiving," she said. "We should all celebrate, especially after the showcase."

David took a healthy drink. "Then I need to drown my sorrows."

Manuel blended gravy with a wooden spoon and spoke with a mellowed accent. "David, are you a funny person like Joyce and the others?"

"No," David said. "I've made one feeble attempt."

Rocco licked whipped cream from his finger. "Hey man, you did a good job," he said. "For a rookie."

David edged close to Sarah. "I had a mental meltdown on Tuesday," he said. "The whole day sucked."

Sarah confiscated David's wine glass. "You're getting buzzed," she said. "No more wine until we eat."

It felt good to be a little tight, David thought, to be with Sarah and Rocco and the rest. His troubles eased with the wine and anticipation of a good meal.

Sarah's friends Grace and Peter joined the party. They brought three bottles of Sauvignon Blanc and Michelle, an attractive olive-skinned art student from France with curly black hair and green eyes. Michelle hung close to Grace. Joyce called everyone to the table where Sarah, Manuel and Fernando presented the food.

Grace counted the place settings. "Who's missing?" she asked.

Sarah set a broccoli casserole on the table. "Turner may come by," she said casually and removed her insulated mitts.

Grace glanced at Peter. "Oh, really," she said.

Rocco reached for the relish tray. "Where's Turner been hiding?"

"I didn't ask," Sarah said. "He called late last night. It's Thanksgiving. I had a weak moment and invited him. I don't want to hear about it. He probably won't show anyway."

David lowered his voice. "Who's Turner?" he asked Rocco.

"The guy I told you about the day we met." Rocco whispered. "The one I got in trouble with in Las Vegas."

"What?"

"We'll talk later." Rocco cut David short and shoved a serving spoon in the mashed potatoes. "Just be cool."

Joyce proposed a toast. They raised their glasses and began the feast of roasted turkey, oyster dressing, candied yams, broccoli casserole, mashed potatoes, and fresh-baked sourdough rolls. David had been on short rations for weeks, so he had his fill. Rocco took second helpings of everything.

When everyone but Rocco had finished, Fernando acknowledged Sarah and Joyce. "The food was wonderful," he said. "Thank you for including us."

"Yes," Manuel agreed. "Thank you for making like we are a part of your family."

"Of course." Joyce lifted her glass. "We're all family."

Rocco nodded. "Praise be to pilgrimage," he said.

"Thank you," Sarah said. "In this crowd everyone is some kind of pilgrim."

Peter stroked his freshly grown beard in professorial fashion. "Speaking of crowds," he said. "We went to the store yesterday. It reminded me of our last trip to Yosemite."

Joyce passed the bread to Rocco. "And what's wrong with Yosemite?" she asked.

"People," Peter said. "Grace and I were there last summer. It's bloody awful. Three million go through the park each year. There are lines for the bathrooms. It's almost as bad as the Beverly Center on Black Friday."

"Okay killjoy," Sarah said. "What's your point?"

"There are too many people," he said. "Grace and I adore nature, but if we really appreciate our National Parks, the best we can do is to stay away. There's smog in the Grand Canyon for god's sake."

Rocco raised his wine glass with a nod to Joyce. "Peter, thanks for braving the crowd at the package store," he said. "We can't resist conquering beauty. It's our destiny."

"And when it's destroyed? All plowed and paved over? When the air isn't fit to breathe and our freeways are impassible?"

"They'll think of something," Rocco said. "They usually raise the price of admission."

Rocco's attempt at levity fell short. Peter rolled his eyes. Grace held Michelle's hand. Sarah and David cleared the plates. In the kitchen David scraped and rinsed. Sarah arranged the dishwasher.

"You seem distracted," Sarah said.

"Lots on my mind." David scraped the last plate. "It's like the two of us take turns."

"You're right. I'm one to talk."

"Cash flow," he said. "That's most of it."

"You need to give yourself a break." Sarah snapped on a pair of rubber gloves. "You've only been in town a couple of months. Despite what you've seen in movies, things here don't happen overnight."

"I know. It's not that hard to figure out."

Sarah set a pan in the sink and closed her eyes. David brushed a wisp of hair from her forehead.

Joyce popped into the kitchen. "How about some pie?"

They helped Joyce serve dessert and coffee from the sideboard. Rocco released a protracted groan then there was a loud knock on the front door. Sarah bolted upright. The knock came again. Joyce glared at Rocco.

"Okay," he said. "I'll get it."

The hardwood floor creaked as Rocco crossed the living room and opened the door. A man in a weathered denim jacket and straw cowboy hat stepped into the room. He slouched like James Dean except he was taller with a pockmarked complexion.

"Look at this," the man said. His pale eyes settled on Grace. "The gang's all here."

"Hey, Turner." Rocco shook his hand. "You rat."

"Come on Roc," Turner said. "You still sore about Vegas?"

"How could anyone stay mad at you?"

Grace addressed Peter and Michelle. "We should be going," she said.

"Don't anyone leave on my account," he said. "I just came to pay my respects to the little woman."

Sarah stepped up to him. "You're drunk," she said. "And you're late."

"Yes babe. A little drunk and a little late." Turner put his hands on her waist then slid them down to her hips.

Sarah grabbed his wrists. "Don't be crude." She pushed him away.

Turner staggered then regained his balance. "But you invited me?"

Joyce spoke up, "Turner, you're an ass all year long. Why not take a break for the holidays?"

David stood behind Sarah. The muscles in his back contracted. His right hand closed into a fist.

"You better leave," Sarah said. "I shouldn't have invited you."

"Whatever you say, babe." Turner's eyes focused on David. "And who is this fucker?"

David stepped forward. "Watch your mouth," he said.

Rocco and Sarah grabbed David's arms.

"He's a friend," Sarah said.

David and Turner stared at each other.

"Come on man." Rocco edged toward Turner. "You better go."

Turner shuffled to the door, stopped short and tipped his hat to Grace. "Always a pleasure."

Rocco opened the door and he was gone.

"I'm sorry." Sarah's voice was barely audible. "Somehow I thought he could behave."

"My dear, that was wishful thinking," Grace said. "People like Turner never change."

Joyce insisted everyone finish dessert. Sarah withdrew to the kitchen. David followed. She snapped on the rubber gloves and cleaned the counter top. The eyes and tail of the Kit-Cat clock clicked back and forth.

"Who was that?" David asked.

Sarah held the sponge above the sink and squeezed. She didn't look up. "Turner is my husband."

A burning sensation struck at the base of David's skull and radiated across his scalp. He should have given her a few minutes. He should have let it go.

"Your husband?"

"That's what I said."

"Why didn't you say you were married?"

"I prefer not to discuss it."

"Well, marriage is worth a mention. And, for the record, that guy is an ass."

"He wasn't always that way. And I'm not sure I like the way

you said that."

"I didn't see much in the few minutes he was here."

"As you should know, hard times in Hollywood aren't difficult to find."

David gathered his thoughts. "You're married?"

Sarah tossed the sponge into the sink. "Yes, legally we're still married. We've been separated for over a year."

David took a deep breath and lowered his voice. "I'm trying to understand."

Sarah turned to David. The fine lines around her eyes deepened. "Well, when you figure it all out then you can explain it to me."

"Okay," David said and left the room.

When Rocco finished his pecan pie he and David said goodbye. Holiday traffic on Sunset Boulevard was light. David rested his head against the Futura seatback and stared into the darkening sky. A cool breeze rattled the blades of the tall palms. Gold foil decorations glittered and swayed beneath the streetlights.

"Why didn't you say Sarah was married?"

"Hey man," Rocco said. "I figured she'd already told you. I'm not one to gossip."

"What's the story?"

Rocco changed lanes, pulled his coat tight around his neck. "I met them three years ago at Bob's Big Boy in Burbank. Sarah seemed patient with Turner. But in Hollywood there's a guitar player on every corner. Turner thinks he has this great voice. He doesn't sing. He growls."

"I thought Sarah was a singer."

"Sarah can really sing. She got that teaching job. Turner tended bar. She worked days. He worked nights. The longer he went without things going his way the crazier he got. Started gambling and drinking and doing cocaine. When he's straight, Turner can be fun. But doing blow makes him nuts."

"How nuts?"

"This is going to piss you off."

"Say it."

"One night Turner came home all messed up." Rocco paused as he rounded the corner onto Laurel Canyon. "They had a fight. Sarah managed to get away. Grace and Peter took her in. The scrape on Sarah's face was bad enough she didn't work for a week. Turner swore he'd get counseling. At first she wouldn't speak to him, but after two months of apologies and anger management she moved back."

"Go on".

Rocco lit a cigarette and flicked ashes into the air as they passed the Canyon Country Store. "Turner behaved. Joined a band and had some paying gigs. Everything was fine until he got fired from the bartending job. When the band's lead singer moved to Nashville Turner flipped out. He got wasted. Sarah claimed he didn't hit her. Anyway, she left and found an apartment. That was a year ago."

"Why would she invite him to Thanksgiving?"

"Who knows?" Rocco pushed his cigarette into the ashtray. "I know most of this through Joyce. Sarah doesn't talk about it. And neither does Turner."

"And why would you go to Las Vegas with him?"

"It sounded like a good idea. I needed the ride. Sort of like how I met you."

Rocco stopped in front of Mrs. Howell's garage. David's room was dark except for the flashing beacon of his answering machine. There were two messages. Liz Edwards asked him to call in the morning and Sarah thanked him for trying to understand.

David didn't return Sarah's call. Enough had been said. He stepped onto the landing. A breeze rushed up through the canyon. Evergreen trees stirred, released the heavy fragrance of hope into the cool mountain air.

FOURTEEN

iz Edwards asked David to work every Angel City Singles event through New Year's Eve. David bordered on optimism as he jogged the fire road. After he paid for the transmission there would not be enough money for December rent. Mrs. Howell would not grant an extension.

He picked up the pace until he broke a good sweat then slowed to a brisk walk. Beneath him the busy city sprawled south and west under a bright sun. His reality became clear. There was no choice but to break the bad news to Mrs. Howell.

Rocco had agreed to take a late lunch and shuttle David to the transmission shop. They stopped at a 7-Eleven and ate hot dogs in the Futura.

"I've thought it over," David said. "I'll accept your offer. I can sleep in the living room with my stuff."

"That's cool," Rocco said. "We'll have a blast."

"This isn't charity. I'm going to pay."

"Whatever, man."

"When I make the money," David said. "I'll pay for half the rent."

Rocco laughed. "Hey, man. Forget about it."

"No," David said. "I won't."

Mrs. Howell stood on her front porch sporting a pink muffler and matching cap. She forced a hollow smile, but the gesture wouldn't last. David hesitated, fearful she would have a stroke.

"I don't have enough to pay you for December."

"No, no, no!" Mrs. Howell shook a boney fist and stomped her feet. "I knew you were trouble. You could've given proper notice. Forget about your security deposit. Call me an old bitch if you want, but that money is mine."

David averted his eyes. "I'm sorry. I don't have a choice."

"You'll get no sympathy from me." Mrs. Howell tossed the end of the pink muffler over her shoulder. "Be gone by Sunday."

It took three trips in both cars to haul David's belongings down the mountain to Rocco's place. In daylight, the two-story building resembled a minimum-security prison with bars on the windows and razor wire wrapped atop of the gate to the underground parking. The neighborhood was congested with apartments and aging bungalows.

David stacked boxes in a corner of the living room. The remaining boxes were placed under the front window and covered with an army surplus blanket where they set Rocco's tiny television. David unrolled his air mattress bed below the circus poster and the move was complete.

Rocco sat at the dinette table and opened a beer. "Home sweet home." He kicked off his sneakers to reveal holes in both of his socks.

David drove the Buick back up Lookout Mountain. Afternoon shadows deepened as he climbed the stairs to the empty room. Lights of the hillside homes on Wonderland began to glow. David cleaned the sink and took out the trash, dropped the key on the counter and closed the door.

Life in the combat zone was anything but tranquil. In the afternoons, small children played on patches of dead grass along the car-lined streets. The children screamed and laughed or walked with their mothers to the corner market to buy meat, produce and sweet breads. At night the lawns emptied. At night families gathered to pray and eat, watch Wheel of Fortune and wait for the lottery numbers to be announced.

Behind the security gate and razor wire the apartment appeared safe. David parked the Buick on the street. The building walls were barely thick enough to mute the murmur of televisions and domestic squabbles. When a door slammed, everyone felt it.

On their second night David taught Rocco how to play gin rummy. Rocco wasn't a card player, but David showed him the basics and kept score. David had ginned six hands in a row when the gunfire began.

BAM-BAM. DAT-DAT-DAT. BAM-BAM. DAT-DAT-DAT.

"Holy shit!" Rocco spun out of his seat. "Get down!"

They scrambled beneath the table. After the first bursts there was silence then voices in the breezeway. Sirens wailed on the way down from Hollywood. A police helicopter hovered nearby. David and Rocco watched from the window as patrol cars cruised past. The helicopter searchlight panned west along Fountain Avenue.

"That's great." David pushed away from the window. "This is why your rent is so cheap?"

Rocco strained to see the helicopter. "Hey, man. It's not that cheap."

The searchlight flashed across the yards and rooftops as the helicopter swooped away. Rocco grabbed a carton of chocolate milk from the refrigerator and sniffed the spout. He took a gulp then offered David the carton.

"Want some?" Rocco asked. "It's fresh."

David surveyed the dirty counter and the dishes stacked in the sink. "No thanks."

"Sorry." Rocco gulped and tossed the carton in the trash. "I'm not much of a housekeeper."

That night David rolled onto the air mattress. In the next apartment voices argued in Spanish. David was almost asleep when he felt something on his ear. He clenched his teeth and slapped himself, caught the cockroach and crushed it. He got up and washed his hands.

The following morning David drove to the Thrifty drug store. Tourists waited in lines outside Gower Studios to watch game shows and sitcoms. David parked near a homeless man asleep in the shade of a mailbox. David purchased disinfectant, scouring powder, paper towels, and roach traps. Outside, the homeless man had awakened. He squatted with a blank stare as the postman retrieved letters and an empty bottle of Captain Morgan's rum from the mailbox.

Back in the apartment, David sanitized the bathroom. The kitchen required two hours including the refrigerator, which had more crusted mold than food and beverages. He walked to the corner market and bought provisions, raw oats, bananas, nonfat milk, spinach, kidney beans, and corn tortillas. David showered and dressed for a meeting with Liz Edwards. As he left the building two Latino boys, about nine years old, occupied the front steps.

"Hello mister," said the smaller one, eyeing David's suit. "Are you going to church?"

"Work."

"My name is Enrique," the taller boy said. "This is my brother Jesus. We're from El Salvador. We live in back with our mother and our cousins."

"I'm David. It's good to meet you."

"We go to the school," Jesus said proudly.

"Are you on television?" Enrique asked.

"No Enrique, I'm headed to a meeting."

"You must do good work," Jesus said.

"That's debatable." David laughed. "But I have to go."

At the Blue Palm Lounge in Glendale David found Liz Edwards in the lobby wearing a strapless gold cocktail dress. She tended herself in a mirror and adjusted the jeweled combs that held her hair. David noted her moist skin and the care with which she applied her makeup.

"How's my hair?"

"Everything looks great," David said.

Liz touched David's shoulder. "I'm glad you're here."

When the first guests arrived, Liz unlocked the cash box. Thirty minutes later the Blue Palm had a line extending out the door. Liz sold tickets and made change as David stamped hands with fluorescent ink and distributed nametags.

"Your crowds are getting larger," he said.

"They're more inclined to go out during the holidays." Liz lowered her voice. "Especially the lonely ones."

In the lounge cocktail conversation drowned the ambient

Christmas music. After the initial rush, Liz rolled her head and pointed to her neck.

"Would you be a dear?"

Obliged, David rubbed his hands together. When his palms warmed he placed them on her bare shoulders, pressed his thumbs gently into the muscles, and moved up to her hairline.

"That's perfect," she sighed.

David massaged her neck and shoulders. When the manager rounded the corner Liz closed the cash box, tucked it into her briefcase and followed him. David stepped outside. Shoppers poured into the mall on Brand Avenue. Despite the decorations this didn't seem like the holidays. Palm trees swayed in a warm Santa Ana wind and made everything strange.

After they closed the event, David rolled the supplies to Liz's BMW. With everything stowed Liz opened her arms. David returned her embrace.

"Thanks for the massage," Liz said softly. "You know what you're doing."

FIFTEEN

David made it back to Rocco's by 10 p.m. His benefactor drank Miller High Life, ate pretzels, and watched *The Gong Show*. When the lack of talent was exposed a gong sounded and the luckless performer escorted off the stage. David loosened his tie, opened a beer and joined Rocco at the kitchen table.

"You have to be warped to do *The Gong Show*." Rocco was indignant. "It's brutal."

"Maybe that's their only shot."

Rocco pointed to the television. "Do you see Ed McMahon? No, because this isn't *Star Search*. *The Gong Show* is a trap."

The curtain parted to reveal the next contestant. Rocco and David gasped. Their friend Elmer mopped his sweating brow and was lost before he began. His lips puckered like a dead fish. The audience showed no mercy. The gong sounded before he reached the "little cowboy" line. Elmer refused to quit. The emcee pushed him toward the curtain. The gong sounded again. Elmer squirmed against the emcee's grasp.

Cut to commercial. An elegant Persian cat ate off a sparkling crystal dish. In a close-up the pristine cat licked her lips as the announcer extolled the virtues of good taste.

"I don't believe it," Rocco said. "Elmer lost his mind."

"He probably thought he was ready."

"Gonged in ten seconds?"

"What should he have done?"

"Get stage time any way you can." Rocco crunched pretzels then wiped his hand on his shirt. "Avoid big clubs until you're ready to be seen."

"I'd like to take another workshop, but I don't have the cash." David sipped his beer. "What do you suggest?"

Rocco thought for a moment. "There's a place called Dharma's over in Los Feliz. They have an open mike, mostly poetry and folk music. If you crack the cappuccino crowd you've done something. A dude named Leonard runs it. Sarah knows him. Have her take you. It doesn't cost a thing." Rocco carried a beer to his room. "And thanks for cleaning the place."

"It was self-defense," David said.

At 7 a.m. Rocco knelt before the shrine, struck matches to light incense and chanted, "Nam-meyoho-renga-kyo." David turned to watch.

"Sorry man," Rocco said. "I need to get this in."

"I wasn't sleeping."

"Want to join me? It's not difficult."

"Thanks, but it's too early."

Rocco completed his ritual and rushed off to work. David recalled the Whole World Expo and Faith Heartwell, how odd that Rocco had concealed this spiritual practice.

David telephoned Sarah before she left for school.

"What a nice surprise," she said.

"Rocco suggested we go to Dharma's for the open mike."

"That happens tonight."

"How about it?"

"It will be good to get out. I'll swing by around 6 and pick you up."

David ate a bowl of raw oats and a banana then opened his journal. He sought redemption after Razor's showcase and spent the day reviewing notes, transferred jokes to index cards then rehearsed in front of the bathroom mirror. His evening meal consisted of boiled spinach, white corn tortillas, and pinto beans. He waited curbside to meet Sarah.

"This was a great idea," Sarah said. "I know you will like Leonard."

Sarah shifted the Volkswagen into gear and drove east on Sunset Boulevard toward Los Feliz. It was dark when they parked on a side street. She held David's arm as they negotiated the buckled sidewalks. In the doorway of an old brick building a man huddled in a tattered bedroll. On Vermont the lights brightened. They passed a Thai restaurant and Chatterton's bookstore. At the threshold of Dharma's Café a motley group drank coffee and smoked cigarettes, tuned guitars or recited poetry.

A large open room with flat gray walls, Dharma's had a high ceiling with a kitchen and service counter in the rear. The artwork resembled decor ideal for The Grateful Dead clubhouse. Track lights illuminated paintings depicting death and resurrection. A laughing skeleton danced on tombstones. An emaciated wolf howled at the moon. Crazed zombies screamed for deliverance. Between the canvases hung several funeral masks painted in primary colors.

At the mismatched tables sat older people and some barely out of their teens. They sipped their drinks, played chess or scribbled in notebooks. An elderly gentleman at the counter squeezed honey into his tea. Beside him a woman with matted gray hair wheezed. She pulled a large bottle of cough medicine from her purse and drank straight from the bottle.

Sarah and David approached a table beside the small stage where a short man with silver hair and a goatee sat with a woman in an ornate embroidered shawl. The woman smiled when she saw Sarah.

"Hello Leonard," Sarah said.

Leonard kissed her cheek and spoke with a raspy Cajun drawl. "Sarah, darling," he said. "How's your sweet self?"

"This is my friend David. We're here for the open mike."

"Hello David. That's fine. That's good." He presented a sign-in clipboard and introduced his companion. "This is Sister Serena, our featured artist tonight."

Sister Serena extended her hand. "I am so pleased to know you," she said. "Bless you both."

"Hey, David." Leonard's sunken brown eyes twinkled in their sockets. "What did you bring us tonight?"

"Five minutes. Hopefully it's comedy."

"Hopefully?" Leonard chuckled. "We don't have many comedians."

Sarah and David ordered green tea and a double fudge brownie. They shared a table with two young poets drinking Jolt colas, an indulgence popular with those who like their caffeine chilled. They said their names were Tom and Dick and confessed these were not their real names.

"It's appropriate to use an alias." Tom's hand trembled as he flipped through the tabbed pages of a three-ring binder. "In poetry duels I smoke Dick's butt."

"A mindless choice of words." Dick pulled a scrap of paper from his shirt pocket. "Tom operates under the delusion that loud poetry is superior. I say he's angry and anal retentive."

"Don't give me any of your vacuous crap." Tom snapped. "With you everything is derivative. Nothing is original. You are behind the curve. You are like a canker sore from *The Canterbury Tales*. You are my friend only because you need someone to envy."

Dick addressed Sarah and David. "The caffeine makes Tom quite animated. He's only correct half of the time."

Tom punched Dick in the arm. "Being correct sucks," he said. "Buy us a couple of fresh Jolts. You owe me."

Sarah and David sipped tea and nibbled at the brownie. Soon the lights dimmed. The crowd applauded.

"We're alive now." Leonard's voice rumbled through the amplifier. "We're here to express ourselves. We're here to listen. We're here to ask, can a humble poem possibly compete with a coffee grinder? Maybe so, but in respect to others, keep your performance brief. Don't carry on like Richie Havens at Woodstock. We don't have all night."

"Hey Leonard," Tom yelled. "I didn't know you were at Woodstock."

"No, I wasn't at Woodstock," Leonard said. "But I did see the movie."

Several people clapped. Some snapped their fingers.

"Okay Tom," Leonard said. "Come up and get it out of your system."

Tom perched on the edge of the stage, removed his worn

wingtip shoes then slapped the soles together. He ranted in a drill sergeant cadence. "People protest when I remove my shoes, it's not my fault they're not amused. Can't be free when I'm leather bound, can't be free unless I make some sound."

Tom continued. David noted the neon light above the exit. No one moved. Tom's allotted time went fast enough to keep David in his seat. Next, a girl with crooked teeth recited five short poems about cherished stuffed animals shredded by her boyfriend's pit bull puppy.

"My boyfriend left me with savage wounds," she concluded. "And I couldn't lick them by myself. My dearest friends are torn to shreds. Now who am I to take to bed?"

David watched as performers offered diverse lyrical turns on unrequited love, the tortures of drug withdrawal, and the singular virtues of masturbation.

A frail young man with dread-locked hair took the microphone. He raised his hands to reveal scars on his wrists. A youthful face belied the depth of his experience. The room hung on every word as he finished with a song for his new lover.

"I've grown weary of remorse, of drowning in pools of sorrow. The sweetest fruit rots the fastest, so our love will know many tomorrows. I've learned dying is not so easy, that water is thicker than air. The secret to surviving our love is knowing which vices to share."

The room convulsed with applause. Tom and Dick pounded the table. Cups rattled in saucers. Fingers snapped in unison. The frail young man bowed.

David studied the unfinished concrete floor. He couldn't explain the attraction that lured him across the desert or his years of running the streets alone or why Sarah sat beside him. But he recognized a connection with these restless spirits and that is when Leonard called his name.

Sarah clapped as David carried his index cards to the stage. "Women aren't necessarily smarter than men," he began. "It just seems that way because they listen."

Two women near the stage nodded their approval.

"I avoid women with motorcycle exhaust pipe burns on their ankles. At a truck stop this biker asked, 'You looking at my woman?' To which I replied, 'My sunglasses don't have wide angle lenses.' That's all of that conversation I recall."

David gazed into stone faces. "Over dinner a blind date confessed, 'I want to get married and have ten kids.' I gave her cab fare. Nancy Reagan gets credit for 'just say no.' Wrong. Republican women have been saying no for a hundred and forty years. That's why there are so many more Democrats. It's 'No, no, no.' versus 'Yes, yes, oh god, yes.'"

Sarah laughed. Several women shook their heads. Tom stood and walked toward the rest room.

"I know a man and a woman can live together without being intimate, I was married. I'm not saying she was cold, but she stored her diaphragm in the freezer."

No one moved. The woman with the cough medicine opened her bottle and took a long drink.

"That's my time," David said. "Thanks for listening."

He left the stage to a smattering of applause and returned to the table. Dick nodded his approval.

"Good stuff." Sarah moved her hand in a reassuring arc across his shoulders. "It's a tough crowd."

"No kidding," David said. "A suicide poet is a hard act to follow."

Sarah smiled. Leonard announced a break and limped toward their table, clothes hanging loose on his frame.

"That was all right," Leonard said. "In the Sixties I watched Lenny Bruce read transcripts from his obscenity trials. That cat was a genius."

Sarah nibbled brownie crumbs. "And your thoughts for David?"

"It's good you want to make people laugh." Leonard pulled close to David and whispered. "But you're holding out on us."

"What do you mean?"

"You are okay, son. Are you coming back?"

"I haven't left yet," David said. "Sure, I'll be back."

"Good." Leonard rested his hand on David's shoulder. "I thought you might."

Sister Serena circled the tables and struck a set of wind chimes with a wooden spoon. She lifted her shawl like a swan spreads its wings to reveal a pair of Egyptian water bearers embroidered in aqua and gold. She raised the shawl like a sail into a breeze. After several long moments she folded her arms and began to sing a wordless song. A string of vowels lingered in her throat. She placed a hand over her heart. Her voice grew stronger as it filled the room. At first David thought this was peculiar, another scene from an alternative universe, but he found himself under her spell.

Sister Serena repeated, "Shanti, shanti, peace. Shanti, shanti, peace."

Onlookers were drawn from the sidewalk. David watched the others surrender to the moment. Sister Serena intoned for several minutes then pressed her palms toward the ceiling. She closed her eyes and continued the incantation, "Shanti, shanti, peace." Serena wrapped the shawl around her body.

"Leonard invited us to express ourselves," she said.

"We've done that. And we have much to be thankful for. And we have much work to do. There is great misunderstanding in our world. There are those who want to drive us apart. But we are here together sharing in this moment."

Sister Serena struck the wind chimes a final time. "One tribe. One people. One spirit."

There was a second of silence then the room rocked with applause. Tom slapped his wingtip shoes. Dick pounded the table. A saucer shattered on the floor. Serena returned to her seat and touched each person that she passed.

"Sister, that was beautiful," Leonard said into the microphone. "Thank her again."

The audience applauded until Leonard raised his hand. "Now please welcome my sweet friend Sarah Fleming."

Sarah waited for the room to settle. "What an inspiration. Thank you." She extended her hand to Sister Serena. "I'm going to sing a song written by someone I once loved."

Sarah sang a cappella. From the first note David was moved by the clarity of her voice.

"I met a man a day ago, his eyes were clear and blue," she sang. "His smile and his laughter reminded me of you. You cared so much for roses, sweet buds of life unborn. I lay down in your garden and crowned myself with thorns. That night when we escaped, we left our bodies far behind, heavenly hallucinations, misperceptions of the mind."

Sarah hummed the melody. "Alone, I wrote these verses, in moments stolen like a crime. In this prison I've constructed such a perfect waste of time. Lovers come, lovers go and some may choose to stay. If I never let them in, then who have I betrayed?"

On the drive home David wouldn't shut up. "You're amazing. You sing like Joni Mitchell. I can't believe it. You were fantastic."

"David, you're totally biased."

"No, I'm completely objective. I wouldn't joke about this. You're brilliant."

"I love Joni Mitchell, too."

"How could you help but love Joni Mitchell? She's so present, so vulnerable."

"Yes, Joni knows what it's like to be alone."

Palm tree silhouettes hung like tropical umbrellas in the night sky. David's mind drifted. He took a deep breath and watched the oncoming headlights, considered how laws, trust and painted lines separate motorists from annihilation.

Sarah shifted gears and began to sing *You Turn Me On I'm a Radio.* David knew most of the words. Sarah encouraged him to sing along. They finished the song as she stopped in front of Rocco's building.

"Forgive me," David said. "I'm not much of a singer."

"You gave it a go." Sarah smiled. "Commitment counts for something."

"Thank you." David stepped out of the car. "That was an experience. You were right about Leonard."

"He's a good man," she said. "And so are you. I'm sorry about that scene at Thanksgiving. I'm grateful you've found a way to forgive my many moods."

Sarah shifted into gear and drove away.

The apartment was quiet. David turned on the kitchen light, opened the journal and slid his hand across the thin blue lines that framed his thoughts. He recalled the polished floors and glass trophy cases of his early school days, classmates eating bologna sandwiches and cupcakes their mothers had made.

David thought about his parents, about the Sixties onslaught of assassinations and riots and war. Somehow hope kindled in the recesses of his mind like that summer day in 1969 when Neil Armstrong stepped onto the moon. A moment of triumph in the Sea of Tranquility symbolized by the otherworldly image of Earth reflected in the mirrored facemask of a man far from home. David recalled how he and his classmates carried their collective dreams into an uncertain future where every hero seemed doomed to the darkest fate.

SIXTEEN

Grace and Peter celebrated the holidays with a Saturnalia party in their warehouse studio. David expected the space to be filled with togas, but Grace's crown of laurel leaves was the only tribute. The guests, dressed in conventional Hollywood black, mingled beneath white parachutes suspended from the ceiling to offer the illusion of an ancient Roman marketplace. Near the end of the evening, in a corner of the living area, a marine biologist entertained Sarah, Joyce and several other women. David and Rocco nursed their beers and listened.

"Dolphins are playful." The biologist fished a piece of cork from his wine glass. "And they are sexually aggressive. The males are easily aroused when tourists enter the water. We're not quite sure why people excite them in that way."

Sarah took a drink. "Are dolphins loyal to their mates?" she asked.

"They're loyal to their pods. Males can be very promiscuous. In the open ocean we've observed young males attacking other males over females, and quite viciously. Fortunately, their libido diminishes with age."

"How do they do it?" Joyce asked. "You know, have sex."

The biologist demonstrated with his hands. "The male swims under the female. They engage, undulate and it's over."

"Really," Joyce said. "That's it?"

"So much for marine romance," Rocco injected. "Wham, bam and thank you very much."

The biologist laughed. The women did not. Rocco and David returned to the kitchen and the California rolls. Grace's art student friend Michelle slipped through the crowd wearing a red Angora sweater and a black beret. Michelle glanced at David, raised an eyebrow and stared disapprovingly at Rocco's belly.

"It appears you have not stopped eating," Michelle said. "Since the day of Thanksgiving."

"You're right." Rocco raised an eyebrow of his own and chewed with defiance. "I can't get enough. I'm feeding my soul. You should try it."

Michelle ignored him and adjusted her beret. David poured her a glass of wine.

"Thank you so much." She touched David's arm. "You are the gentleman, unlike your friend who eats like the pigs."

Michelle excused herself and settled onto the couch beside Grace. They kissed on the cheeks.

Rocco ate a handful of grapes. "Man, no matter how cool I get, I'll never wear a beret."

"I'm certain Michelle has similar feelings for you."

"Yeah, so who cares?"

"I like French women. Strange how she seemed so reserved at Thanksgiving?"

"Well, the shrew has escaped from her cage."

Rocco pushed a knife through a block of Provolone cheese. In the corner, the marine biologist made clicking dolphin sounds. The women laughed. David noticed how Sarah cradled the wine glass in her palms. She gestured and David crossed the room.

"Don't look," Sarah said. "Promise?"

"What?"

"Don't be difficult."

David stepped closer. "You're drinking too much."

"Promise you won't look."

"Okay, I promise."

"Michelle has a thing for you."

David waited then turned. Michelle and Grace held hands on the couch. Sarah yanked his arm.

"You promised."

"And what gives you that idea?"

"She asked about you."

"And what'd you say?"

"I said I thought you were available."

"What's this, high school? You must be looped."

Sarah took the last of her wine. "I am not," she said. "But Michelle did ask. And I don't know. You must meet lots of women hosting those single parties."

David glanced at Michelle then turned to Sarah. "Those parties are work. And that singles crowd is sad. It's not a place I'd recommend to meet someone."

Sarah searched David's face. "But if you were attracted to Michelle, I'd understand. She's stunning."

"I'm not interested. Besides, she's too young."

Peter interrupted their exchange. He carried a candlestick and shielded the flame with his hand. The candlelight exposed tiny capillaries that spread across his nose like a spider web.

"I seek the truth." Peter raised the candle to David. "What do know that's true?"

"You are Peter," David said. "And you are wasted."

Peter extended the candle to Sarah, her blue eyes bright beneath the flame. "And you, dear Sarah. What do you know?"

Sarah blew out the candle. "I know," she said. "When it's time to leave."

"You're right." David took her hand. "Let's go."

A light rain began to fall. The Buick's windshield wipers, dried from lack of use, squeaked against the glass. David detoured through a residential neighborhood lined with mature sycamore trees. Antique streetlamps glowed in the mist. Soft light shimmered off the wet asphalt.

Sarah grabbed David's shoulder. "Pull over," she said.

"Now what?"

"Don't be a drag. Pull over."

David steered to the curb. They sat quietly and watched the mist collect and streak down the windshield.

"Look to the end of the street." Sarah tugged on David's jacket. "You can't see because of the darkness, but it's there."

"You've had too much wine."

"No, I haven't. Just go with it."

"What? I don't see anything."

Sarah lowered her window and gazed down the street. Cold, damp air filled the car. "The light from the lamps," she whispered. "The shadows and the trees and the misty rain. It's like an impressionist painting. Like we're someplace far away. At the end of the street, out of our sight, is a bridge across a river. You can't see, but you can almost smell it."

David played along. He lowered his window and extended his

head like a Golden Retriever.

"Can you smell it?" she asked.

The mist hardened to rain that rapped against David's head and the roof of the car. A gust of wind lifted sycamore leaves into the air. Oily puddles rippled on the street. Soft light glistened.

"Yes." David cranked his window and wiped his face. "I smelled it."

Sarah smiled, rolled up her window and released the seatbelt. "That makes me happy." She moved next to David. "If you can imagine then anything's possible. Right?"

"I imagine tonight you needed a designated driver."

"Be quiet or you'll spoil it."

Sarah leaned against David and fixed her eyes on the darkness ahead of them. The rain fell. A succession of cars crossed the intersection two blocks away. Sarah was first to breach the awkward silence.

"When I was a girl, back in Texas, on rainy days I'd go up into our attic. I had a secret place beside my mother's old dollhouse. I'd hide with a flashlight and read Edgar Allen Poe. I loved being up there."

Rain peppered the roof of the car and flowed down across the windshield.

"One night, the summer I turned sixteen, I smoked hashish with a neighborhood boy named Kevin. We were up in my bedroom singing along to Pink Floyd's *The Wall* with the window open waiting for something to happen."

Sarah stared down the street. David watched her lips form each word.

"All of a sudden my bedroom came alive. Music poured from

the speakers like in *Fantasia.* Tiny liquid notes swam through the air like a school of sea horses. The room was full of them. Tiny sea horse notes flapped their fins, curled their tiny tails and sailed out the window into the summer night. Kevin couldn't see them. He just sat there saying, 'far out' over and over. That was a one-time teenage thing, but after that I saw music everywhere. Singing elevates the human spirit. That's always been true for me."

Their breath fogged the windows. David remembered once as a teenager he climbed an old elm tree beside Aunt Mary's garden. He climbed as high as he could and rested his face against the rough bark. Clouds grew dark and threatening. With the first rumble of thunder he found shelter on the porch until the storm passed. Afterward the air was charged with electricity.

"I never wanted to do drugs like that," David said. "I've had similar experiences watching summer clouds sweep across a lake or running cross country."

"That's what I mean," Sarah said. "It's a moment etched in our memory that stands out among a lifetime of moments."

David slipped his arm around her waist. She rested her head on his shoulder then turned to him. They kissed carefully, each of them probing the intentions of the other. A breath was finally taken followed by a heavy sigh. David's dark eyes met hers, a hazy shade of midnight blue. For several seconds there was only the tap-tap-tap of raindrops on the roof.

They kissed. Sarah's lips grew impatient. David pulled off his jacket. She unbuttoned his shirt. The fogged windows created a steamy cocoon. Sarah fumbled to unbuckle his belt. David raised her dress. The Buick rocked gently in the rain. In time David braced himself. Sarah pressed her body against his. For several long minutes there was nothing but the retreating rhythms of their breath and the falling rain. David cracked a window. They straightened their clothes.

"So much for how dolphins do it," he said.

"Don't make jokes. Not right now."

Sarah rested quietly in his arms, satisfied, and on the verge of slumber. David knew she was tired, but he felt invincible. In that moment, he thought he should be quiet, but he wanted to know.

"Why Michelle?"

Sarah stared into the fogged windshield. "She asked about you. You should be flattered. What's your point?"

"So you don't care?"

Sarah bit her lower lip. "Of course I care, but I'm not jealous if that's where this is going."

David recalled their conversation at the observatory about the synergy of light and darkness and how, in the twilight of that day, the fading sun played upon her face.

"I'm not asking about jealousy," he said. "I want to know what you're thinking. About what this means."

"Can't you just let that be?"

David was willing to face the consequences. "Not tonight," he said.

"Haven't you been paying attention?" Sarah's tone sharpened. "I'm separated from my fucked-up crazy husband, but I'm still married. It was bad and I'm working through a lot."

Sarah turned away. She extended a hand, pressed her fingers against the fogged window and let them slide down the wet glass. David closed his eyes and waited.

"You've been good for me." Sarah's voice was low and resigned.

"I haven't allowed anyone to get close in more than a year. I trust you. I love our conversations. I love your patience, how you're slow to touch me and gentle when you do."

"So what are we doing?" David opened his eyes. "Is that a reasonable question?"

Sarah touched David's face. Her moist fingers traced the ridge of his lips. "It's wonderful, being together like this. You make me feel wanted and desired in all the right ways, but this just isn't the right time to consider pairing up. It wouldn't be fair to either of us."

David shook his head in disbelief. "So why make love?"

"It's what I wanted," Sarah said. "It's what we both wanted. But now I feel irresponsible and like I've let you down again. And I don't want to let you down. I want us to be in a better place."

The rain paused. David yielded to a sudden need for self-preservation. He moved behind the steering wheel and turned the ignition. The windshield wipers and defroster slowly cleared the view of the rain-soaked asphalt, the streetlamps and the sycamore trees. What was once a faraway imagining became a familiar reality.

"Everyone longs for some better place," he said. "Most people never get there. What's it going to take for us?"

Sarah ran a brush through her hair. "I'm not sure," she said. "First, I need to find another job so I can pay my way. The big one is filing for divorce from Turner."

David pulled away from the curb.

"Then what?"

"I have to take my time." Sarah dropped the brush in her purse. "It's the only way I know. Right now, maybe it's wrong for me to want to be your friend and your lover, and I do, but I don't want to hurt you. And I don't want to be hurt. Not anymore."

"No one wants that."

"I know, but it's not fair for me to ask you to wait around. I wouldn't do that."

"That's why you mentioned Michelle?"

"I don't want to think about you with another woman. Or hear anything about it, but it's unfair for me to ask you to wait even if you wanted to do that."

The rain resumed. David drove into Hollywood. When they reached Vista Del Mar David held his jacket over Sarah as they hurried through the rain. The courtyard fountain gurgled. Raindrops rapped against the red tile roof. Puddles formed on the garden flagstones. They stopped in the hallway short of her door.

Sarah tugged at David's wet shirt and kissed him on the mouth. "It's best," she said. "That you don't come in."

"Of course. You're right. And don't worry about anything. I don't think that helps."

The streets were slick and blackened by the rain. David drove and recalled what he had learned from books and the larger lessons of life. Noreen had told him women came into the world as divine beings. They are born with their spirits intact while men must journey on a quest for completion. At the time, being Noreen's husband, David was compelled to agree with her proclamation of innate divinity. He was never convinced.

The passing rain brought a measure of relief from the recurring Southern California drought. Nature's unquenchable thirst had been satisfied if only for a few days. The rain cleared the auburn haze. Cracks in parched hillsides filled with silt washed from higher ground. Patchy clouds floated over distant snow-capped mountains under an indigo blue sky. Autumn leaves, refreshed and supple, played against the cool northern breeze.

At Dharma's Café the paintings of death and resurrection appeared less menacing in the light of day. The funeral masks yawned with merriment. A crystal prism suspended from the ceiling cast rainbows across the gray walls and concrete floor.

David ordered a large green tea, took a table and opened his journal. Across the room a young woman in an army fatigue jacket sat beside the window. She checked her watch then stared at the traffic on Vermont. After several minutes she leaned close to the window and exhaled. Her breath clouded the glass. With a finger she drew a heart as large as her hand. David scribbled notes in his journal and recalled Sarah's hand sliding down the fogged window of his car. He imagined two people tossed together like a pair of flattened stones, skipped across a watered-down dream. When he looked up the young woman was gone.

The waiter played *In My Tribe* by 10,000 Maniacs. Natalie Merchant's voice vaulted through the room as a yellow taxi stopped in front of the building. Leonard turned off the service light and exited the driver side wearing a pair of dark sunglasses and a fedora with the brim turned down. His passengers were the poets Tom and Dick. Leonard removed his hat as he walked through the door.

"Thanks for the lift, Leonard," Tom said. "You're a public servant."

Leonard waved to David then turned back to the poets. "I was headed this way. Next time you'll pay for the privilege."

The poets ordered Jolt colas. Leonard bought a coffee and joined David. They watched Tom and Dick search the reading notices on the bulletin board then settle for a game of chess.

"Crazy kids." Leonard removed his sunglasses and squinted into the skylight. Dark pensive eyes disappeared into loose folds of skin. "What's on your mind, little brother?"

"Your story."

"That's a good one." Leonard laughed and raised his cup of coffee. "Almost funny."

"I'd really like to know."

Two girls with spiked green hair entered the room. Leonard's eyes followed them as they ordered Italian ices and took a table near the door.

"I'm from Louisiana. Creole country. Came to California in 1956 as a teenager riding in the back of a Greyhound bus with my mother. Couple years later I graduated Fairfax High School. Always wanted to be an actor. Took night classes. Went on a hundred auditions. Landed a couple of films. Made some money. The Sixties was a wild time to live in Los Angeles and be making some money."

Leonard stared beyond the green haired girls to the taxi. Afternoon sun crawled up the gray walls. "In the Sixties it was cool to be an artist and to be your self," he said. "That should always be the case. Hosting these open mike nights keeps me connected."

"The performers are grateful," David said. "I'm grateful."

"Thanks little brother, but what's really on your mind?"

"Am I that transparent?"

"Call it what you want."

Leonard tilted his head and waited. David stirred his tea.

"The other night when I was here with Sarah, what did you mean when you said I was holding out?"

Leonard sipped his coffee. "Your comedy bit was all well and good, but I suspect there's something deeper going on. I'd like to hear some of that."

David thought about the song Sarah sang, about Tom and Dick, the suicide poet and Sister Serena. "I've been in Los Angeles about three months," he said. "I've been making notes in my journal. It's like purging, mindless wanderings that don't make sense."

"There's no rhyme or reason or how or when." Leonard coughed into his fist. "If you let your mind wander long enough, maybe some sense will come of it. But don't keep it bottled up. You got to let that shit out. Can't be any harder than telling jokes. That's rough, especially for a serious guy like you."

"You don't mince words."

Leonard cleared his throat. "Mincing words is something to avoid when you realize you only have so much time."

"I've been seeing Sarah," David said. "It's complicated because, as you probably know, she's married to Turner. I met him briefly at Thanksgiving and can't imagine what she ever saw in him."

"Some people handle a rough patch better than others." Leonard dipped a spoon in his coffee. "Remember Sarah's song about love and betrayal? Turner wrote that a few years back when he was sober."

"Those lyrics were tight. Or maybe it was Sarah's delivery."

"It's all good," Leonard said. "Turner's a boy who once had a good heart and talent. But he's all screwed up. I call him a boy because that's about all he'll ever be. I'd stay clear of Turner."

David straightened in his chair. "I'm not afraid of him."

"In the interest of all concerned, I'd stay clear. That's my best advice."

"Thanks Leonard. I needed to hear that."

"No doubt, little brother. No doubt."

That night David sank onto his air mattress. Beams of light pierced the tattered blinds and fanned out across the ceiling. He curled into a fetal position. The pace of his breath calmed. Heartache was a self-inflicted wound he thought. Shades of doubt entered his mind. He wasn't certain he could, but he would somehow let Sarah be.

SEVENTEEN

David dressed for the New Year's Eve party amused by the illusion of success his business suit presented. Liz Edwards would never suspect that he slept on the floor in a combat zone building surrounded by razor wire.

Something heavy crashed in the next apartment. A male voice screamed. "Damn you!"

"Are you possessed?" A woman pleaded.

"Damn it, I want forty dollars."

"I work all afternoon for forty dollars."

"Please mama? I will pay you. I swear."

Voices quieted. A door slammed. Windows rattled in their frames. Footsteps hurried down the walkway.

David put on his suit coat and locked the deadbolt. Through the window of the next apartment a woman slumped on a couch, her head in hands, an elderly man's arm draped across her shoulders.

The Manhattan Beach Marriott Hotel was a forty-five minute drive from the frayed fringes of Hollywood. A dense fog trundled in from the Pacific and clung to the sleek aluminum streetlights. David parked in an adjacent lot. Plumes of water gushed from a fountain in the center of the hotel circle drive. Valets rushed to greet hotel guests.

David found Liz Edwards wearing a black evening gown with thin straps and a slit that revealed her left knee with each stride. They accompanied a bellhop who rolled a luggage rack piled with party favors to the ballroom.

"New Year's is huge," Liz said.

David smelled wine on her breath. He didn't comment on the absence of Harold Ames. DJ John tested the sound system. Workers hurried to finish the ballroom decorations. The caterer hoisted a net filled with balloons to the ceiling.

At 9 p.m. the ballroom lights dimmed and the disco ball turned. Within an hour the room filled with middle-aged engineers and management types, the recently divorced and never married, people with nowhere else to go. Some circulated cautiously carrying cocktails and appetizer plates.

David scouted the ballroom. Sobriety sharpened his senses. Flares of disco ball lights animated the scene. DJ John busted moves. Drinkers made fast friends. Strangers embraced. Laughter poured from the dance floor. An older woman shook loose her long red hair. Her partner pulled her close.

Liz smiled when David returned. A couple followed from the ballroom.

"We want a refund," the man said. "How dare you call chips and dip food? How dare you call this crowd sophisticated?"

David stepped up. "I'm sorry, we don't offer refunds."

The man turned to Liz. "This is outrageous. There's no place to sit. A long line at a cash bar."

"You're right." Liz pulled fifty dollars from the cash box. "We want you to be happy."

The man took the money and left.

David looked at Liz. "What about your policy?"

"It's been a good year. I feel generous." Liz squeezed David's hand. "By the way, I like it when a man's tight with my money."

Shortly before midnight Liz and David followed the catering crew into the ballroom to distribute party favors and bottles of cheap champagne. DJ John counted down the New Year. When the balloons began to fall Liz collared David and pressed her fingernails into the back of his skull. Her lips were slick, her tongue thick with Chardonnay. David hesitated then accepted what she offered. It was a new year after all.

Early the next afternoon David reclined on his air mattress in front of the television.

"It's the 1988 Rose Bowl," the announcer declared. "The granddaddy of them all. The Trojans of Southern Cal and the Spartans of Michigan State."

The telephone rang.

"Happy New Year," Sarah said. "How was your party?"

David crawled to the television and lowered the volume. "A complete triumph. No food fights. No one threw up."

"Big crowd?"

"Packed. How was Grace's?"

"Casual, but we had fun. Grace and Peter are buying a home on some land out near Agoura Hills. They want to get away from the city."

"I'm sure the city will move to them soon enough."

The television revealed a man shaving. A model caressed his chin. Her fingers morphed into the animated tread of an all-weather tire on a stretch of wet highway.

"Something bothering you?"

"No. I was about to watch the football game."

"You should have said so."

"I didn't want to interrupt. But it is the Rose Bowl."

"Well, call me later."

David hung up. USC cheerleaders with perfect white teeth tossed girls skyward. Tommy Trojan thrust his short sword into the air. The blimp-view camera panned the Rose Bowl, framed divided sections of crimson and green. Team captains shook hands at midfield. Rocco opened the door.

Fevered fans shoved index fingers into the camera. "We're number one," they screamed. "We're number one."

"People say that before every game." Rocco stared at the screen. "How can you watch this?"

"I'm an American," David countered. "Watching football is my birthright."

Rocco shrugged, dumped his overnight bag on the floor and went into the bathroom. "Hey, man," he said. "Are you really going to watch that?"

"Why?"

"I'm going somewhere. Thought you'd want to tag along."

"I had a decent night's sleep." David thought for a moment. "I don't have a hangover. Why should I sit on my ass in front of the television?"

"Right." Rocco clapped his hands. "Let's get the hell out of here."

Rocco drove the Futura. They stopped for the light at Santa Monica and Vine. Across the intersection a few demonstrators stood in front of the California Surplus Store. A bearded man with a megaphone held a sign: JUDGMENT DAY IS NEAR.

The bearded man raised the megaphone. "Now hear this. The Lord's mighty vengeance is at hand. Beware the wretched beast. Beware those who conceal their horns with a disguise of great beauty. The beast is a sodomite. He worships the forest and copulates with animals. He crowns his dark throne with evil doings and eternal damnation."

The light turned green. The bearded man pointed at the passing cars. "Jesus is coming," he said. "Save yourself. This is your last chance. This time we're not kidding."

Rocco stepped on the accelerator.

"What a freak," David said. "Can you believe that?"

"On any day in Hollywood there are zealots who claim to channel Jesus. They probably have a support group, Saviors Anonymous."

"I'm certain they need one."

Rocco turned into the Hollywood Memorial Park Cemetery. He drove slowly between the tombstones and urns, obelisks and mausoleums. To the south, the Paramount Studios soundstages rose above the cemetery wall. To the north, the mountains and the Hollywood sign overlooked the family plots and stately celebrity graves.

Rocco parked the car on the narrow road. They went down two short flights of steps to a large reflecting pool.

"Here," Rocco said. "We'll wait here."

Rocco lit a cigarette. David walked the length of the hundred-foot pool and stopped at the white marble tomb of Douglas Fairbanks, 1883 to 1939. Between the lily pads a school of tiny fish darted through the murky water. He returned to where Rocco waited.

"Here she comes," Rocco said. "Don't make any sudden moves."

The woman shuffled down the knoll wearing a knit cap and dragging the belt of her long wool coat. David thought she was older, but as she moved closer he could see she was probably early forties. Auburn hair streaked with gray.

"Gayle, this is David," Rocco said. "He's with me."

Gayle stepped forward, cracked lips pressed tight. Rocco presented an envelope. When Gayle opened it she began to cry.

"Everything's going to be all right," Rocco said.

She muttered, shoved the envelope in her coat pocket and closed the collar beneath her chin.

"Thank you." Her cracked lips barely moved. "Rocco."

Gayle hung her head. Rocco lit two cigarettes. She took one and puffed, looked to the south where palm trees towered above the cemetery wall. A trail of smoke dissolved into the air. Gayle offered a final tight-lipped smile. She shuffled up the knoll beneath the broken branch of an evergreen and was gone.

"What the hell was that?"

"I've known Gayle for a while." Rocco ground his cigarette butt into the road. "I see her on the street sometimes and give her food. She was napping on a park bench. Some scumbag stole her teeth."

"Her teeth?"

"A partial plate. She can't sleep with it in her mouth. Afraid she'll choke. I promised to help her."

"And you agreed to meet here?"

"New Year's Day. Two o'clock. Near Douglas Fairbanks' grave."

"Why here?"

"This is where we met." Rocco cupped his hands and lit a cigarette. "Isn't she beautiful?"

"Could be. Hard to tell."

"She's shy."

"Why didn't you offer her a ride?"

"She's afraid of cars. Traumatized by an auto accident. That's how she lost the teeth. She's on disability. It was an ordeal for her to accept the money. You should see her smile. That's something."

"I'll take your word for it."

David stared across the cemetery lawn at the gravestones and monuments, the aged evergreens and lofty palms. He thought how easily tragedy strikes and how quickly one reality becomes another. He wasn't much different than Gayle, a traffic accident away from disaster and sustained for the moment by Rocco's good will.

"It's righteous that you helped her," David said. "And that you have helped me. I want you to know how much I appreciate everything."

"Hey man, forget about it. Let's go eat. My treat."

"I can't let you do that."

"Of course you can. Come on, I'm starving."

Rocco drove to El Pollo Loco. For David dining out was an extravagance, but Larry's Hollywood Lube Job paid Rocco well enough to cover bills, save a little money and do good deeds. For twelve dollars they ate their fill of flame-broiled chicken, corn tortillas, pinto beans, and Spanish rice.

On the way home Rocco stopped for cigarettes and bought a 12-pack of Miller High Life. Hollywood sidewalks welcomed hustlers, hands shoved in their pockets against the evening chill. Wayward tourists in Michigan State sweatshirts and shorts waited to cross Santa Monica Boulevard. A police squad car cruised up a side street and flashed a searchlight into a row of hedges.

Back at the apartment David and Rocco listened to jazz on KCRW and toasted the New Year. They debated the merits of resolutions and resolved to be more productive.

"Hey man." Rocco struck a statuesque pose. "I haven't changed my underwear in three days."

"Please, don't burden me with such thoughts."

They agreed to do laundry, bundled their dirty clothes in bed sheets, and marched outside like refugees. As they neared the Buick Rocco dropped his bundle.

"Hey man. There's someone in your car."

A figure sat behind the Buick steering wheel. Adrenaline rushed through David's body. He dropped his laundry and sprinted to the car. Shattered glass crunched under his shoes as he ripped open the passenger-side door.

"What the hell?" David shouted.

The teenaged boy froze, eyes wide with terror. The driver's side door was blocked by Rocco's stomach. The boy turned to David. Dirty hands clutched the steering wheel.

David's first impulse was to drag the intruder onto the sidewalk and extract a full measure of revenge. Then he saw the fear. "It's okay." David backed onto the sidewalk. "Just get out of the car."

The boy didn't budge.

"We should call the cops," Rocco said. "This little shit should be locked up."

"There's no need for the police." David held the boy's gaze and stepped back. "Just get out. We aren't going to hurt you."

The boy released the steering wheel.

"It's okay," David said. "Come on, get out."

The boy looked back at Rocco's stomach then scooted across the seat. David raised his open hands. The boy stepped out of the Buick, his right sleeve torn, the elbow bleeding. A steel blade flashed. The boy pointed a knife at David's chest.

"You don't need that." David moved back. "Put it away."

Rocco came around the front of the car. The boy extended the blade and stood his ground.

"Get out of here," David said. "Go on. Go."

"What the fuck," Rocco said. "If you needed money, you could've asked. He has to pay for the window and you pull a knife. This is bad karma for you, man."

The boy inched back down the length of the car and staggered into the street.

"Go on," David said.

The boy turned and disappeared into the shadows.

"You suck!" Rocco yelled after him. "Dirt bag."

David's rage only lasted a few seconds. He had looked into those desperate eyes and witnessed a horrible possibility. Rocco helped sweep broken glass from the car. They shoved their laundry in the back seat. As David drove west on Fountain Avenue his hands began to shake. He stopped at a package store and bought a pint of Jack Daniel's, broke the seal and offered Rocco the first drink.

"He pulled a knife. It could have been a gun." Rocco drank, wiped whiskey from his lips. "He could have killed both of us."

"You're right," David said. He took the bottle. "It could have ended just like that."

EIGHTEEN

L iz Edwards opened the door in a silk dressing gown. Her jet-black hair fell soft and straight against her powdered face. A purple scarf hung loose around her neck.

"It will take me a few minutes." She handed David a glass of Chardonnay and withdrew to her bedroom. "Make yourself comfortable."

David couldn't refuse Liz's invitation. The Buick's shattered window cost $200, about what he'd make in two weeks working Liz's parties. The New Year's Eve kiss concerned him. Nothing good would come of it, yet he found himself in her living room drinking her wine.

An etched glass coffee table held a fresh floral arrangement, copies of *Fortune*, *Vanity Fair*, and the Victoria's Secret catalog. David settled into the overstuffed sofa and admired the late afternoon light that fell across the UCLA campus. He was deep into the pages of the Victoria's Secret catalog when Liz's hands found his shoulders.

"The models are so young," she said.

Liz massaged his neck. David closed his eyes.

"We better go," she said. "I made a reservation."

Liz drove her BMW up Highway 101, the Ventura Freeway, exited at Topanga Canyon and raced along a winding road. Twilight slipped from the mountains and left the valley cool and dark. At the Inn of the Seventh Ray the hostess seated them on the patio where, in daylight, the brook may have been a pleasant sight. But it was evening and they sat beneath space heaters and trees wrapped with strands of festive white lights. The brook gurgled faintly as the waitress filled their wine glasses.

David watched the patrons in the cottage-style shop across the patio. "Have you been in the store?"

"Once," she said. "I don't care for self-help books."

Her eyes fixed on the candle shielded in hurricane glass. She raised the bottle and refreshed David's wine.

"I have a proposition." Liz forced a smile. "Harold has been dismissed. I want you to be my lead assistant."

"What happened?"

"That's not worth discussing." Her expression hardened. "Other than Harold couldn't be trusted."

A smile returned. She reached for David's hand.

"This comes with a considerable raise: $18 an hour for each four to five-hour shift, three evenings a week."

Candlelight glistened in her dark eyes. David calculated a minimum of $216 a week. He would have more than food and gas money for the first time in two months.

"How could I refuse?"

Liz's moisturized grip closed on David's hand. "That's wonderful." She raised her glass. "Let's toast."

"To friendship," he said.

"To partnership." Her grip softened. "But that's all the business we'll discuss tonight. The rest of the evening is just the two of us."

They ordered then sat quietly. David listened to the brook as it wandered toward the Pacific. An awkward silence was broken when their food arrived.

Liz had lobster bisque and endive salad, a spinach soufflé and pouched halibut. David ate sirloin steak with red potatoes and asparagus. They emptied the bottle of wine and Liz ordered another. David felt compelled to drink. The less she drank, he figured, the better their chances of getting home alive. They shared a slice of cheesecake with strawberries. Liz fixed an empty look on the candle and toyed with the scarf around her neck. She paid the check.

Outside, they waited for the valet. When the car arrived, Liz took a step and the heel of her shoe twisted in the gravel. David caught her.

"Are you okay?" he asked.

"What do you mean?"

"We've had some wine. Are you okay to drive?"

"Don't be ridiculous." Liz climbed into the car. "I know what I'm doing."

David buckled the seatbelt. Liz drove fast. The headlights swept neatly through every turn. When they reached Liz's place she insisted they have a nightcap. Liz lit candles scented with vanilla then went off to her bedroom. David admired the lights of the UCLA campus and the hillside homes, the traffic on Wilshire Boulevard ten stories below. He retired to Liz's sofa and the Victoria's Secret catalog. The cover model struck a seductive pose, a plush robe slipped off one shoulder. David relaxed and considered what was about to unfold. A gentleman would have excused himself. A gentleman would have gone.

Liz assumed a position in the middle of the living room wearing a sheer black negligee, the purple scarf tight about her neck.

David rose from the sofa. For a moment they stood like gunfighters in a high noon showdown. Liz rested her palms on the sheer fabric, slid them over her hips and down to her thighs.

Her freshly painted lips parted. "I love it when a man calls my name," she said. "Say my name."

There was no turning back. David crossed the room. Liz lifted her lips. They kissed, her tongue thick with wine. David strained to lift her then carried her into the bedroom careful not to bang her head on the doorjamb and dumped her on the down comforter.

Frantic wine-laced kisses followed. David unbuttoned his shirt. Liz battled to unbuckle his belt then rolled on top and straddled him. She paused to admire herself in the dressing table mirror then lurched into action like Mr. Toad's Wild Ride. Liz gripped his shoulders. An awkward rhythm escalated. Her grinding grew into urgent convulsions. Liz twisted the scarf tight around her throat. Her face flushed red and cocked sideways like a primitive Cubist painting.

"Call my name." Liz raked her nails across David's chest. "Say my name. Say it."

"Liz," David said. "Liz."

"Louder. Slower." She tightened the scarf. Her voice strained. "Do it now."

The grinding escalated. Her face turned red. David thought her head would explode.

"Say it. Say my name."

"LIZ." David called. "LIZ. LIZ. LIZ."

She groaned and tossed her head like a wounded animal fighting to escape the bondage of her skin. Liz bucked faster and faster then, with a final desperate surge, released three high-pitched squeals and collapsed. Her knees trembled. Her heart pounded. David loosened the scarf.

He had known women who laughed or screamed, but Liz's asphyxia fantasy was something new. She passed out with an arm across his chest. David considered the consequences of this transgression. He considered the burden of trust and being awake while his satisfied employer snored blissfully by his side.

Late the next afternoon, David relaxed at Rocco's drinking water to recuperate from the night before. The telephone rang.

"Hello stranger." Sarah's voice was cheerful. "Joyce said you guys had a close encounter with a car thief."

A sinking sensation washed over David like a high-rise elevator in a rapid descent. He gathered his thoughts.

"That was a wake up call. I need to move to a better neighborhood."

"Don't we all."

"That requires resuming my search for a real job." David paused. "Working these parties won't make rent."

"Something will come through. You can count on it."

David felt the pointed curse of guilt. "Sorry I haven't called," he said. "I've been distracted."

"Hey, Joyce wants to hit an open mike in Northridge tonight. Rocco and I are going. Come along."

David visualized a smoke-filled bar with drunks hurling rotten cabbage at the stage. Another stand-up attempt could serve as worthy penance for his sins.

"Sure," he said. "We can all ride in the Buick."

A drive north into the San Fernando Valley off the 405, Muldoon's Saloon was crowded with local contractor types, workers from the Budweiser plant, open mike comedians and their friends. Neon beer lights buzzed. The floor was littered with discarded peanut shells. Near the makeshift stage, four men wearing Budman bowling shirts drank beer at the bar.

Joyce and David added their names to the sign-up sheet. Rocco secured a booth near the door and order a round of drinks. Joyce gave the waitress a five-dollar tip. She filled their basket with roasted peanuts and hurried off.

"This place is a dump," Rocco said. "And you two are at the bottom of the list. We'll be here all night."

"I told you we'd be late." Joyce jabbed him in the ribs. "We should've been here thirty minutes ago."

"Don't worry." Sarah slipped a straw in her diet soda. "You'll both get on."

A burly man tapped the microphone. "Hello and good evening. My name is Mike. Welcome to Muldoon's comedy night."

The men in bowling shirts booed and tossed peanut hulls at the stage.

Mike pleaded. "Can't you bowling league losers do better than that?"

The men protested. "Hey Mike," one of them yelled. "Your shoes are untied."

"Have another beer, Tony." Mike didn't look at his shoes. "I'm sure your wife won't mind since she's probably home fucking your pool boy."

The drunken bowling teammates laughed and slapped Tony on the back.

Rocco nursed his beer. "This could get weird," he said.

"We'll soon find out," David said.

Mike introduced a man in his late twenties. He jumped on the stage in a white T-shirt with sleeves rolled tight above his biceps.

"I'm Bobby from Brooklyn. New York is tough. They do CPR like this." He stomped his boot against the floor. "They kick your gut and scream, "Get up 'fore yo fuckin' die.'"

The bowlers howled.

"Ever hear a New York echo? Yell 'Hello.' Then some asshole screams, 'Shut the fuck up.' How do New Yorkers learn the alphabet? Fuckin' A, fuckin' B, fuckin' C. You know the card game go fish? We played go fuck yourself."

The bowlers laughed, raised their beer mugs. Peanuts sailed across the room.

Next, an aging librarian from Chatsworth pulled two homemade hand puppets from her purse. The crowd stared in silence as the puppets chatted back and forth. The woman closed with puppets singing: "That's just how it goes when your best friend has a button nose."

"Go granny. Go," a bowler shouted. "Really, just go."

Rocco shook his head. "That was so weak."

"Stop with the play by play." Joyce studied her note cards. "I'm trying to concentrate."

Rocco took a drink. "What would Faith Heartwell advise in your situation?"

"Adjust to your environment," Joyce said. "Isn't that obvious? Don't make fun of me. Not now."

Rocco ordered more beer.

Sarah pressed her hip against David's and dropped her hand

beneath the table. Their fingers entwined. The bitter taste of remorse rose into David's mouth. Neon lights reflected in Sarah's eyes, accentuated the highlights in her hair.

Over the next hour and a half, they shared a few laughs. The laughter lessened as the crowd thinned. When a comedian finished the allotted time, most would sit for one more act then leave with their friends. Rocco and Joyce drank several beers while Sarah and David sipped sodas. Near the end Muldoon's was nearly empty except for the drunken bowlers.

Joyce abandoned her notes and walked to the stage with a bottle of beer. Two of the drunks at the bar continued their conversation. Joyce glared for a couple of seconds, but the men kept talking.

"Hey. You guys," Joyce yelled. "I'm working here. Give a girl a break. Shut up, will you?"

The men turned to watch.

"What happens to a woman's breasts when you hit a speed bump?" Joyce adjusted the cups of her push-up bra. "You guys don't know, because you're drunk. You don't know, because you're too stupid. Yeah, that's right, I'm talking to you."

Joyce took a drink. "Men have a one-track mind, 'Me horny. Me very horny.' I'm not prejudiced. I've dated lots of dumb guys. 'Me horny. Me very horny.'"

Mike escorted Joyce off the stage. "Thanks Joyce," he said. "You're a classy chick. Here's our last performer, David Bishop."

Rocco and Sarah clapped. Peanut hulls crushed under David's feet. He faced the drunks at the bar.

"Forgive my friend Joyce," he said. "She has unresolved issues with men. The best advice I can give a woman looking for a man is to lower your expectations."

The drunks stared.

"Sure, men are predictable. We think about sex every sixty seconds. Women think about sex every other day, that's why gay guys seem to have so much more fun. Women have other things on their mind, but don't ask what they're thinking. Because you can't keep up."

David looked out across the empty tables to the booth in the back where Sarah, Rocco and Joyce waited.

"Women love to say things like, 'You can tell me anything.' No, we can't. We want to live. Women love to dance. I tried country line dancing. I got stomped. I took a swing dance class and dislocated my partner's shoulder. I'm not a swinger."

Mike approached the stage and pointed at his watch.

"Hey, you guys at the bar," David said. "Have some coffee before you hit the road. Or at least wait until we leave."

The stream of red taillights on the 405 Freeway flowed like molten lava toward Sepulveda Pass. David slowed for the transition to the eastbound 101. Sarah rolled down the passenger window. The wind blew her hair across her face.

In the back seat Rocco coached Joyce. "I told you that place was a dump," he said. "And never drink before you go up. It's unprofessional."

"Unprofessional?" Joyce objected. "You're the one that ordered the beer. Like I care. Like I'm ever going back."

Sarah gathered her hair. "Hey, miss congeniality," she said. "Be grateful you got some stage time."

"Thanks for the reminder," Joyce said. "David, did you really dislocate a woman's shoulder swing dancing?"

"It wasn't quite that bad."

"Hey man, your delivery was good tonight," Rocco said. "Too bad there wasn't a crowd."

"I agree," Sarah said. "Your material was revealing."

David drove down into Hollywood, dropped Rocco and Joyce at her house. As he approached Vista Del Mar Sarah hummed a melody David didn't recognize.

"I'd invite you in," she said. "But I have to be at school early tomorrow."

David pulled to the curb. Gentle light from the building angled across Sarah's face. She twisted an index finger through her hair.

"My hair's going gray," she said. "Have you noticed?"

"Not at all."

"You're diplomatic. My mother and grandmother went gray before they reached forty. I'm thinking of letting it turn."

"A wise man always withholds comment on a woman's hair. It's too perilous."

"You're Confucius now?"

"I wouldn't worry over a few gray hairs. Like Ingrid Bergman, you'd be beautiful even if you shaved your head."

Sarah's smile broadened. "Ingrid Bergman? That's sweet." She kissed David's cheek. "You want to talk?"

"It's late," he said.

Sarah opened the car door and paused. "Call me if you change your mind."

"We'll get together. I'm working through some things."

"We're all doing that." Sarah stepped onto the curb. "Good night."

David watched her walk into the courtyard. It was unwise to

confess current events. Whether acknowledged or not, he knew women had keen instincts that bordered on paranormal.

At Rocco's apartment, David raised his hands toward the light over the kitchen table. The shadows of his fingers played on the blank page of his journal. The backs of his hands appeared to have aged, skin stretched across a web of tendons and thick veins. Closed, his fists revealed the scars that crowned his knuckles. He grabbed a pen and began to write.

As a teenager, David rowed a skiff across an inlet on Lake Texoma. He set the oars into the locks and shoved off, the water glassy beneath an autumn sky. The boat veered right and left until he focused on a point behind him. He stopped and watched his wake ripple and fade. He drifted, contemplating the chaos of a cold and expanding universe described in a lesson by his ninth grade science teacher. He thought about his parent's modest graves, the rumble of freight trains on the tracks near Uncle Buck and Aunt Mary's. That day David learned the importance of keeping his eyes on the point of departure. He learned not to sink his oars in too deep.

NINETEEN

The following Sunday David found a notice in *LA Weekly*, gathered his journal and drove west to the Beyond Baroque Literary Art Center. Late afternoon sun cast a golden veil upon the Spanish colonial-style building that once housed Venice City Hall, a remnant of California's romantic past surrounded by aging apartments and beach cottages with iron bars over the windows. A brisk onshore breeze carried the Pacific's primordial fume and, for David, a lingering sense of familiarity.

He crossed the lawn where a couple played with their Labrador Retriever. At the entrance birds of paradise guarded the flowerbeds. A tall woman with purple hair opened a pack of Marlboros and offered a cigarette to her young male companion. She produced a lighter from the pocket of her chain-laden leather jacket. A serpent tattoo consumed what was visible of her left breast.

Inside, David approached a thickset man at a table. "Is this where we sign up?"

"I'm Carlos." He offered his hand. "You've come to the right place."

David found a seat in the rear of a room painted flat black, dark except for track lights above the stage. The ocean breeze poured through the windows along with the intermittent drone of Venice Boulevard traffic.

Folding chairs squeaked. Readers sorted papers. A woman knitted, balls of yellow and red yarn nestled in her lap. A platinum-haired woman cleaned her eyeglasses with the hem of her skirt. Carlos brought the gathering to order and called the first reader.

An elderly man named Benjamin opened a folder. Abundant eyebrows mocked the frailty of his slender frame and ruddy complexion. He spoke with the controlled manner of a college professor.

"I'd like to congratulate those of you living a contemplative life," he said. "Creativity is often jeopardized by our myriad obligations to work and marriage and children, the seduction of drugs, booze, and copulation. I've survived my distractions and, more recently, my solitude. I am alone, except for moments like these." Benjamin read softly.

> *She is called beautiful*
> *my silver bird about to fly*
> *her hungry tongue tapping once again*
> *at my brittle old veins.*
> *She awakens me from abandoned dreams*
> *reminds me I've come too late*
> *to my calling. I cannot sleep*
> *now the final chapter has begun.*
> *I will write what I know.*
> *Filling empty pages until life*
> *is taken from me and my heirs,*
> *blinded by what they refuse to see,*
> *toss my papers into some dumpster.*

They will weep for me and wonder
why they could never understand.

The audience applauded. A pair of pigeons landed on the windowsill. One took flight while the other cocked its head with curiosity. A battered Chevy sedan cruised by on Venice Boulevard. Windows vibrated from the bass beat of the car's music.

Carlos called the list. Poets and performance artists took their turn. Unlike the rowdy crowd at Dharma's, this audience listened quietly.

Toward the end, Samantha with the serpent tattoo removed her leather jacket and let it fall. Chains clanked against the wooden floor. She began to shimmy, opened her arms and sang.

"It's all the rave of fashion, to be a slave to passion; as lovers learn to listen, they'll do just what they're told. With heavy chains or leather, no matter how they're bound; the men that I've encountered insist I wear the crown."

Samantha's companion sat in the front row. She stopped to mess with his boyish hair then buried his head in the abundance of her inked bosom.

"What's a woman to do?" She feigned disgust and pushed him away. "You want a girl, just like the girl, who subjugated dear old dad."

The audience responded with polite applause. Samantha announced performances at Club Lingerie and Poecentric Lounge. She distributed flyers. A ragged man crept into the room and squatted on the floor near David. He drank from a bottle that smelled of peach brandy.

Carlos called David. When he reached the stage, he paused

at the lectern. Samantha zipped her leather jacket. The knitting woman folded her hands. Benjamin cupped palm to ear. The ragged man capped his bottle.

David felt compelled to tell a joke then noticed the curious pigeon perched on the windowsill. Expectant faces waited. He opened his journal and began to read.

> *They hide their scars well*
> *beneath beautiful facades*
> *whispering of the past to confidants*
> *behind shuttered blinds.*
> *Security access to an empty room*
> *with a futon on the floor.*
> *The first steps to stardom.*
> *Drinking red wine in the evenings,*
> *telling clever stories*
> *left over from the Sixties*
> *when they were younger,*
> *and thought about things*
> *besides making a fortune*
> *and retiring to Hawaii.*
> *Blue skies, big surf,*
> *making love with a stranger.*
> *Paradise must be earned,*
> *one deal can do it.*
> *I played chess when I was a child,*
> *now I have forgotten how to set the board.*
> *White queen on her own color?*
> *It is unimportant unless you are in the game.*

Street people on Sunset Boulevard,
talking to themselves, seldom seem bored.
They have found their paradise,
so what makes them
less sane than you or me?

With the sudden applause the pigeon took flight. David watched the faces before him and felt a tremor of emotion.

"David's a first-time reader," Carlos said. "Thank him. I pray you will all come back for our next reading."

Benjamin winked at David. The knitting woman nodded. The ragged man offered his brandy. The crowd mingled, spoke in hushed tones then moved out into the evening darkness. Samantha stopped, lit a cigarette and handed a flyer to David.

"I liked your stuff," Samantha said. "It was raw."

She shared the cigarette with the young man who puffed and stared into the flowerbed.

"You're outrageous," David said.

"Nice." Samantha grabbed her companion's hair. "That's the response I'm going for."

"Good luck," he said. "To both of you."

David's stomach growled as he crossed the lawn, the cool damp air filled with memories. He recognized the proximity to Santa Monica and the beach where he and his parents once walked. He recalled the indifferent force of the surf and how his parents held his hands.

The eastbound traffic flowed on Interstate 10. David exited and headed north on Highland. By 9 p.m. he reached Vermont, parked and found Leonard in a corner of Dharma's, his face buried in *The Los Angeles Times*. David ordered a bowl of hearty vegetable soup and joined him.

"Look who's here?" Leonard peeked over his reading glasses. "Hello little brother."

"What's in the news?" David said.

Leonard's brow furrowed. "Says here Nancy Reagan's running the White House with the aid of an astrologer." Leonard lowered the newspaper. "I don't favor political affiliations, but we should acknowledge when our fearless leaders are aware that Jupiter has aligned with Mars."

The waiter presented David's soup with two slices of crusty dark rye bread.

"Are you hungry?" David asked. "I'll order another bowl."

"I ate already." Leonard examined David's face. "You look like you found money."

"I went to the Beyond Baroque reading."

Leonard folded the newspaper. "How was it?"

"Surreal. The space and what the people had to say." David lowered his eyes. "Venice Beach is where I first saw the ocean. I was a little kid on vacation with my parents." David spooned his soup, stirred carrots and new potatoes. "We ate on the boardwalk. I remember men fished off the end of the pier. Couples walked on the beach, their footprints in the sand then the surf came and washed them away."

Leonard took the last of his coffee. The waiter brought a fresh pot and filled his cup.

"I read a piece today," David said. "I don't know if it was good or if that even matters."

"It should matter to you." Leonard stirred sugar into his coffee.

"And for that you should be proud."

"Since that night when you challenged me, I've been up late writing. At first nothing made sense. I have folders with scribbles on scrap paper and cocktail napkins. I've filled a journal."

Leonard sipped his coffee.

"Voices call to me in dreams," David said. "I've written poems, at least I think they're poems. And love letters. It's like they're writing themselves."

"Sounds like you got it going on." Leonard added cream to his coffee. "But be careful with love letters. You can't take them back."

"I'm holding on to them."

"Sit on those until they hatch." Leonard coughed. His thin frame shook. "Eat little brother. Your soup is getting cold."

David finished his meal, thanked Leonard and returned to the combat zone in an elevated mood. The night smelled like rain. Cool air and fog rolled across the city with the false promise of an end to the drought. In the distance a siren wailed. David entertained the prospects for contentment. He unlocked the security gate and climbed the stairwell. When he opened the door, Turner bolted from the table.

"Fuck, man." Turner reached under his denim jacket. "You scared the piss out of me."

"Hey David." Rocco's eyes narrowed like slits in a happy face. "Have a beer, man."

Smoke filled the room. Beer bottles, an ashtray of butts, and a bag of marijuana cluttered the table. David's euphoria evaporated at the sight of Turner. He thought of Thanksgiving and the crescent scar on Sarah's lip.

Rocco made the introduction. "Remember David, Turner?"

David walked into the kitchen. "Thanksgiving," he said. "At Joyce's house."

Turner dragged a denim sleeve under his nose. "I don't remember." He reached for the marijuana and rolling papers. "Probably best. November was a fucked up fade to black month for me."

David opened a beer. "Tell us all about it," he said.

"No, man." Rocco countered. "We do not want to know."

Turner rolled a joint, licked the paper and struck a match.

"My life's not that bad." Turner inhaled, held the smoke and offered the joint to Rocco. "It's been worse."

"We don't want to hear about it." Rocco grinned. "If Turner talks we'll be incriminated."

David considered leaving, but he wanted to know what possible virtue had earned Sarah's forgiveness. He searched for a redeeming quality in Turner's pockmarked face and cold gray eyes. Rocco hit the joint and handed it to David. He passed.

"Maybe Turner needs to open up," David said. "Maybe he needs to share his feelings?"

Rocco twisted the cap off a fresh beer. "Hey man, forget about it. Turner's beyond help."

Turner took the joint. "Rocco, who is this guy?"

"I told you. David is crashing here. That's his stuff."

"Another gypsy on the road to find out." Turner glanced at David's boxes stacked in the corner. "Well, god's speed wherever the fuck you're headed."

Rocco pulled David close in the kitchen. "Turner came to pay me some money," he whispered. "He'll be gone in a minute."

Turner dropped the bag of marijuana on the table. "I promised I'd pay you," he said. "And with some killer weed for interest."

"How about those Lakers?" Rocco said to David. "Is Magic Johnson great or what?"

"You know I hate basketball," Turner said. "I can take a fucking hint. I'll leave you two faggots alone."

Turner stood, his jacket opened to expose a .38 Special holstered in his waistband.

"A gun?" Rocco slammed his beer bottle on the counter. "I told you. Never bring guns around me. I told you, man."

"I wouldn't live in this shit neighborhood," Turner said. "Not without a fucking gun."

"Imagine," David said. "How we've managed to live so long."

Turner lifted the flap of his shirt pocket like nothing had happened and set a gram of cocaine on the table. "Probably your dumb luck," he said. "I've never been lucky. Hey, let's do a couple of lines before I go?"

"No way," Rocco said. "I have to sleep tonight."

Turner fumbled with the vile. "Are you tripping?"

"No," Rocco said. "Do your thing and get out. I've had enough of you for one night."

"Sure," Turner said. "You're the boss."

Turner shaped two neat lines, rolled a dollar bill and snorted. He licked a finger, wiped the residue from the table then massaged his gums.

"Sweetness." Turner dropped the vile of cocaine in his pocket. "You don't know what you're missing."

TWENTY

David's expanded Angel City Singles duties covered food and enough to ease the pressure of underemployment. On free nights David dropped into Razor's club with Rocco, to Dharma's for the open mike or a chess match with Leonard. In sharp contrast with the Bohemian neo-caffeine cultural vibe, three evenings each week he worked with Liz Edwards. On Thursday nights they would have dinner, discuss business and, when she insisted, retire to her apartment.

One Thursday Liz and David sat in a booth at Miceli's, L.A.'s oldest Italian restaurant. Liz nibbled spinach ravioli and sipped Chianti. When she finished eating Liz slid onto the bench beside David and kissed him on the mouth.

"That doesn't do it for me."

"Well, it turns me on," Liz said. "Loosen up."

David drove to Liz's apartment with her fingers on his thigh. At traffic stops she taunted him until the light turned green. When they reached her apartment, Liz left him in the kitchen to open a bottle of Cabernet. She returned with a heavy black portfolio.

"Want to see my book?"

David delivered her glass of wine. "What book?"

"My former life. When I was a model."

Liz drank wine. David turned the pages. Thick plastic sleeves held photographs and advertisements from the Seventies and early Eighties. A girl in bell-bottom jeans struck a confident pose. In a bikini, Liz reclined on a surfboard and flashed a convincing smile. A young woman with long legs straightened her pantyhose.

"In 1972 I had a great figure."

"Clearly," David said. "And everything remains completely functional."

"That's not funny," she said. "Keep going."

Hemlines rose and fell with passing seasons. Pastels in spring, earth tones for fall, and eveningwear in basic black. On successive pages the smile faded. Near the end only her legs were revealed, an ad for hosiery, a half-page for an electric razor, and a spread for orthopedic slippers. David closed the portfolio.

Liz tugged at his sleeve. "What do you think?"

"The camera loves you."

"Well, a woman likes to hear that." Liz took a drink. "I started the networking parties on the side. There will always be lonely people. It took me five years to build the business."

"You've done well. Far beyond self-heating orthopedic slippers."

"Those slippers were not self-heating." She emptied her glass. "You made that up."

"It wasn't a big stretch."

When Liz drank an excessive amount of wine a predictable pattern of humorless behavior prevailed. She stood, loosened her hair and began to unbutton her blouse.

"You like my breasts, don't you?" Liz whispered. "Call my name."

Liz unzipped her skirt and let it fall to the floor. She hurried to open David's shirt.

"Liz." His enthusiasm waned. "Liz. Liz."

She fumbled with his belt. David's pants dropped to his ankles like leg irons. Liz twisted his shirttail into a leash and led him toward the bedroom. David shuffled like a penguin, trousers tangled about his shoes. In the absence of adoration David accepted that men and women make choices. In this context Liz and David stripped themselves of pretense. Pleasure presented a process unlimited by haggling. They agreed on their intentions. They plundered.

By late February the afternoons warmed enough to sun by the swimming pool. In the back corner of Rocco's building, the pool was framed on two sides by overgrown hedges and a cyclone fence crowned with rusted razor wire. Untreated through the winter months, the pool had degenerated into an emerald swamp.

David entertained the idea that the pool area resembled an abandoned white-collar prison. He spread a towel on a chaise lounge and made notes in his journal. The warm sun shined. He relaxed for an hour in solitude until the boys came home from school.

"Hello, Mister David," Enrique said.

Jesus mimicked his older brother. "Hello, Mister David.

"Hello my friends," David said. "What did you learn in school today?"

"To duck." The boys covered their heads and giggled. "When the earthquake comes."

"Yes," Enrique added. "And to say no to the drugs. The police came to teach us."

"Enlightening." David gathered his papers. "Listen to your teachers. And the police."

"Please, Mister David, don't leave." Enrique hiked the stairs to their apartment. "Stay and swim with us."

"Not today," David said. "The water isn't safe. It will make you sick."

"But today it is warm. We waited all winter."

"You have to wait. When the water is treated it will be clear. Then you may swim."

Late that night the telephone rang. Sarah's sleepy voice reminded him of the possibilities that for several weeks he had ignored. He pulled the telephone onto the floor. Shafts of light from a streetlamp pierced the blinds.

"We haven't spoken for a while," Sarah said.

"You're right." David rested his back against the wall. "I've missed your voice."

"And I've missed yours." Sarah sighed. "I've been blue."

"When you feel that way it helps to write it down."

"Then I'd have writer's cramp," she said. "Do we ever grow tired of longing?"

"What do you long for now?"

"Something you can count on. To be more grounded, more satisfied."

"You'd be bored."

Sarah paused. "I wouldn't know."

"How do we know anything for certain? If longing provides some measure of inspiration or motivation it has value. Otherwise, it's useless."

"That's kind of harsh."

"Beyond longing, what can it be?"

"A sense of place, a home, maybe out in the country." Her voice brightened. "A vegetable garden."

"None of that should be difficult."

"I love teaching children. I love the angelic pitch of innocence in their voices." She paused. "You should come to our class recital Thursday and hear for yourself."

"I love your voice," he said.

"You're impossible."

"Sing for me, Sarah."

"No, you have to wait."

Rocco accompanied David to Sarah's recital, but insisted they attend a meeting on the way. Rocco drove the Futura north into Hollywood and stopped in front of a palatial residence off Franklin.

Rocco grabbed a tote bag. "Just follow my lead," he said.

"Whatever you say Sherlock."

They entered a spacious living room and huddled by the door near an industrial-strength incense burner. Sandalwood smoke billowed from the bowl and curled toward a vaulted ceiling. Near the front of the crowded room several women in check-patterned tunics sat cross-legged on the floor and meditated. Like stripes on a herd of grazing zebras the checkered tunics unified the group and obscured the individual. Even the swiftest predator would be unable to single out an easy target.

The room fell silent as Darla entered adorned in an orange robe and a necklace of yellow flowers. She raised her hand. The assemblage closed their eyes and chanted in unison, a deep sigh that grew in volume until it echoed like a collective grown from the bottom of a waterless well. Engaged by the rapture that swirled around him, David sank into the depth of experience and began to hum like a model airplane.

"Snap out of it, man." Rocco shook him. "You're here to help me out."

"Sorry, I was going with the flow."

"That's not why we're here. Stay sharp."

Darla led three chants followed by sharing and the collection of offerings. When the meeting concluded Darla floated through the congregation. Enthusiastic young females introduced themselves to newcomers extending handshakes and eye contact as long as possible.

Darla approached. Rocco clutched the tote bag. Darla's flowered necklace flattened as they embraced. When Rocco pulled back Darla tightened her hold.

"I've been asking about you," she said. "You've missed meetings and our Ojai retreat last month."

Rocco presented the bag. "Here's my tunic and the shrine."

"But Rocco, to withdraw you must address the elders."

Rocco edged toward the door. "This is it," he said. "I'm not a group guy."

Darla reached for Rocco's arm. "It's not that simple. You can't break your agreement without a consultation."

"I won't argue," he said. "Good-bye."

Darla's eyes fixed on David. He shrugged and followed Rocco through the door. They passed two women with flowers in their hair.

"Why are you boys rushing off?" one woman asked.

"Can't talk." Rocco pulled at David's collar. "We're in a hurry."

"Then come back." The women waved like enchanted Sirens on a rocky shore. "We'll be here."

Rocco revved the Futura and squealed the tires as he pulled onto Franklin then east toward Sarah's school. Palm leaves rustled in the breeze above them, cast bladed shadows across the topless car. Rocco lit a cigarette and checked the rearview mirror.

"Those women were unbelievable," David said. "How could you just walk away?"

"Don't jack around. It's a trap, man."

"They were so eager." David growled like a tiger. "You've been holding out on me."

"Eager, but those chicks aren't easy. No smoking, no drinking, no fooling around."

"But there were so many of them."

"Hey, man, don't mess with me. And keep this between us. Okay?"

David laughed. "If you say so."

Rocco parked the Futura. They crossed the lot to Sarah's school and joined the crowd filing into the ivy-covered building. In the auditorium, proud parents prepared their cameras.

Sarah stood center stage in a long blue dress. Parents applauded then readied their cameras. The curtain parted. A dozen choir-gowned children perched on a set of risers. Cameras flashed. Video cameras rolled. Sarah tapped a wand on her music stand. The children sang *The Wheels on the Bus*.

Three songs later, near the end of *Do-Re-Mi*, a chubby boy in the second row began to reel. He raised his arms. The gown ballooned. The girl beside him reached out, but it was too late. He hit the stage with a thud. The children stopped singing. Sarah rushed to his side. The audience strained to see. For a few seconds the boy lay motionless then he sat right up. When he realized everyone watched his face blazed red with embarrassment.

"It's okay, Michael." Sarah straightened his gown. "You had a fall. It could happen to anyone."

Michael hopped to his feet and darted off the stage. Sarah went after him. The audience waited. Sarah returned with Michael in tow, spoke loud enough for everyone to hear.

"We can't go on without you Michael," she said. "You can stand next to me."

They stopped at the risers. Sarah leaned over. Michael said something, let go of her hand and climbed back into position. Everyone applauded and the choir sang two more songs without incident. Cameras flashed and video cameras rolled until the end.

Sarah's Volkswagen was in the shop for repairs. She joined Rocco and David as they climbed into the Futura, sat between them with a white wool cape draped across her shoulders. David rested his arm on the seat behind her. Rocco drove east beneath a flat moonless sky.

"That was very kind," David said. "How you handled that situation with Michael."

"Yeah," Rocco added. "That kid's a riot."

"Michael's a good boy," Sarah said. "He requires a lot of attention."

"Tell Michael I think he's cool," Rocco said.

When they reached Vista Del Mar, Rocco shifted into low gear to make the incline. He set the parking brake in front of Sarah's building.

"Thank you both for coming tonight," she said. "And for the ride home."

David escorted Sarah through the courtyard and into the hallway. She slipped her key in the lock. Instinct told him to turn away, but he thought of her sleepy voice calling in the night. In that moment he couldn't think about Turner or Liz Edwards. David lowered his hands onto hers. Their fingers closed together.

"You were wonderful with the children," he said.

"It meant a lot to have you there."

Sarah turned to him. They kissed. Their lips clung together then she responded with a sudden tenderness that surprised him.

"I've been thinking about that," she said.

"About kissing?"

"About being kissed by you."

"You asked me not to do that."

Sarah smiled. "That doesn't mean I don't think about it."

"You're such a tease," he said.

"Then you must enjoy being teased." Sarah pressed her fingers to his lips. "We shouldn't keep Rocco waiting."

TWENTY-ONE

David sat at a window table in the Gaucho Grill and waited for Sarah, Joyce and Rocco to return from the bathroom. Late afternoon traffic on Sunset surged past a construction site. A tall plywood enclosure was plastered with posters for psychic counselors over which a graffiti artist had spray painted DECLARE MARSHAL LAW.

A young woman in a pink summer dress hurried beneath the scaffolds. Construction workers whistled and waved when she crossed the side street. David made eye contact. A gust of wind lifted her dress. She entered the restaurant, went to David's table and removed her sunglasses.

"Did you get the good look?" Her accent was Swedish.

"Sorry, we can't stop the wind from blowing."

She curled her lips. "And the woman, she can't help that men look?"

"Unfortunately, that is also like the wind."

"I come from audition. I like that people notice," she said. "To be in movies is all I ever want."

"Good luck." David reached for the basket of bread. "In Hollywood beauty is a fleeting commodity."

"I know this. My mother taught me."

The manager waved to the woman.

"I must change to work clothes. Goodbye."

Sarah, Joyce and Rocco returned. Sarah and Joyce split a salmon salad. David ate grilled chicken breast with vegetables. Rocco had flank steak. They ate in a rush. Joyce had purchased tickets to the Jackson Browne concert at the Greek Theater.

David drove the Buick east, merged with traffic on Los Feliz then north on Vermont into Griffith Park. Joyce sat in the backseat singing *Lawyers in Love*.

"I hope he sings all of the old songs," Joyce said.

"If he doesn't," Rocco said. "You probably will."

Joyce laughed. "I love Jackson Browne."

Police and attendants directed cars. David parked and they joined the crowd headed toward the gates. Sarah's hand found David's. Their arms swung together as they walked.

Stately evergreens framed the amphitheater. To the north and west the mountains rolled into a fading violet sky. Joyce and Rocco finished their second beer before the opening act concluded. In front of them a burly man in a sharkskin suit sipped from a silver flask. His female companions drank from red plastic cups.

"Have drink." The man spoke with a Russian accent. He offered David the flask. "We have party in limousine."

"No thanks," David said. "It's okay."

Jackson Browne opened with *Running on Empty*. The drinking women screamed and danced. Half way through the song Rocco nudged David.

"What's this guy's secret?" Rocco asked.

"Women love limousines," David said.

Sarah scoffed, "Not all of us."

During *Fountain of Sorrow* Sarah excused herself and stepped into the aisle. Two songs later she hadn't returned.

"I'll go check," Joyce said.

Ten minutes later, Joyce waved. "Come quick," she said. "Turner's flipped out."

The threesome raced through the aisles, down a ramp and found Sarah and Turner on a flight of stairs overlooking the line for the bathroom. The waiting women stared. A security guard watched from the landing.

When Turner saw Joyce, he shouted, "I told you to beat it, bitch."

David called to Sarah. "Are you all right?"

"Yes," she said. "I just need a few minutes."

Turner glared at Sarah then turned to David. "What the fuck is this?"

Sarah touched Turner's arm. "Lower your voice."

David took a step.

"Please," Sarah said. "Give me a minute."

David, Joyce and Rocco waited beside a concrete retaining wall. A minute passed. Turner reached for Sarah. When she resisted Turner pounded his hands against his head. "I'm not going to lose you," he screamed.

There was a moment of silence then Turner grabbed Sarah. David rushed the stairs. Sarah broke free and with surprising force punched Turner squarely in the nose. The security guard hustled down from the landing. The waiting women applauded.

"Right on girl," a woman yelled. "Show him you're the man."

Joyce ran up to Sarah. A second security guard arrived. They searched Turner's pockets then guided him down the stairs with his arms behind his back. Blood ran from Turner's nose. He glared at David.

"Better watch your back, fucker," Turner said.

David didn't budge. "Stay away from her."

"This is our business." Turner spit blood at David's feet. "Me and my wife. So fuck off."

"Take a hike, Turner," Rocco said. "You dumb ass."

"Fuck you, too," Turner said.

Jackson Browne began to sing *Stay*. Turner lowered his head. The guards escorted him past the concession stands and released him at the gate. Turner wiped blood from his mouth, flipped the collar on his denim jacket, and disappeared.

Late the next morning David found Leonard at Dharma's reading a dog-eared copy of Charles Bukowski's *War All the Time*. Sunlight blazed through the skylights. David shared Sarah's confrontation with Turner.

"Think she broke it?" Leonard asked.

"Broke what?"

"Turner's nose?"

"Hell, Leonard, his nose was already crooked."

Leonard reached for his coffee. "Sarah's been trying to make that work for a long time."

David looked up into the skylights. "I've loved her since I first heard her voice," he said.

"Love?" Leonard coughed into his fist. "Have you mailed any letters?"

"Those letters are secure."

"Wait it out."

"I've waited for months." David stepped up from the table. "I have to go to a meeting."

"I'm pulling for you." Leonard returned to his book.

David met Liz Edwards in Sunset Plaza, a lunch spot favored by the fashionable and unhurried. They took a table with crisp white linens that faced the sidewalk, ordered lunch and discussed expanding to Orange County. David noticed a couple strolling.

"Is that Jessica Tandy and Hume Cronyn?"

"Oh, please." Liz protested. "Don't gawk at celebrities. That's so common."

"Look, they're like teenage lovebirds."

Liz turned to look. "They're old." She reached for her wine. "Sometimes you worry me, David. They're only actors."

"I'm making an observation."

"Let's stay on topic." Liz ordered a second glass of wine. "Today that is Orange County."

After lunch David walked Liz to her car. In the lot behind Sunset Plaza he could see Westwood through the haze and to the east almost to downtown. David recalled, back in the fall, the glimmer of Century City buildings as he ran the dusty fire road that crested Lookout Mountain.

"Call me tomorrow with the revised schedule." Liz rummaged through her purse. "And don't forget."

David watched Liz drive away and walked back through the lot. When he neared the building he saw a familiar face with an elegant Eurasian woman.

"Hello Richard," David said.

Richard Knox's face went blank.

"David Bishop." He extended his hand.

"Right, of course. It's been some time."

The companion smiled. Knox didn't offer an introduction.

"Whatever happened with Quincy's?"

"Those people?" Knox winced. "I haven't the slightest idea. I've been preoccupied since the Stock Market collapse. I'm producing a documentary."

"You're not consulting?"

"With a few clients, but certainly not Quincy."

Sunlight flared off a building across the street. "Then you wouldn't mind," David said. "If I called on them?"

"Why waste your time?"

David repeated the question. "You wouldn't mind?"

"No, not in the least." Knox checked his watch. "I hate to break this off, but we have to go."

"Good luck with the documentary."

"Film is where the real money is," Knox said. "You should get into it."

David did not hesitate. His mind cycled through multiple scenarios as he navigated Sunset Boulevard. By the time he reached Rocco's apartment he had his pitch. The receptionist put him through to Alice Quincy.

"Yes, of course," Alice said. "I remember that meeting. You were the quiet one."

"That was Knox's presentation," David said. "But I've given your business considerable thought. I have some suggestions."

"To be blunt, Quincy did not care for Mr. Knox."

"This has nothing to do with Richard Knox. It's a practical extension of your current program."

She paused. "With Quincy, practical is the right approach."

David spent two days in the Hollywood library researching articles on menu and marketing trends. Joyce recommended a graphic artist who helped produce layouts. David finished Quincy's marketing plan, made copies and mounted the layouts on black poster board.

Quincy sat behind the table wearing a green polo shirt. Alice smiled when David entered the room. He placed the layouts on the table.

"What do you have for us?" Quincy said. "Don't have much time."

"Then let's get to it." David placed a hand on the marketing plan as if swearing an oath. "This is an operational outline to test menu extensions in six of your stores. All related development and marketing costs are budgeted including outsourcing some of the food preparation."

"Outsourcing?" Quincy glanced at Alice. "What would we be outsourcing?"

"The Quincy's-Lite menu." David presented a layout. "Soups and single-serve salads, low-fat turkey sandwiches and veggie burgers."

Quincy laughed. "Veggie burgers? Son, our customers don't eat salads and veggie burgers."

"You're right," David countered. "But diet-conscious people do. There's no compelling reason for people counting calories to eat in your restaurants now. This menu will attract them. And they'll come back, once they taste your sauce."

Quincy nodded. "Our sauce is damned good."

"I was raised on barbecue. Your sauce is exceptional."

Quincy examined the menu. "You aren't suggesting we change

our logo?"

"That's unnecessary. The diet-conscious menu is what needs to be tested. I helped create a similar program for a franchise in Dallas a few years ago. It was a big success."

Quincy studied the menu then passed the layout to Alice. "We're not keen on outsourcing," he said.

David sensed the momentum shift. "That's an option. It's your call, but outsourcing allows greater flexibility for testing the menu with minimal up-front costs."

Quincy reclined in his squeaky chair. "Let's see the rest of it."

David presented layouts for window banners, table-tents, take-out menus, and direct mail coupons. The concepts were straight-forward, the graphics tight.

Quincy scratched his sunburned forearms. "What's all this go-ing to cost?"

"Everything's here including references for the Dallas restau-rants I mentioned." David pushed the proposal across the table. "Budgets are net with production, printing and direct mail billed to you. My consulting fee is $500 a day. The program will require three to four weeks to set up, then approximately two weeks a month to coordinate. After ninety days we'll evaluate based on sales and feedback. Your downside is break-even."

Alice scribbled notes on a legal pad. Quincy swiveled in his chair. "Veggie burgers." Quincy stood and shook David's hand. "Son, that's pretty good. We have a manager's meeting on Friday. Call Alice Monday morning after ten. She'll have an answer for you."

David left Quincy's office. He accepted the likelihood of suc-cess and, for the first time in months, had cause for celebration.

When he reached Rocco's apartment he phoned Sarah.

"I knew something good would happen," she said.

"Let's have dinner. I'll tell you all about it."

David took Sarah to Tommy Tang's on Melrose for Thai food. David recounted the presentation. Sunlight slipped through the window. Sarah's gaze shifted from steaming noodles to a retirement home across the street where, behind a picture window, elderly people slumped in wheelchairs.

Sarah returned to her noodles. "I hope the deal goes your way."

"You can never be sure. I'm grateful Joyce referred her designer friend. Those layouts made a difference."

"Joyce and Rocco are good friends to have when you need one." She stirred her noodles with a chopstick. "Guess I'm not that hungry."

"They'll box it. Come on, let's go."

Outside a woman in a long coat carried a bag of aluminum cans. David recognized Gayle, Rocco's friend from the graveyard New Year's Day. Sarah offered the leftovers.

"Noodles with shrimp," Sarah said. "It's not too spicy."

"I love shrimp," Gayle said. Her face transformed into the smile Rocco had promised. "Thank you." She took the noodles and bag of cans to a nearby bus bench.

"There's a showcase at Dharma's tonight," David said.

"I don't feel like singing," Sarah said. "Not tonight."

"Let's stop and say hello to Leonard."

David drove into Loz Feliz. Dharma's filled with singers and guitars. On the sound system Edie Brickell and the New Bohemians performed *What I Am*.

Freshly painted walls featured frescoes of crazed dancing musicians. White doves flew from their mouths. The spotlight cast a wide arc across the stage. Leonard wedged through the crowd to greet them.

"Little sister. Little brother."

Sarah kissed Leonard's cheek. "We're celebrating," she said. "David thinks he's landed a client."

"Good for you, David. I trust prosperity won't dull your sensibilities. You were making progress."

"No need for concern." David hitched his jeans. "Not tonight anyway."

"He sounds cocky." Leonard turned to Sarah. "What do you think?"

"Cocky looks good on him."

"You might be right." Leonard poked David's stomach. "Solid as a rock. Could stand to gain a few pounds."

"I've been on short rations," David said. "But I'm ready to get on with my life."

Leonard rested a hand on David's shoulder. "I wager you will," he said. "I better kick this show in gear. You kids be good to each other."

Performers packed the room. After two acts Sarah seemed restless. David motioned to the door. At the threshold they waved to Leonard. David drove west on Sunset then up Laurel Canyon and onto Lookout Mountain until they were alone on the narrow road. When the pavement ended David parked.

They leaned against the Buick and looked to the south. The lights of Los Angeles sparkled like gemstones spilled on black velvet. Puffs of fog strayed with the onshore breeze and dissolved beneath them. Faint stars twinkled above. A car came up the road.

Headlamps swept across Sarah's face. She smiled then her eyes wandered back to the west where, in the distance, city lights yielded to the ocean.

"In the country the stars are so much brighter." Sarah gazed into the sky. "Living in the city with all the people tends to obscure everything. It's easy to lose your way."

David pulled Sarah close. "You're not lost."

"Sorry." Sarah shook her head. "You're all happy and I'm trying to catch up."

David pointed. "There's the Big Dipper and the North Star. When it's clear you're never really lost."

"When school's out in June I'm giving up my apartment." Sarah's attention returned to the west where the light surrenders to darkness. "Grace and Peter asked me to sit their new house near Agoura Hills. They've rented a place in Tuscany for the summer."

David had never considered this possibility.

"I learned this morning that the school is not renewing my contract," she said. "I didn't want to tell you earlier. I didn't want to spoil the evening."

"Now you've done it."

"Please, don't try to make me laugh."

"It's too late."

Sarah shivered. "It's getting cold," he said. "I'd better take you home."

"I'll make hot tea."

David drove down to Vista Del Mar. As they crossed the courtyard a wrench of sadness struck David knowing that soon he would no longer have cause to visit here. Summer would come and, without her, the tranquil fountain and mellowed walls of her place would fade into memory.

Sarah cleared laundry from the love seat and put the kettle to boil. Outside, the security light illuminated the stained-glass window, cast patches of color that skipped over the wooden floor, climbed the wall and disappeared into the gauze-draped sleeping nook.

Sarah poured lemon ginger tea, sat on the floor and cradled her porcelain cup like an injured bird. Footsteps echoed down the hallway. A heavy door closed. Sarah blew across the teacup and peered through the stained-glass window.

"You're my dear friend," she said. "I trust you and that means the world to me."

"I feel the same."

"Then I want to tell you something that I've never shared with anyone."

David focused as if each word could be her last. Sarah took a deep breath. Her nostrils flared.

"Back in Lubbock my grade school friends called me giggle box," she said. "I laughed all the time. In third grade I had a friend named Bobby, sweet and sort of funny. He was afraid of my mother especially when she was drinking. One day I was on the front porch when Bobby pedaled by on his bicycle, shouted 'I love you Sarah' and tossed a box on the lawn. Inside was a small heart-shaped charm. That made me so happy. I still have it."

Sarah extended her legs on the wooden floor. Colored light played on her bare feet. The edges of her mouth dropped. Her jaw tightened, eyes fixed on the window.

She struggled to form the words. "When I was twelve, my mother had a boyfriend named Walter. One day after school, when mother was at work, I climbed the stairs to my secret place in the attic where I could be alone and read. I heard Walter stumble into the house. The attic stairway moaned under his weight. At first I wasn't afraid. I couldn't imagine he would hurt me. He promised he wouldn't. I remember he smelled of whiskey. When he touched me, he said that I was beautiful. I asked him to stop. I begged him, but he didn't."

Tears welled in Sarah's eyes, but she held them. David could not breathe. It was as if a great stone had been placed upon his chest. He wanted to destroy Walter, to grind his flesh and bones to dust. In so doing he would erase that horror from Sarah's life to somehow reclaim what had been stolen and make her world right.

"I'm sorry," Sarah whispered. "I wanted you to know. I wanted someone to know."

"What do I say?" David's voice cracked. "What do I do?"

A patch of colored light illuminated the watery blue of her eyes. "There's nothing to be said or done."

David knelt beside Sarah. A tear meandered down her cheek and lingered on her lips. He realized in that moment he could not reconcile her loss any more than he could his own.

TWENTY-TWO

Monday morning David paced the floor. He paused to study Rocco's circus poster of a trapeze artist suspended in mid-air. The audience froze as the man lunged for the bar. David made the call.

"Well son," Quincy said. "Your client back in Dallas had fine things to say."

"They're good people," David said.

"Well, I hope we have as much success."

"I won't let you down."

Early that afternoon David met with Quincy to review the budgets. They sealed their agreement with a handshake. When he returned to Rocco's he called Sarah.

"They approved everything," he said. "I'm back in business."

"That's wonderful. I knew it."

"Now I have to produce."

"You will, just stay on top of it."

David recalled the tears in Sarah's eyes, how he didn't know what to say.

"This business with Quincy is a ton of work," he said. "I'll be swamped for a month."

"You have to make this happen," she said. "You don't get many opportunities like this."

David thought about summer, how Sarah would be moving.

"By the way, Friday I signed my divorce papers," she said. "I spent the weekend cleaning out my closet. I feel much better."

"Cleaning house will do that."

"It's like therapy," she said. "Only afterward you have more room in your closet."

"We should be celebrating."

"There will be a time for that," she said. "For now, we both have work to do."

Later that week David and Quincy presented their plan to the store managers. The new menu items, pricing and logistics were well received. David's days and free nights were consumed with the launch. After depositing his first proceeds, he wrote Rocco a check for $1,500 and stopped at Larry's Hollywood Lube Job to make the presentation.

"I can't take this," Rocco said. "You crashing at my place had nothing to do with money."

"I promised that I'd pay," David said. "I wouldn't have made it without you."

"Of course you would."

"Just take the money."

"Man, if it squares your karma. I'll put this to good use."

"Do what you like. I am grateful for everything. And the beer is on me."

"Beer sounds good."

"Not tonight," David said. "I have to work an event in Marina Del Rey."

After the party David waited outside the Rusted Pelican. Rows of sailboats lined the marina beneath a flamingo pink sky. A brisk onshore wind blew. Rigging clink-clink-clinked against masts. Sailboats motored toward their moorings. Cars circled the lot searching for parking spaces.

David and Liz set the supplies into her BMW. She slammed the trunk.

"Something's wrong," she said. "Admit it?"

"I told you about my restaurant project," David said. "That hasn't impacted our work."

"I'm not talking about that." Her eyes narrowed with speculation. "Don't put me off. It's been weeks."

"What is it Liz?"

"Please, come up to my place." Her tone softened. "We need to speak in private."

"I'll follow you."

As he drove, David thought how sexual desire fosters a dependency that impedes judgment. The consequences of casual affairs are damned when the distance between two people widens and truth emerges like a splinter from a wound.

Liz's possessions were perfectly arranged. Magazines on the coffee table, signed lithographs on the wall, an etched crystal vase filled with orchids on the dining table.

"Cocktail?"

"Not tonight," David said.

Liz began to unbutton her dress. "Really?" She stepped toward the bedroom. "Make me a vodka martini."

David removed his sport coat and found vodka in the freezer. He chilled a glass and stirred a splash of vermouth, speared three olives then brought the drink into the living room.

Liz's black silk robe hung to her knees. She dimmed the lights, tuned the radio to a classical station and eased onto the sofa. The robe slipped up her thighs. She took the martini with breathless slurps and saved the olives for last. When she finished David set the empty glass on the table.

"Just what I needed," Liz said. She thrust her feet into David's hands. He massaged her insteps. Minutes passed. Her head rested on the cushions. Liz crossed her legs. The robe crept up her thighs.

The radio played Schubert's *Wanderer's Fantasy*. One would expect, after a certain hour, that classical selections would promote a tranquil mood yet Schubert's composition vaulted toward high anxiety. After a few somber passages the music convulsed like the soundtrack of a melodramatic silent film. David imagined a villain lashing the helpless woman to the railroad tracks. The villain laughed a silent laugh, twisted his handlebar mustache. The train roared around the bend. A silent whistle screamed. The orchestra played on. Surely, the woman would be rescued and the day would be saved.

"Ouch." Liz pulled her feet from David's grasp. "What are you doing?"

"I apologize." David chuckled. "It was the music. I was carried away."

Liz returned a foot to David's keeping. He pressed lightly. The music mellowed. The robe fell open. Liz's hand moved up a thigh.

"That's more like it." Her body shifted on the sofa. "Please, go on."

But David could not. Candlelight fluttered across her legs and offered a convenient refuge. David paused and merged with the flickering flames, floated up the wick to where vapors rise into the ethereal plane.

"Hello." Liz snapped her fingers. "What are you doing now?"

David didn't answer. Liz sat up and closed the robe.

"Hello!"

David abandoned the flame and faced reality. "I don't want to do this."

Liz stared in disbelief. "What are you saying?"

"It's not right to be like this with you. I'm involved with someone else."

Liz blinked several times. "You bastard," she said.

"You wanted to talk. But …"

"But nothing." Suddenly Liz's robe wasn't long enough. She raised her voice. "You've been leading me on."

David paused, collected his thoughts and spoke as clearly as he could. "Liz, no one leads you anywhere."

She punched him in the arm. "You're all bastards," she said and punched him again.

David refused to argue.

Liz fumed. "Are you just going to sit there?"

"No," David said. "I'm going to leave. And when you cool off, we can discuss business. I care about you and our friendship. But the sex part is over."

"Friendship?" Liz snatched the martini glass from the table. "How presumptuous can you be?"

"I consider that we're friends," he said.

"Friendship?" Liz stood. "There's no friendship. And there's no business. For you, it's over and done."

David grabbed his coat and headed for the door expecting the martini glass to smash into the back of his head. He turned. Liz waited in the middle of the living room, her robe twisted sideways. David expected her anger to fade, but that didn't happen.

"I hope we can work this out," he said.

"You're nothing to me." Her eyes widened. "You're nothing at all."

It was 10:30 p.m. when David returned to the apartment and found Rocco hunched over the dinette table clutching a letter. Grease-stained fingers stroked his freshly clipped flat top. His face was riddled with concern.

"Oh brother," David said. "Has Darla and the tunic cult sent a summons?"

Rocco dropped the letter on the table, went to the kitchen and returned with a pint of Jim Beam bourbon and two glasses.

"Man, I should check the mail more often." Rocco poured. "Have a drink with me."

"Rocco, what is it?"

Rocco pushed a glass into David's hand. His face cracked a smile that bordered on concern. "It's clown school," he said. "They accepted me. I'm headed for the big top."

They raised their glasses and emptied them.

"Rocco, that's unbelievable."

"Yeah, man. It's pretty damned good."

"It's your dream."

"Man, I need a hug."

David gave Rocco the biggest hug he could. "You'll be the best damned clown," he said.

Rocco danced a flat-footed jig into the living room. The windows rattled. A neighbor pounded on the wall. Rocco pounded back. His face transformed into a rubber mask. He cycled through a range of goofy expressions then sang like the lion from *The Wizard of Oz.*

"Makeup and a big nose will help," David said. "And you need exercise. You're not in clowning condition."

Rocco stopped to catch his breath. "You're right, man." He poured a round of drinks. "School starts in Florida in six weeks. I can drop some pounds by then."

The telephone rang. Rocco shuffled through a stack of *LA Weekly* newspapers on the floor. He found the receiver and answered.

"Rocco's place. Rocco speaking."

His forehead furrowed. He sipped whiskey and listened.

"No, man." Rocco shook his head. "We've been through this. I don't have money. I don't care when you can pay me, 'cause I'm not loaning it." He waited. "No. No way."

Rocco hung up the telephone.

"Who was that?"

"Turner. Imagine calling me after that stunt at the Greek. He must be desperate. Forget Turner. This is my night."

Rocco produced two cigars from a kitchen drawer. "One of Larry's lube guys had a baby," he said. "Let's smoke these."

They lit the cigars with ceremonial resolve. Rocco blew smoke rings above the table. "I prefer cheap cigars," he said. "Don't you?"

David puffed and coughed. "I'm not much for smoking," he said. "The price was right."

"Imagine me traveling cross country on a circus train." Rocco clenched the fifty-cent cigar in his teeth. "Imagine cruising with the clowns."

David contemplated their good fortune. In exclusive clubs adorned with hand-carved paneling, wealthy men toasted victory with fine Cognac and hand-rolled Cuban cigars. In the cluttered confines of Rocco's humble quarters, unburdened by formalities and dress codes, their tribute proved just as true. They recognized the significance of this moment and tended the ashes of their cigars with great care.

"Hollywood won't be the same without you," David said.

"That's a fact." Rocco puffed until his cigar glowed. "But you'll find your way."

"It's time for me to look for an apartment."

Rocco exhaled a narrow stream of smoke. "There are some cool places up Beachwood Canyon. Have Sarah show you around. That's her neighborhood."

When they finished their bourbon and cigars Rocco retired to his bedroom to call Joyce. David brushed his teeth and collapsed onto his air mattress heartened by Rocco's good news. Sleep came easily as an ominous silence fell upon the combat zone.

TWENTY-THREE

The following Saturday morning, beneath another flawless April sky, David and Sarah toured Beachwood Canyon, the street that leads up to the Hollywood sign. On the top floor of a newer building, they found an apartment with a modest view of the city and the tall palms lining Franklin Avenue. In the living room a sliding glass door opened onto a wide balcony. Padded carpet cushioned their steps as they moved through the empty rooms.

"This is perfect, clean and quiet." Sarah walked into the bathroom. "Look, a shower and a bathtub."

"What every bachelor needs."

"I love long hot baths."

"Maybe on the weekend after a run."

Out on the balcony they admired the palms down on Franklin.

"You're right," he said. "It's perfect."

"And a good deal for the area," she said. "I'd jump on it."

"You'd make a great real estate agent."

"Maybe." Sarah smiled. "I'd make a bundle if every client was as easy as you."

David's move to Beachwood Canyon required most of a day. He started early, made several trips and loaded the last box in the Buick as the boys came home from school with their mother. When they saw him, they hurried along the sidewalk ahead of her.

"Mister David, you are leaving?" Enrique asked.

"Yes. I have a new place. Not far from here."

Jesus stood quietly. "But David, the water in the pool is clear." He shielded his eyes against the sun. "I am a good swimmer."

"I know. I've watched you." David crouched and looked into his soft brown eyes. "You've done very well."

Jesus' gaze dropped to the sidewalk. "You will not forget about us?"

David looked up at their mother. She placed a hand on Jesus' shoulder. "No, my friend," David said. "I will never forget. Promise you will study hard in school and mind your mother."

Enrique stood tall. "That is easy Mister David," he said. "We do these things already. You have our promise."

In the weeks that followed into late May, Quincy's restaurants sold truckloads of veggie burgers, pre-packaged salads and barbecue sauce. "More than I'd ever have believed," Quincy said the day he agreed to David's contract extension. "You were right. There are no losers in this deal."

The next morning David purchased an Apple computer, a small stereo, a fax machine and a queen-size futon. At a resale shop in Burbank he bought a table, two side chairs and bookcases large enough to hold his mother's library. The following day, with the furniture delivered, David unpacked boxes. On top of a bookcase he placed the photograph his father took of David and his mother wading into the surf.

It was late afternoon when David finished unpacking and went for a jog. He labored up Beachwood's incline noting the cracked and buckled sidewalk with automobiles parked head to tail along the way. The road narrowed and turned. He moved through the Hollywoodland stone gateway and passed the neighborhood market. A short distance further he pulled up with muscle cramps, stretched and walked back down the hill.

The living room was dark and filled with shadows. He went onto the balcony. Traffic from the 101 Freeway produced a faint and sustained buzz. An ambulance siren shrieked. On the balcony of an adjacent building a woman watered houseplants and sang Puccini's *Che Gelida Manina* from *La Boheme*.

David recalled Sarah's comment about hot baths. He filled the tub, opened a bottle of Miller High Life and lit the lavender-scented candle Sarah had given him as a housewarming gift. David eased into the steaming water. He forgot about his cramped legs, closed his eyes and held his breath. Beneath the water the thump-thump-thump of his heart reverberated. David broke the surface, sipped the beer and watched the candle flame.

The water had cooled and his toes were wrinkled like prunes when the telephone rang. He ignored it, but the phone continued to ring. David grabbed a towel and dashed into the bedroom.

"Hello."

There was no reply.

"Hello. Who's there?"

David was about to hang up.

"It's me," a voice sobbed. "Sarah."

The muscles in his back tightened. "What's wrong?"

She sobbed. David's heart pounded.

"It's Leonard. He died last night."

Agony struck the pit of David's stomach. He suppressed the

urge to scream and rolled onto his futon bed.

"It was a heart attack," Sarah continued. "Tom found him parked in his taxi. The engine was still running."

David couldn't speak. His eyes searched the blank walls.

"Are you there?"

"Yes," David said. "I'm here."

He tucked the towel around his waist, carried the telephone into the living room and found the family photograph. He studied the smile on his face and his mother's face. A strange sense of clarity came over him.

"It's not fair," Sarah said.

"Life is not intended to be fair."

They held Leonard's memorial at the Heliotrope Theater, a venue south of Melrose Avenue popular with performance artists and poets. Set among aged commercial brick buildings, the Heliotrope offered a beacon of hope. Beyond where the poets gathered, most of the streetlamps were shattered. Across the street a meeting hall filled with Koreans held an evangelical service. The doors were open wide. The congregation sang and clapped. David didn't understand any of it.

A photograph of Leonard wearing a fedora welcomed them. The Heliotrope stage was dressed for a production of Hair, the rear wall blacked out and the midnight blue ceiling splattered with hand-painted planets and stars. Sarah and David squeezed into the theater. Everyone huddled together, the open mike crowds from Dharma's and Beyond Baroque, the poets Tom and Dick, Sister Serena, Carlos and Samantha.

Sister Serena opened the program, rang her chimes and sang

Amazing Grace. "Leonard wasn't a religious person, but he loved that song." She lowered her head for several seconds. "He did so well by all of us, creating a place where we could be ourselves. That's a beautiful legacy. Leonard thought that no one should deny the wonder of their truest calling, that this life is all what we make of it. Thank you Leonard."

Everyone paid tribute. When Tom and Dick went up Tom removed his well-worn wingtip shoes.

"Leonard would want me to do this," Tom said. He slapped the soles together for a few seconds then, unable to continue, covered his face and cried.

Dick tapped the stage lightly with his drumsticks. "Suck it up," he barked. "Take a stand. Let's do our thing already. Let's do it for Leonard."

Tom righted himself. They slapped shoes and tapped drumsticks in a synchronized beat then bowed gracefully.

"We love you, Leonard." Dick pointed his drumsticks to the star-splattered ceiling. "You're like our father."

"What?" Tom said. "That would mean we're brothers."

Dick glared at his friend. "Only metaphorically."

Sarah stepped to the stage and sang Joni Mitchell's *California.* She never missed a note. At the end of the song everyone stood and cheered.

"Leonard was a dear friend." Sarah wiped her tears. "He was always there to listen and offer a few choice words. I know you probably feel the same way. I loved him so much. Goodbye, my friend."

David waited for the audience to settle. He took a breath and thought about the man he had come to honor.

"Leonard challenged me," he said. "Leonard challenged all of us. This piece was one of his favorites."

David pulled the paper from his jacket and read.

A leader of the moral majority
stood blow-dried, beaming
a big-toothed smile in the middle
of the Republican National Convention,
broadcasting in the name of salvation.
He is a political shepherd, a master
of television marketing and financial urgency.
His stomach shows little sign of suffering
and while some may laugh,
millions listen intently, believing
they send him money
so he can fuel his jets,
air-condition doghouses
and broadcast.
I wonder if Mother Teresa's dogs
are comfortable at night
as she blesses millions with quiet miracles.
I can see saints like her comforting small children,
rocking back and forth,
I hear true salvation whisper:
We owe nothing. We own nothing.
All we have is strength, intellect
and love to give each other.
All we have is love. Don't be shy.
Give it away. I'll go first.

The audience applauded. Tom slapped his shoes. Dick rapped his drumsticks. David nodded, held his emotions, and returned to his seat. Everyone stayed until the end.

David and Sarah stopped at his apartment and went onto the balcony. Palms swayed in the cool breeze. In the distance, jetliners approached from the east and descended toward LAX.

"How many palm trees do you think there are?" Sarah gestured to the south. "Along Franklin and down on Hollywood."

"You'd tire of counting."

The breeze freshened. In the alley below a pair of cats grappled. Sarah peeked over the railing. A cat hissed. A garbage can lid crashed against concrete then it was quiet.

"How are you?"

"I'm not sure." Sarah gripped the railing. "I'm trying very hard not to be sad."

"Let yourself have it, sadness or whatever comes next. Death is a curse. We're all cursed. No one is ever prepared."

TWENTY-FOUR

anta Ana winds brought waves of crackling heat down from the high desert. The evening before Rocco was to depart for clown school David met him at the apartment. Rocco's possessions fit into a duffel bag and two suitcases. The room was empty except for the luggage and the dinette set.

Rocco opened windows and grabbed the last two beers from the refrigerator. They sat down at the table for the final time.

"Sorry, man. It's like an oven in here."

"A cold beer will help." David raised his bottle. "Here's to you, Rocco. My life won't be the same."

"I'll miss you, man. I'll miss Los Angeles and the mountains. Florida is so flat."

"I've heard some of the bugs in Florida are as large as your hand," David said. "And they fly."

"That's why they have screened in backyards. Those bugs are like hawks. They'll snatch a Chihuahua."

Something crashed against the door. A large man, his face scarred like a boxer, appeared in the front window. A fist pounded the door.

"Hey Rocco. Open up. It's Turner."

"That's great." Rocco turned to David. "Be cool. Can you do that?"

David braced himself. Rocco opened the door. Turner edged inside. The white T-shirt beneath his denim jacket was twisted and torn, his lip cut and swollen.

"What the hell?" Rocco said.

The scar-faced man moved from the window to the door, his face without expression.

"This will only take a second," Turner said. "Can we have a second?"

The man folded his arms across his chest. Rocco tried to close the door.

"Leave it open," the man said.

David moved to the rear window and looked down at the street. In front of the building a red Mercedes convertible was parked with the top down. A thin man in a linen sport coat smoked a cigarette. Rocco followed Turner into the bedroom. Their voices were easily heard.

"No, man," Rocco said. "I told you. Forget it."

"All I need is five hundred."

"Five hundred! You're crazy."

Turner pleaded. "You don't understand."

"I don't want to know."

"These guys aren't fucking around."

Voices quieted. They returned to the living room. Rocco backed away. Turner cast one last hopeful glance then stepped to the door. In front of the building, the thin man checked his watch and lit another cigarette.

"Fuck you, Rocco," Turner said. "Fuck you all."

"Time's up." The man collared Turner. "Let's go tough guy."

Rocco grabbed his stomach. "I feel sick," he said and headed to the bathroom.

David stayed by the window. The thin man flicked his cigarette to the curb. His accomplice ushered Turner into the back seat of the convertible. The two men slid into their seats when the LAPD squad car rolled up behind them. Red and blue lights flashed across the Mercedes, Turner and the two men.

"Police," an officer shouted. "Freeze."

Two officers opened the squad car doors and drew their weapons. The second officer made a call on the police radio. The first officer shouted again. "Don't move. Put your hands in the air. Keep them where we can see them."

Turner and the two men complied.

"Driver, open your door. Slowly from the outside," the officer said. "Do it slowly. Do it now."

The driver extended his left arm outside the Mercedes.

"Step out slowly. That's it. You others sit tight. Don't even breathe."

The thin man opened the door with his hip.

"Now step away from the vehicle. Step into the middle of the street. Get down on your knees. Put your hands behind your head. Keep them there."

The thin man kneeled. The officers aimed their weapons.

"Okay big guy. You're next. Open the door from the outside. Keep your hands up. Move slowly. Put your hands behind your head. Move into the street. Now, down on your knees."

The man locked his fingers behind his head. Turner remained seated in the Mercedes. Sirens wailed in the distance. The deep-throated drone of a police helicopter approached from the north.

"You, in the back seat. Keep your hands where we can see them. Step out of the car. Take your time."

When Turner's boots touched the pavement, he froze.

"Okay. Step away from the vehicle. Get down on your knees."

Turner didn't move.

"Down on your knees. Get down. Do it now."

Turner started to kneel then jumped up and sprinted across the street toward the hedges, arms pumped wildly, denim jacket flapped against his sides.

"Stop!" The officer shouted. "Stop or we'll shoot!"

Turner didn't stop. At the curb he dropped his right hand inside the jacket.

"Gun!" The second officer shouted. "Gun!"

BAM-BAM. Shots fired. BAM. The third shot smashed into Turner's left shoulder and spun him sideways. He stumbled onto the sidewalk and lunged forward. BAM. The fourth shot struck him in the chest. Turner staggered, then collapsed against a chain link fence. The helicopter hovered, whirling blades sliced through the scorched night air. A searchlight illuminated the scene. Turner's head twisted to one side against the fence. A dark stain spread across his shirt. Empty hands formed fists. His chest rose and fell. He gasped, the right leg straightened, and he didn't move again.

By 11:00 p.m. the coroner had removed Turner's body and the police had cleared the street. As the only forthcoming witness, David gave a lengthy statement then the detective said he and Rocco could go. They went up to the apartment and waited for Joyce to get off work. When she learned what had happened, she cried uncontrollably.

"I told Turner he was dark." Joyce sobbed. "I told him he was evil. I wish I hadn't said those things. I wish I could take them back."

They sat at the dinette table in the heat. David went to the kitchen, turned the faucet and cupped his hands. He brought the water to his face, soaked his hair and the back of his neck.

"I should tell Sarah," he said. "Before she gets a call from the police."

"One of us should do it," Rocco said. "That's only right."

"Maybe we should all go," Joyce said.

"That's too much." David shook his head. "I'll go to her. You guys need to rest for tomorrow."

They carried Rocco's duffel bag and suitcases to the street and loaded them in Joyce's car.

"I'll see you in the morning," he said. "Try to sleep."

When David reached Sarah's place, he tapped softly. Sarah cracked the door. When she saw David's face she unlocked the latch and secured her robe.

"Something has happened, hasn't it?"

"It's Turner," he said. "I was at Rocco's. Turner came by, asked for money then went with these two guys. The police came. Turner ran."

"He's dead, isn't he?" Sarah retreated toward the stained-glass window. "That's why you're here."

"Yes. He's gone."

Sarah froze, immobilized as if an anonymous messenger had delivered long awaited news, the shock tempered by years of expectation. Her gaze fell to the floor, to the patches of scattered colored light.

"I'm sorry," he said.

"Don't be. Not about this."

Their eyes met briefly then Sarah pulled away toward the window. She stood tall with her shoulders square.

"I knew you'd want to know right away," he said. "I didn't want you to learn about this from the police."

A fan churned in the corner, forced warm air around the room. Sarah stared through the window at the security light and the small tree alive with freshly budded leaves.

"Thank you for coming. I know that wasn't easy, but I really don't want to talk."

David opened the door. "Take care."

"I will," she said. "I need some time."

During the night the Santa Ana heat surrendered to a subtle on-shore breeze and a gloomy June morning. Rocco stowed the Futura at the end of Joyce's driveway with the blue tarp tied down tight. He promised Joyce four days at Disney World in Orlando before he began clown school. Little was said as they loaded luggage into the Buick and headed for LAX.

"It's dreary," Joyce said. "I don't like dreariness."

"The sun will shine in Florida," Rocco said.

Rocco and Joyce checked their luggage curbside while David parked in the short-term garage. Together, they walked into the terminal, down a hallway and stopped short of the security gate. Their collective embrace created an island midstream in a rushing human current. Passengers moved around them, tourists and business people, mothers with strollers, soldiers in uniform. Rocco welled up.

"I thought you were a happy clown," David said. "You'll trash your image."

"Screw that." Rocco held on tight. "I love you guys. And I'll cry when I want."

"We'll always be close," Joyce said.

David savored their last few moments of solidarity. Rocco and Joyce walked away. At the gate Rocco turned to David. "Hey man," he said. "Don't pick up hitchhikers. They'll only get you in trouble."

"Don't worry," David said. "I've learned my lesson."

A line formed. People passed single file. Beyond the checkpoint, Rocco and Joyce waved then disappeared into the crowd. David waited as strangers swirled about him. The experience was magnified by the significance of every goodbye. He considered the weight of that moment, of how one life may alter another with a single word.

TWENTY-FIVE

June mornings produced a progression of gloom. By noon a welcome sun burned through the marine layer and David had worked three or four good hours. He would take a break and jog up Beachwood Canyon through the steep winding streets. After a quick shower he'd drive down to Franklin or Melrose for a late lunch. Sometimes he would dine outside and read the papers or write in his journal, grateful as he recalled those days in the fall when he was uncertain of his next meal.

David had given Sarah time. This became increasingly difficult as the last days of spring rolled past. His thoughts always returned to the reassuring sound of her voice. He waited patiently until early one evening his telephone rang.

"Hey stranger," Sarah said.

"How's everything?"

"Well enough. I finished school and that was hard. I'm leaving tomorrow for Agoura Hills. I wouldn't go without seeing you."

"It's not like you're moving to Alaska."

"Right, even with traffic, Agoura Hills is not that far."

David looked toward his balcony and the open sliding glass door. A fresh breeze animated the vertical blinds, made them twist and clatter. On Franklin the palm trees leaned against a fading burnt orange sky.

"I put most of my stuff in storage," she said. "All I'm taking are summer clothes, a few good books and my music. Grace expects me before dark."

David listened intently, considered her words resembled a series of coded messages that he must decipher.

"I'm sorry that I haven't called." Her voice was clear and more familiar. "I wanted to call. You know?"

Twilight played between cracks in the vertical blinds, palm trees pitched against the encroaching darkness.

"I look forward to seeing you."

"We'll have lunch tomorrow. Then I'll be off."

They met at the Rose Café in Venice. Sarah parked her Volkswagen in front of the restaurant. She wore white jeans, a Pink Floyd T-shirt and a light jacket. Freshly trimmed blond hair hung just above her shoulders. On the patio summer sun battled low gray clouds rolling off the Pacific. They drank iced tea, shared grilled albacore and mixed green salads then split a slice of vegan chocolate mousse pie.

David didn't know what to say. He was only sure that he should not probe beneath the fragile surface.

"How about a game of pool?" he said.

Sarah's eyes sparkled. "They don't have a pool table."

"The Oar House does. It's right down the street."

"You want to shoot pool with me?"

"I feel lucky."

"You must," she said. "Sure, let's go."

They walked north along Main Street. Sunshine surrendered to gray clouds as they entered the tavern. Beyond the ambient light from the front windows the room turned dark. A heavy wooden bar ran along one wall. The rafters were cluttered with dusty relics, an antique bicycle, a wagon wheel, vintage surfboards, and Route 66 signage. Three men huddled over pints of beer at the bar. Long-billed fishing caps shielded their eyes. David and Sarah stepped into a room with a pool table. A Budweiser light hung low over the worn green felt. David went to the bar and returned with two glasses of beer.

"A proper game requires refreshments," he said.

Sarah chalked a cue. "Apparently."

"Go ahead and break," he said.

Sarah smiled confidently. "You must feel lucky."

The cue slid precisely through the bridge of her left fingers. David gave her a tight rack and she nailed it, made two balls on the break, a solid and a stripe, called the five-ball in the side and played shape on the seven. Three more balls dropped before she left one short down the rail.

David scouted the table. Sarah sipped her beer and watched as David ran the twelve ball, made the ten and fifteen then banked the eleven in the corner down the length of the table.

"Nice shot," Sarah said.

David's attempt at the nine rattled the side pocket, but did not fall.

"That's a shame." Sarah studied her next shot. "By the way, you never said what we're playing for."

"We're playing for fun." David opened his arms. "For the joy of competition."

"Yeah, sure. Joy won't put gas in my car."

"Ten dollars."

Sarah smiled. "You're on."

She returned to work, made the four and six easily. The eight ball hooked behind the fourteen. She evaluated her options then played a safe shot that cleared the eight.

David surveyed the situation. The nine-ball fell in the side pocket. He cut the fourteen in the corner, but it wouldn't go. The eight ball remained clear with a straight shot in the side pocket.

"This is too easy." Sarah smiled and finished her beer. "Are you letting me win?"

"No. I'd never slack off. Not even for you."

Her bridge was solid, the stroke confident and the game was won. David placed a ten-dollar bill on the table.

Outside, the sun vanished behind leaden clouds. On the corner a man strummed his guitar and sang *Norwegian Wood*.

David took Sarah's hand. "Let's walk," he said.

They crossed the street, passed condominiums protected by high walls then reached the beach. On the strand people jogged, skated and rode bicycles. Sailboats bobbed on the choppy gray water. Further out, an oil tanker crossed slowly. Sarah and David removed their shoes and sank their toes into the loose sand. At the shore flat waves crested and fell.

Sunbathers appeared bewildered by dull clouds and a chilled breeze. They covered themselves, read magazines or talked with their companions. Two lovers wrestled playfully on a beach towel. An attentive mother applied sunscreen on teeth-chattering children.

David and Sarah headed north on the packed sand. In the distance, a band of brilliant sunlight burst through the clouds, struck the water and swept east along the length of the Santa Monica Pier and over the buildings on Ocean Avenue.

This was the beach David had shared with his parents where he discovered the unforgiving force of nature. He imagined his parents there ahead of them, talking and laughing.

"Dark clouds don't bother me," Sarah said. Wind swept the hair from her face. "I love walking the beach. I guess everyone does."

"It's primal." David pulled a pebble from the sand and tossed it into the water. "The ocean is like fire in that way. We're drawn to the edge of our experience."

A wave collapsed. Sandpipers scattered. Cold water surged around their ankles.

"It's getting late," she said. "We'd better go back."

David stared at the Santa Monica Pier and the Ferris wheel. He closed his eyes and imagined that sunny day a lifetime ago. In the recesses of his memory David heard seabirds call, felt the warm sun against his face. He opened his eyes and turned away.

They crossed the sand. Sunbathers folded umbrellas and shook their beach towels. Gluttonous gulls hopped spot to spot scavenging discarded scraps. Sarah and David stopped to wash the sand and beach tar from their feet. They put on their shoes and walked side by side. Neither spoke until they reached Sarah's car.

"I'm not good at this," she said.

David touched her face. "You don't have to be."

Her hand folded over his. A tear escaped and trickled across their fingers.

"You've been so good," she said. "I couldn't ask for a truer friend."

"I'm right here." David drew her close. "You don't have to ask for anything."

Sarah wrapped her arms around David's shoulders, kissed him on the lips then stepped into the street.

"It's like this." She wiped a tear from her chin. "I won't say goodbye because I don't want to. I'm pathetic, I know, but I felt I was strong and now I'm not. I'm thinking too much and my mind is still processing everything that's happened."

"It may take awhile," he said. "But you'll get there."

David checked for traffic then opened Sarah's door. She rolled down the window and tucked a note into David's hand.

"That's the address and telephone number." Sarah started the car. "I want you to drop me a note. Then I could write you back. Or you can call. Or I'll call you."

"We'll figure it out."

David leaned through the window. One wind-chapped kiss followed another.

"Drive safely," he said.

"I will." Her voice cracked. "I miss you already."

Sarah made a sharp turn then drove north on Main Street. David touched his lips and waited on the curb until long after she had gone.

TWENTY-SIX

Early morning light served as David's wake up call. He arose weary from a restless night in which the resolution of his recurring dream of human bondage had once again been denied.

Breakfast consisted of a banana and a bowl of granola with low-fat almond milk. He ate cereal and noted the palms along Franklin Avenue. Pointless to count palm trees, he thought, yet he had counted them each of the ten days since Sarah's departure. Months of patience and resolve had morphed into a mental state David diagnosed as separation anxiety.

Sarah had shared her telephone number and address, but David would not call. A telephone call could be intrusive, that would be too much. She had suggested a letter not knowing David had composed several for her. After breakfast he found those pages and read them out loud.

"Your tears shine like diamonds in the noonday sun. I surrender to your sorrow, but my heart does not race. My heart does not pound. Its beat is slow and steady."

David gazed out over Hollywood and affirmed every word.

"I have tasted these lips, known the warmth of this embrace, the sound of laughter, the joy of surrender to this divine neurosis. This grinding of flesh and bones which transforms me into a beast who has lost its soul, who must now wait quietly among the shadows, licking its wounds and longing for completion."

He sorted the pages and placed them in order, the opening piece inspired by that first night in Sarah's apartment.

IN THE BEGINNING
The world turns slowly
and the rain falls softly on the City of Angels
when it falls.

She tosses her long blond hair
against pillows well placed
in our darkened corner, and she laughs
a lonely lover's laugh and sighs,
"It's always better in the beginning."

I laugh with her
and in this moment we find each other
again in fragile pieces,
beautiful stained-glass reflections
hidden from the light.

I touch her skin
smooth and warm and willing
and through the evening we uncover
those fragile pieces of ourselves.
Sleep finds us close together,
wounds healing, we dream of flight.

It's always better in the beginning
and the world turns without a thought.

Late that afternoon David slipped his work into a manila envelope, drove to the Hollywood Post Office on Wilcox, and waited
in line. The clerk reported first class mail would take two business
days. David clutched the envelope and recalled Leonard's warning.
He knew the letters were a risk. They revealed too much. Perhaps
better to burn them as a sacrifice.

"Hey, you there." The elderly lady behind him rattled her
walker. "I don't have all day."

David returned to the Buick and tossed the envelope in the
back seat. He drove aimlessly down to Sunset Boulevard, passed
Cross Roads of the World and the Cineramadome where he
stopped and checked show times for *The Accidental Tourist* and
A Fish Called Wanda. It was Friday, a weekend when friends and
family gather to celebrate, but he had no cause.

Back on his balcony, David witnessed another day slip away.
A vivid sunset dissolved into hazy bleakness. The city of light with
millions of people surrounded him yet he was alone. David meditated on the toll of loneliness, the pervasive hunger, and the desire
to fill an undeniable void. Across the living room the telephone
waited on the counter. From the creeping shadows a shrill sound
interrupted his scattered thoughts. He raced inside.

"Hello."

"Hi." She paused. "It's Sarah."

David closed his eyes, visualized himself suspended in a tropical sea of embryonic fluid, the glorious maternal bliss from which
all humanity emerges.

"Are you there?"

David opened his eyes. "Yes, of course."

"What are you doing?"

"Thinking of you."

"How odd," she said. "Because I was thinking about me, too. And you."

David laughed. He refused to restrain his happiness. "And what could be on your mind?"

"Well, I'm ready for some company." Sarah's voice quieted. "If you are."

A breeze coursed through David's balcony and rattled the blinds. On Franklin palm trees swayed beneath a moonless sky.

"When?"

"Now," Sarah said. "Why don't you come right now?"

"But ..."

Sarah interrupted. "There will be plenty of time to talk when you get here."

David drove north on the Ventura Freeway and merged with the crush of Friday night traffic crawling out of the San Fernando Valley. He gripped the steering wheel and focused on the flow of crimson taillights as he passed the exits for Encino, Woodland Hills and Calabasas. Traffic eased steadily with each passing mile until suddenly there were no more neon fast food beacons or liquor stores, no sprawling apartment complexes or stilted homes or lights on the rolling hillsides. When David reached Lost Hills Road he exited and traveled on a dark two-lane street until his headlights found a mailbox decorated like a Jersey cow. He veered up a gravel road to a cheerful ranch-style home.

Sarah appeared on the porch wearing a thick sweater, jeans

and hiking boots. She skipped merrily down the steps. The music of Johann Strauss' *The Blue Danube Waltz* floated from the house.

"Hey, stranger. Have you lost your way?"

"I knew where I was going."

"Oh yeah?" Sarah took his hand. "Then you better come along with me."

Sarah led him on a path beside a weathered barn into a broad meadow where they stopped and gazed up into the clear radiant splendor of the star-filled heavens.

"Isn't it beautiful?"

"Yes," David said. "More than I could imagine."

"I knew you would love it out here."

Sarah smiled. Faint light from the porch illuminated her face, her eyes an aqueous midnight blue. David's heart beat slow and steady. Far from the longing and chaos of the city they embraced the rapturous singularity of that moment. The chill of night closed in around them and, as if the universe became a ballroom, David took her gently in his arms and they began to dance.

THE END

Thank you for reading *Angel City Singles*.

Your Amazon, Goodreads or other review
will be greatly appreciated.

MR

ACKNOWLEDGMENTS

I am grateful for my mother and father, both great storytellers, for giving me this life, their unconditional love and support. I thank my brothers Frank and Mike, my sister Carol, and my son Russell for sharing our adventures. To Aunt Joan, and my mentor Frank Natale, thank you for introducing me to the power of presence and the writer's journey. I acknowledge stand-up comedy guru Greg Dean, and his students, for our years of friendship and laughter.

Thank you to the UCLA Extension Creative Writing Program, and instructor Jamie Cat Callan, the Los Angeles Writer's Block including Janet Fitch, Diana Wagman, Cat Bauer, Marlea Evans, Charlotte Laws, and Charles Parselle. Thanks to Leslie Schwartz for her editing guidance and to readers Melissa Brevetti and LeeAnn Holmberg. To the Beyond Baroque Literary Arts Center in Venice, and performance art venues everywhere, thank you for creating space where inspired voices may be heard.

ABOUT THE AUTHOR

Angel City Singles is Ralph Cissne's first novel. An award-winning poet, his short stories have appeared in publications such as *American Way* and *Playboy*. His poetry collection *Don't Be Shy* was published in 2015.

A native Californian, Cissne grew up in a military family and is a graduate of The University of Oklahoma School of Journalism. He lives in Oklahoma where he writes and volunteers as a creative life skills mentor. Cissne is a member of PEN America, The Author's Guild, and is a lifetime member of the National Eagle Scout Association.

For more, visit RalphCissne.com

CPSIA information can be obtained
at www.ICGtesting.com
Printed in the USA
LVOW11*2001040518
576084LV00001B/3/P

9 780999 853719